"Goodbye, Joe."

Pip walked down the hall toward the elevator with dragging steps. Why was she so loath to let him go?

He was the kind of man—arrogant, wounded, stubborn—who never drew her. Why work that hard? She pushed the elevator button, conscious of his gaze still on her. But there was so much more to him. Glimpses of depths she wanted to plumb. Integrity. Hurt she could soothe. Pip was instinctive in her emotional choices; her family said impulsive. But she trusted the big insights.

The elevator doors opened; she turned and strode back to Joe. She refused to spend the rest of her life regretting the "what if."

"I have to do this, at least once." Hooking her hands around his neck, she drew his head down and kissed him.

Dear Reader,

This is the first time I've been privileged to share a miniseries with other writers. The most fascinating part of the process for me was seeing how Tara Taylor Quinn, Kathleen O'Brien and Janice Kay Johnson used a character I created—Joe Fraser—in their books. I never got over the wonder of seeing Joe striding through their manuscripts, talking, interacting, *alive*—and completely independent of me. I mean, how typical of the man.

And it really brought home how powerful a writer's imagination is. No wonder we're all a bit crazy. We truly come to believe our imaginary friends are real.

This book forms part of THE DIAMOND LEGACY miniseries, one of the many celebratory events around Harlequin's sixtieth anniversary. That's sixty years of delivering imaginary friends to readers.

One thing I *never* imagined when I was a teenager devouring Harlequin romances was that one day I'd be working for the dream factory. Sometimes I wish I could go back to that book-struck kid and say, *Guess what your future holds*! Many thanks to my wonderful editor Victoria Curran for playing the fairy godmother.

If this is the first book you've read in THE DIAMOND LEGACY series and you'd like to read more of Joe's history, I encourage you to pick up *A Daughter's Trust* by Tara Taylor Quinn and *For the Love of Family* by Kathleen O'Brien.

And I certainly hope I've intrigued you enough to read how the Carsons and the Frasers resolve their last differences in Janice Kay Johnson's *A Mother's Secret*.

Here's to another sixty years of Harlequin romances enriching women's lives.

Karina Bliss

Like Father, Like Son
Karina Bliss

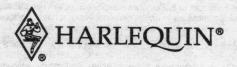

HARLEQUIN®

TORONTO • NEW YORK • LONDON
AMSTERDAM • PARIS • SYDNEY • HAMBURG
STOCKHOLM • ATHENS • TOKYO • MILAN • MADRID
PRAGUE • WARSAW • BUDAPEST • AUCKLAND

To my oldest friend, the incomparable
Ros Lakomy, and all our shared adventures.
Let's eat to many more.

ISBN-13: 978-0-373-71596-1

LIKE FATHER, LIKE SON

Copyright © 2009 by Karina Bliss.

ABOUT THE AUTHOR

New Zealander Karina Bliss was the first Australasian to win one of Romance Writers of America's coveted Golden Heart awards for unpublished writers, and her 2006 Harlequin Superromance debut, *Mr. Imperfect,* won a Romantic Book of the Year award in Australia. It took this former journalist five years to get her first book contract, a process, she says, that helped put childbirth into perspective. She lives with her husband and son north of Auckland. Visit her on the Web at www.karinabliss.com.

Books by Karina Bliss

HARLEQUIN SUPERROMANCE

Don't miss any of our special offers. Write to us at the following address for information on our newest releases.

Harlequin Reader Service
U.S.: 3010 Walden Ave., P.O. Box 1325, Buffalo, NY 14269
Canadian: P.O. Box 609, Fort Erie, Ont. L2A 5X3

The Diamond Legacy Family Tree

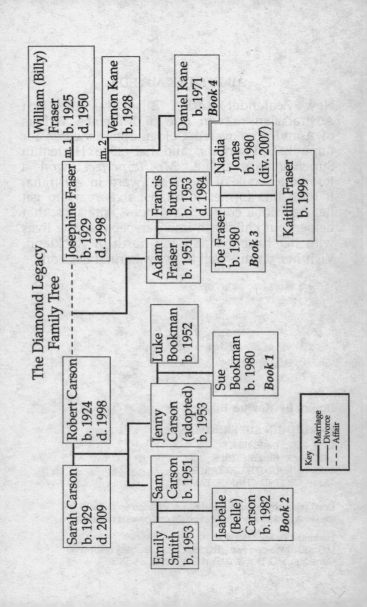

Key
— Marriage
— Divorce
- - - Affair

Sarah Carson
b. 1929
d. 2009

Robert Carson
b. 1924
d. 1998

Josephine Fraser
b. 1929
d. 1998

m. 1

William (Billy)
Fraser
b. 1925
d. 1950

m. 2

Vernon Kane
b. 1928

Daniel Kane
b. 1971
Book 4

Sam
Carson
b. 1951

Jenny
Carson
(adopted)
b. 1953

Luke
Bookman
b. 1952

Adam
Fraser
b. 1951

Francis
Burton
b. 1953
d. 1984

Emily
Smith
b. 1953

Isabelle
(Belle)
Carson
b. 1982
Book 2

Sue
Bookman
b. 1980
Book 1

Joe Fraser
b. 1980
Book 3

Nadia
Jones
b. 1980
(div. 2007)

Kaitlin Fraser
b. 1999

CHAPTER ONE

"MR. FRASER, I'm your daughter's teacher, Philippa Browne. I'm calling because—"

"My ex-wife deals with school matters, Miss Browne." The man had a deep voice—impatience dragged over gravel. "I'm in a meeting."

Pip doodled a frowny face on the blotter on her desk with a blue pen. "Nadia and her fiancé are out of town for a couple of days." She wondered fleetingly why his daughter was staying with a friend and not with him. "And this isn't a social call. Kaitlin's just been involved in a fight with another student and we need you to come pick her up."

"Is she hurt?" Now Joe Fraser sounded like a concerned dad.

"No, though unfortunately the other girl will have a black eye."

"Good."

Startled, Pip dropped the pen. Then she realized the man was laboring under a very natural misapprehension. "Perhaps I should clarify…Kaitlin started the fight."

There was a brief silence on the other end of the line. "We are talking about Kaitlin Josephine Fraser, aren't we?"

"This is a shock to us, as well, Mr. Fraser. This makes three misdemeanors in the space of a fortnight."

Another silence. He didn't know.

"How about we talk when you get here," she suggested. "Can you come before lunch recess is over?"

"Hang on." There was the sound of a muffled conversation on what must be his landline. Pip had rung his cell. She caught the words *"...my father...best treatment... that's for me to worry about."* She started as his voice suddenly barked in her ear, "I'm on my way. What's the address?"

His daughter had been coming to this middle school for just over a year and he'd never picked her up, dropped her off?

After giving him directions, Pip hung up. Standing, she studied the girl through the window in the classroom door. The ten-year-old waiting in the corridor, knuckling away tears, did not look like a playground scrapper. Or someone who carved her name into trees.

She looked like the A-grade student she was, with serious brown eyes, tidy dark braids and a prepubescent coltishness that would have sent Pip's farm-bred grandmother reaching for the worming tablets. Sensitive, quiet and conscientious, often lost amidst her boisterous classmates, Kaitlin Fraser had aroused Pip's protective instincts since she'd first taught this class last year.

Pip opened the door. "Come and sit down, Kaitlin. Your dad's on his way."

If anything, the girl blanched paler, but obediently she crossed to the chair indicated, next to Pip's desk. Outside, children raced past the open window in noisy, happy play.

Pulling her lunch bag out of her desk drawer, Pip unwrapped her ham-and-cheese sandwich and offered half to Kaitlin, who shook her head miserably. "I insist." Kaitlin accepted the sandwich and they ate.

Pip needed information, but she waited until they'd finished, deliberately cutting up the chocolate cake and apple with her letter opener. Kaitlin smiled. Color came back into the child's cheeks.

Balling the paper bag around the apple core, Pip lobbed it into the bin and sat back. "Did you really start it?"

She'd been on playground duty when she came upon the fight...more a flailing of hands with eyes shut than the roll-around-on-the-ground punching and biting that Pip had once inflicted on her older brothers. At her shout, Kaitlin had swung around and her elbow had accidentally connected with Sophia's cheekbone.

Possibly in shock that she was the victim for once, Sophia kicked up such a squawk that a remorseful Kaitlin had accepted all the blame. Which was a shame—Pip had been trying to nail Sophia for weeks.

"I did hit her first," Kaitlin said. "I mean, she was calling me a geek and saying the giraffe wants its legs back, but she always does that." Her voice started to wobble. "I'm just sick of people acting like my feelings don't matter."

Pip frowned slightly. Kaitlin might be quiet, but she was well liked. "Are there other kids that make you feel that way?"

"No...not kids." She hesitated. "You know, you shouldn't have called my dad. His work's very important."

Now that was an interesting connection. "I'm sure you're important to him, too."

Kaitlin began to straighten the pleats of her uniform over her bony knees.

Pip's counselor instincts kicked in. "While we're waiting for him, why don't you tell me about your dad."

The girl's eyes met hers. "He's not someone you mess with." There was pride there and a warning.

Pip hid a smile. She could handle tough guys. "I'll

keep that in mind.... Remind me how long your parents have been divorced?"

Kaitlin returned her attention to the pleats; her fingernails were chewed ragged. "Since I was eight. Mom loved Dad, but he didn't love her," she added matter-of-factly. "He always loved someone else. That's why they split up. They only got married because of having me."

Pip blinked. "They told you that?"

"No." She hesitated. "Remember that genealogy project we did last semester? My birthday was only six months after their wedding." A deep blush colored her cheeks; she'd realized she was making an indirect reference to *S-E-X*. "And when you're an only child you hear stuff...you know, if you're quiet enough."

Pip didn't know. She was the youngest of four and the sole female. "How much time do you spend with your dad now?"

"Sundays...when he's not working. I don't sleep over because he only has a one-bedroom apartment." There was defensiveness in Kaitlin's posture, as though she was used to justifying it to her peers. She shot Pip a suspicious glance, then relaxed a little when she received an encouraging smile. "And Dad doesn't have much furniture," she confided, "or stuff to cook with."

"Guys can be a bit hopeless like that," agreed Pip. But she was puzzled. King's Elementary was a private school and Kaitlin lived in one of San Francisco's affluent neighborhoods. Kaitlin's mother, Nadia, didn't seem the vindictive type who'd demand a steep divorce settlement. Through her daughter's recent troubles, they'd shared several heart-to-hearts, and Pip liked the woman.

In character Nadia was very much like her daughter except that Kaitlin's shyness had become composure in the mother. Pip always left their meetings thinking ruefully, *Next life I'm coming back impeccably groomed and dignified.* The downside of being sporty and gregarious was a wardrobe of sweats and a distinct lack of mystique.

"Your mom's getting married again soon, right?" Maybe this acting out stemmed from adjustment problems.

But Kaitlin brightened. "Yeah, and it's because of me they met. Mom made me do a team sport and Doug's my soccer coach. He's so cool he can even make *that* fun."

Pip hid a smile. Kaitlin was notoriously hard to motivate with sport.

"So, who's acting like your feelings don't matter?"

Kaitlin started gnawing at her chewed nails. "I wasn't meant to be listening."

"Is it your dad?"

The girl's eyes filled with tears. "I shouldn't have told Mom I wasn't enjoying my Sundays with him."

Pip removed Kaitlin's fingers from her mouth and held them gently. "She repeated it to your dad?"

"Yeah." Kaitlin gulped. "But that doesn't mean I don't want to see him, which is what he thinks now. It's just… awkward because we run out of things to talk about. He enjoys sports and I don't. I love fun parks, but he gets sick on the scary rides. We always eat somewhere expensive as a treat and I have to pretend to like the food. Sometimes we go to movies, but he always falls asleep. Mostly we go to the mall—he gives me some money and I spend it while he sits at Starbucks doing work."

Disapproval must have flickered across Pip's face because Kaitlin added loyally, "I mean, I tell him to. He always offers to shop with me, but I know he hates it and I don't want him to be bored. But now I've ruined everything because I heard him say to Mom…" Her voice trailed off, her hand tightened on Pip's.

"You can tell me, sweetie."

"He said maybe he should step aside for Doug," Kaitlin whispered, "since he makes me and Mom happier than Dad ever could."

With difficulty, Pip maintained her nonjudgmental expression. What a whiner Joe Fraser was.

"I see the problem," she said. "You feel like you have to choose between your dad and Doug."

Kaitlin nodded.

"When what you really want," continued Pip, "is to have them both."

"And to keep seeing Dad on weekends," Kaitlin said in a rush, "but…"

She looked pleadingly at Pip.

"But to have more fun doing it?"

She nodded again.

Pip thought hard. "Why don't I ask your dad to join us at camp next week?" The four-day adventure retreat was the only activity where dads out-volunteered moms, and places were so hotly contested, the school usually held a draw. But as camp organizer she could pull a few strings.

"He'll be working. He always is." The child's stoicism had a strained adult quality to it. "I mean, he can't even make concerts and sports days and stuff like that."

Pip experienced a strong urge to give Joe Fraser a swift kick in the derriere. "Let me handle your dad."

Kaitlin looked doubtful.

"Trust me," Pip assured her. "I'll have your father sorted out in two shakes of a lamb's tail." She used a colloquialism common in New Zealand to make Kaitlin laugh.

As they beamed at each other, a grim voice said, "I thought I was here to discuss my *daughter's* behavior."

She and Kaitlin jumped. Pip's immediate thought upon facing the door was *Who blocked the light?* Her second: *This guy isn't the whiner type.* With close-cropped black hair, a square jaw and crooked nose he looked like a linebacker for the San Francisco 49ers—despite the impeccably cut suit. Although his bearing and the laser focus of those deep-set navy eyes were more military.

And right now, decidedly hostile.

JOE REMEMBERED TEACHERS as nosy and meddlesome, and it appeared nothing had changed. He looked at his crestfallen daughter. "You okay?"

She gulped and nodded. His gaze swung back to Miss Browne, who'd stood up behind her desk and was assessing him with equal candor. She barely looked old enough to have graduated teachers college. Her short, blond hair and dewy-eyed prettiness made the confident assertion she'd just made to Kaitlin laughable. No one managed Joe Fraser.

Unsmiling, he held out a hand. "Miss Browne."

"Mr. Fraser." She had a surprisingly firm handshake for someone barely taller than Kaitlin. She smiled suddenly, as though he'd passed some kind of test. For a moment the surprise of that open, friendly smile nearly disarmed him. Then he frowned.

"I'd prefer to talk to the principal." He let his tone fill in the gaps. *Someone with authority.*

Miss Browne's eyes widened slightly, accentuating the ingénue effect. They were the color of the sky on a clear July day. "She's mollifying Sofia's parents right now, but of course, you're welcome to wait." Her accent suggested she was the Kiwi teacher Kaitlin raved about. "It could be some time."

Resigned, Joe sat down. "What happened?"

As Miss Browne outlined events, he watched Katie, who started to squirm. Didn't she know he was on her side? Only a few years ago she would have crawled into his lap for comfort. Now he couldn't even bring himself to put a supportive hand on her shoulder for fear of doing the wrong thing.

On the cusp of womanhood, his baby girl was guarded, sensitive and quick to tears. Joe felt like a testosterone-charged bull in a china shop. Her cheeks were still damp, and a stab of tenderness made him reach into his suit jacket for a handkerchief. His grandmother had raised him to carry one for emergencies. Tentatively he held it out.

Kaitlin shook her head and looked away. "I am *trying* not to be a crybaby," she muttered.

Wincing, he put it back in his pocket and met Miss Browne's luminous gaze. He interrupted her explanation. "So you're saying my daughter stood up for herself against a bully and *she's* the one being sent home? What kind of crackpot reaction is that?"

"Exchanging slaps isn't a solution to problems, Mr. Fraser," the teacher replied calmly, "and both girls are being sent home early to reflect on their behavior."

"Perhaps the school should be made to reflect on *its* behavior in allowing an aggression issue to get to the stage where the victim has to defend herself."

Miss Browne didn't even blink at the threat of litigation. Or else she didn't recognize his threat. Frustrated, Joe leaned forward and planted his forearms on her desk. "Do you even *have* a procedure for handling bullies?"

"Dad," said Kaitlin, squirming in her chair.

"It's okay, sweetie," her teacher said. "And yes, Mr. Fraser, I know *exactly* how to handle bullies." She leaned forward and planted her forearms on her desk until the two of them were eye to eye. "Zero tolerance."

CHAPTER TWO

SUPPRESSING AN involuntary smile, Joe sat back. Maybe the school could protect his child. "You mentioned other misdemeanors?"

Miss Browne turned to his daughter. "Kaitlin, would you mind waiting outside while your dad and I talk?" She sounded kind...an ally not an enemy.

Kaitlin glanced at him. "Do you have to tell him *everything?*"

"Yes. But don't worry, he'll be fine." Miss Browne looked back to him for confirmation. Heartsick that his daughter obviously saw him as *her* enemy, Joe could only manage a nod. For the hundredth time he wondered how they'd come to this. At the door, Kaitlin hesitated, then inadvertently twisted the knife. "I'm sorry you had to get involved, Dad."

"I'm not," he said, but she'd already gone.

Feeling exposed under Miss Browne's continued scrutiny, he got up and strode to the window. September was San Francisco's warmest month now that summer's blanketing fogs and biting winds had finally given way to blue skies and moderate temperatures.

But like the kids in the playground, Joe dressed in layers and wouldn't dream of abandoning his suit jacket.

Every local knew the weather could turn on a dime. "So what didn't my ex-wife tell me?"

"Kaitlin hasn't been doing homework. Her grades are suffering. She's inattentive in class, even miserable. And at home, too, according to Nadia."

Blindly, Joe watched three boys use their drink bottles in a water fight, laughing as they dodged arcs of water. He might be first call when the media needed an expert to comment on commercial real estate, but he was dyslexic when it came to emotional problems.

"And then there's the graffiti," she added.

He spun to face her. "My daughter wouldn't do that. Hell, she's so law abiding she makes me clip my seat belt before I start the engine."

"She admitted she carved her name in her desk and on a Monterey pine in the play—" Miss Browne broke off with an arrested expression. "Of course, it makes sense."

"What does?"

"Kaitlin Fraser…she's announcing who she wants to be."

"Excuse me?"

Her teacher looked at him with a glint in those Bambi eyes. "Let me be frank, Mr. Fraser. *You're* the problem with your daughter."

He folded his arms. "And what's your basis for that sweeping statement?'

"She told me."

Joe's heart sank. Rock bottom was deeper than he'd thought.

Only six months earlier, he'd discovered that the beloved grandmother who'd raised him had been the other woman in a love triangle going back sixty years. And that the married man involved, Robert Carson, had fathered two of his grandmother's three children, including Joe's father, Adam. Which meant his dad had gone from being the son of a war hero to the unacknowledged bastard of a philanderer.

Two strokes later for his father, Joe was still picking up the pieces. And now this.

"Kaitlin overheard you talking to Nadia about having less contact," Miss Browne said softly.

Joe's response was instinctive and heartfelt. "Shit." He realized he'd sworn out loud and apologized. "That's not how I wanted her to find out."

"I see." Miss Browne seemed to choose her next words very carefully. "I was hoping she'd misheard."

Formulating tactics, Joe barely registered her disapproval. "Thanks for telling me," he said abruptly, and strode toward the door. "I'll deal with it from here."

"Now you're doing it to me," she complained. "Mr. Fraser, walking away does not solve problems."

Stung, he released the door handle and turned around. "For your information, Miss Browne, I'm always the last man standing."

She raised her eyebrows. "Yet you've just admitted you intend to walk away from your daughter."

"Because it's too painful to lose her by degrees!" Damn, why had he let her provoke him into saying that? Exhausted, he passed a hand over his face. "Look, it's complicated. But believe me, my daughter's interests come first."

Head tilted, the teacher assessed him. "I believe that *you* believe that."

His patience snapped. "With all due respect, Miss Browne, what qualifies you to lecture me? Because it sure as hell isn't experience."

She stood up. "You mean apart from an ability to listen and keep an open mind?"

Was it his imagination or did everything she say contain a barb?

"I may look young," she continued, "but I'm twenty-six and I've been a teacher for five years. Prior to coming to the States on a teacher exchange program I completed extramural papers in counseling and family therapy."

As she talked, she put a hand under his elbow and steered him back into the room. He found himself distracted by her fragrance, subtly evocative of spring. "I've been counseled myself," she finished, "so I understand your trepidation."

Joe stopped dead. "*My* trepidation? And if you need counseling, then why are you even teaching?"

"All counselors are obliged to undergo personal therapy." With gentle pressure she propelled him forward. "You have to know your own shortcomings in order to deal effectively with *other* people's." Damn it, the woman was doing it again.

Joe saw a definite glint of amusement in her eyes. "Let me guess," he said sourly, "your shortcoming is charging in where you're not wanted or needed."

"No, I'm usually needed," she said cheerfully. "I'm told I suffer from a lack of diplomacy, Mr. Fraser. Something we have in common." She patted the seat of the chair and, reluctantly, Joe sat down.

He felt as if he was fighting with a rubber sword. Every time he thought he'd made a hit, it bounced back on him. But however guileless she acted, the woman had a dimple that gave her away when she was trying to hold back a smile. He narrowed his eyes. "You're the kind of person who'd try to pat a tiger through the zoo bars, aren't you?"

She grinned. "They're so cute." She walked back to her desk and sat down. The male part of him noted Miss Browne had great legs. "Now on the subject of feelings—"

"I'm not good at them," he interrupted.

"Nothing that a little practice can't fix, surely?"

He had been practicing; it hadn't been enough. He and Kaitlin could barely communicate. He'd put it down to the incompatibility of a ten-year-old girl and a twenty-nine-year-old workaholic. He'd always thought if he was patient, sooner or later their planets would realign. Then Doug had come into her life. With Doug, Kaitlin was animated, giggling…happy. And Joe needed his little girl to be happy.

"The old 'If at first you don't succeed' motto?" he said with acid politeness. "Right up there with 'Those who can't, teach.'"

She smiled. "You know what my definition of a cynic is, Mr. Fraser? An idealist who gave up."

"I've never been able to afford the luxury of idealism, Miss Browne. I've been supporting a family since I was nineteen. And before you accuse me of it, I didn't give up on my marriage. My wife did."

"I imagine it was because you didn't love her, but loved someone else," she said briskly. "Kaitlin mentioned it. And that you only got married because you had to. *And* that you're a workaholic. Honestly, it's not surprising that little girl wonders whether you really love her."

For a moment Joe could only stare at her. "Do you talk to all your kids' parents like this?"

Her eyes widened. "Of course not. Most of them don't need an intervention as badly as you do."

Joe felt as if Alice had pushed him down the rabbit hole. "You're one of the strangest people I've ever met. I'm amazed the school even lets you *near* children."

"I expect you're always apologizing for thoughtless remarks," she said kindly. "Fortunately, I can see past the rudeness. What I think, Mr. Fraser, is that you're having a crisis of parental confidence because you perceive Doug as more suitable for the job."

"He *is* more suitable for the job." Goaded by her frankness, Joe dropped his guard. "Look, it's selfish to insist on spending time with Kaitlin when she's so obviously unhappy about it. The best thing I can do for my daughter right now is to back off and let her settle in with her new family. We'll still see each other."

Miss Browne shook her head. "She wants to keep spending Sundays with you."

"She's a softhearted kid who feels sorry for me." Torturous to say, tortuous to believe, but Joe wouldn't flinch from the truth.

If only he'd worked less and eked out more time for his family. But his childhood had made financial security an imperative. His wife and child would have the best. And Nadia had never complained. Joe hadn't even known she'd been unhappy until she'd told him she wanted a divorce.

All he knew was that since then his clumsy attempts to forge an independent relationship with his daughter had been disastrous.

"Perhaps Kaitlin was following your lead," said Miss Browne. It took a moment to remember they'd been talking about his daughter feeling *sorry* for him!

"Are you accusing me of self-pity?"

"If the hair shirt fits…"

With an exclamation of disgust, Joe stood up.

"I can help you with your daughter, if you'll let me."

He hesitated, despising himself for his neediness. Lately he was a blind man stumbling through a minefield of emotions, his own and other people's. How low was rock bottom that he would even consider taking hope from this crazy woman?

But all the challenge had left her expression. Instead her smile was so understanding he had an urge to lay his head on her lap and weep for everything he'd lost. But Joe wasn't that kind of man.

"I always thought—" he paused to clear his throat "—that the reason I wasn't good as a father was because I never had a good role model. But Doug lost his dad young and he's a natural with my daughter." Joe hauled in a breath, then made the hardest, most painful concession of his life. "I think Katie's better off without me."

Miss Browne's gaze never wavered. "As Kaitlin's dad, you'll affect your daughter's life for good or bad, and right now she sees your wanting to leave as a sign you don't care."

"Of course I care," he said harshly.

"The situation's not irredeemable. I can help you," the woman repeated.

He remembered when he'd had that kind of unshakable confidence. Before his divorce, the return of his prodigal father and the shock of discovering his heritage was a lie. "What are you suggesting?"

"A four-day school camp, seventy-five tweens and—" the dimple flashed "—me."

TENSE AND UNHAPPY, Kaitlin sat in the passenger seat of her father's BMW, staring out the window at the passing San Francisco cityscape. Dad navigated midafternoon traffic with one hand while he told Melissa's mom on his cell phone that Kaitlin had got into a situation at school and wouldn't be staying at their house as arranged.

"I think it's better if she stays with me tonight, Yvonne." A cable car clanged into sight and he paused, waiting for it to pass.

Normally, Kaitlin would wave and smile at the tourists clinging to the end poles, their cameras swinging from their necks as the trolley lumbered up Nob Hill.

Miss Browne told her the States was the friendliest place she'd ever visited, but Kaitlin watched CNN every morning as she ate her granola, and she knew some countries thought the last president had been a bit pushy. She felt an obligation to help the new one.

Kaitlin was going to be a diplomat—after she'd been a missionary—because she was good at including kids that mostly got ignored, either because they were shy or geeky or odd. Knowing herself to be a borderline case, she took this responsibility very seriously. Miss Browne had once told her she had a kind heart.

Right now she didn't feel kind. She felt…scared and…bewildered…sulky and defiant. These feelings had been plaguing her for some weeks, and when she was in their grip she wasn't Kaitlin Fraser who did all her homework and was a nice, quiet girl. She was someone she didn't like very much.

The cable car rumbled into the distance; Dad resumed his conversation with Melissa's mom. "No, Yvonne, don't worry about returning her overnight bag. We'll drop home…by her house for clothes. Katie, do you have a key?"

She nodded, still staring out the window, because she could feel a prickle of tears behind her eyes. She hated reminders that he didn't live with them anymore even though it was two years since he and Mom had gotten divorced. But she didn't want Dad to see her being a baby. She'd caused enough trouble today.

Since they'd left the school grounds he'd already fielded four calls from clients and staff, and one of them had been mad that he wasn't available. She could tell because Dad always got cold and calm and reasonable when someone was yelling at him.

Like Mom.

Kaitlin couldn't remember them fighting when they were married—not like Melissa's parents, who seemed to yell at each other all the time. But Mom was getting mad at Dad a lot lately and telling him to be a better father. But then Mom was doing heaps of things differently since the divorce.

Like getting a career as a professional organizer and doing salsa classes with Doug. And being happier. Most of the time Kaitlin preferred how Mom was now, but sometimes—like today, when she really needed her—she wished she still had a stay-at-home parent.

"So your mother gets back from the Sacramento conference around three tomorrow," Dad said when he'd ended the call to Yvonne. He disapproved of Mom working, which was odd because he'd set up some maternity leave thing at work and said he'd bankroll Kaitlin's presidential campaign.

Kaitlin started to feel sick. Only last week she'd promised Mom she'd stop getting into trouble. But her anger had boiled over before she could control it.

"Do we have to call Mom right away? I mean, she has to know and everything, but couldn't we call her tonight instead of bothering her during the conference?"

"No," Dad said. "What if the school's already left a message or Yvonne calls her?" He held out his cell phone and, reluctantly, Kaitlin took it, knowing there was no budging him. Dad always made such a big thing of accepting responsibility for your actions.

When she was six she'd accidentally left the latch open on the neighbor's rabbit hutch and it escaped. Dad had docked her allowance until she'd paid for a new one. "It's not about blame," he'd said at the time. "It's about accountability."

He was kind of old-fashioned like that. Mom said it was because his grandma, Nana Jo, had brought him up after his mother died when he was four, and his dad—Grandpa Adam—had gone to make his fortune fishing crab in Alaska.

Kaitlin wasn't surprised *that* hadn't worked, which made Grandpa Adam laugh. "Honey, you're smarter at ten than I am at fifty-eight."

He hadn't been in her life long, not even a year, but Kaitlin loved him. For his wild stories and his willingness to break rules—like having ice cream for breakfast. But mostly she loved Grandpa Adam for never being in a hurry. For always having time to spend with her.

She and Mom often had him to stay, which was one of the things Mom and Dad fought about. Mom said Dad needed to "get over it," whatever "it" was.

Except now Grandpa Adam was in some special hospital and Dad said he was still too sick for her to visit. They were going to the hospital later this afternoon and she'd have to sit in the car.

"I just remembered, I need to finish Grandpa Adam's get well card," she said.

"Quit stalling and make that call."

Kaitlin dialed her mother's cell. To her intense relief it went straight to message. "Mom, it's Katie. I… It's all okay now but…" She took a deep breath, then expelled the words in a rush. "I-got-into-a-fight-at-school-nobody's-hurt-and-I'm-not-suspended-and-Dad-came-and-picked-me-up."

The worst over, she breathed again. "I'm gonna stay with him tonight and go back to school tomorrow. Melissa's mom knows and everything." She swallowed. Okay, maybe the worst wasn't over. "I'm really, *really* sorry, Mom."

"Tell her to call me later."

"Call Dad later."

They pulled up to the house, a canary-yellow mission-style duplex on the eastern side of Russian Hill. Dad had bought it three years ago when he'd made his biggest deal. He was a partner in some important commercial brokerage firm downtown, but all Kaitlin knew was that they gave lame family Christmas parties at Napa vine-yards and places that were boring for the kids.

"Got your key?" asked Dad. Kaitlin dug around in her schoolbag and produced it. "Let's go then." Inside the front door he stopped. "I'll wait in the hall, honey."

She knew it was because it wasn't his house anymore and he felt funny being there with Mom away, so Kaitlin didn't argue. Upstairs, she changed out of her uniform into a short-sleeved green sweater and jeans, and combed out her hair, trying not to cry, because if she started she'd never stop.

Her sneakers must have been quiet on the carpet because when she started down the stairs Dad didn't look up. He was staring into the living room where a bunch of photos sat over the fireplace. He used to be in all of them, but now he was only in one, holding Kaitlin as a baby. He looked so sad that she said, "I have them in my room…the others."

The family ones when they were all together.

But he only nodded and said briskly, "Ready to go?"

Rebuffed, Kaitlin continued down the stairs with her overnight bag and pink denim jacket.

"We're going to have to drop by a couple of sites before we go to the hospital," he said. "And afterward there's an investors meeting I can't get out of at the office." They got back into the car. "Negotiations are at a critical stage. I'm sorry, honey."

Gesturing to Dad's seat belt to remind him, she said in a small voice, "That's okay." She'd hoped things were going to be different after his talk with Miss Browne, but they weren't. He hadn't even asked for Kaitlin's version of the fight or why she'd done it or anything. At first she'd been glad, now she decided he didn't care.

"It's a working day, honey," Dad said gruffly, "and I have com—"

"Commitments. I know." She looked out the window, not seeing anything. There was a moment's silence before she heard the click of his seat belt, then he started the engine.

"My place is being remodeled so we'll be staying in a hotel on Geary."

Kaitlin felt a flicker of interest. "When it's finished will there be room for me?"

"Renovations are going to take a while." His voice sounded strained as he pulled into traffic.

He hadn't answered her question. Kaitlin leaned her head against the door and closed her eyes.

"Tired, baby?"

She didn't answer. Strong fingers brushed back her bangs.

"I thought maybe…" He cleared his throat. "I mean, how would you feel if I came to camp with you next week?"

Kaitlin's eyes snapped open; she bolted upright. "Promise?"

CHAPTER THREE

JOE SAT ON THE sage-green couch with his gaze firmly fixed on a landscape print, trying not to look at the bed.

It could have been a room in any good business hotel, right down to the big-screen TV, humming air-conditioning unit and token rubber plant to his left.

It even had the same impersonality, despite the brochure claim of "home away from home." Except this room was costing Joe thirty-five thousand dollars a month.

A groan emanated from the bed. Instinctively, he looked toward it, then quickly away. But the pale, naked form of his father had already imprinted on his brain, along with the straw-colored urine in the catheter's drainage bag as the nurse removed it.

Abruptly, Joe stood and walked to the picture window. Today the large pond was a glassy mirror reflecting its surroundings—overhanging willows, the two-story stroke rehab unit, a girl on a bench reading. Sensing his scrutiny, Kaitlin lifted her head and waved. Her smile still radiated excitement, and some of Joe's tension eased. He'd done the right thing in committing to go camping.

"I'm ready to move him now," said Nurse Elaine.

His father kept his eyes resolutely closed as, with the ease of practice, Joe helped her shift Adam's semiparalyzed body, then reposition the foam pad from midcalf to ankle and tent the bedsheet over the toes. Their patient grunted in protest.

"We don't want bedsores, do we?" Elaine chided him with the relentless cheerfulness of a professional caregiver.

Adam opened his eyes. As always, Joe experienced a jolt of shock to see so much life in them. So much life despite that ruined body. His father's once powerful chest heaved to expel the words, "Get...out." The left side of his mouth remained immobile.

Her plump face shiny from exertion, Elaine only laughed. "You're always grumpy after occupational therapy, so I won't take offense." Picking up the detritus of her patient's recent bed bath and change, she nodded pleasantly to Joe and departed, taking the faint smells of peppermint and human waste with her.

They were left with the receding sound of rubber heels squeaking on the polished floor, the very hospital trademark that Joe was paying a fortune to eliminate.

One side of his father's face twisted. "Hate...hospit..." He stopped, exhausted.

"I know, Adam," Joe answered briskly. "That's why you're in a private rehab center, remember?" Mom had been in and out of hospitals all Joe's early childhood. An aversion to them was the only bond father and son shared.

But no matter how little he felt for Adam, the guy was still his father, and Joe, at least, understood loyalty. It amazed him that they'd been brought up by the same woman, yet Adam hadn't picked up any of the values Josephine Fraser had drilled into her grandson. Though that implied *some* strength of character, Joe thought wryly.

Adam seemed to be dozing, and Joe glanced at his watch. Lifting his head, his gaze collided with his father's, and he felt his face flush. But his guilt quickly became annoyance. He was doing enough for this man. "I had a meeting with your case manager yesterday," he commented. "He's not happy with your attitude."

Adam shut his eyes again. Even bedridden, he found a way to run from his problems.

"He says you're not cooperating with your various therapists," Joe persisted.

One corner of Adam's mouth twisted. Another agonized chest movement. "No...use."

God, he'd always hated his father's defeatism. "The case manager says a key factor in improvement is the patient's determination."

Another was strong family support. Joe could still remember the horror on the faces of his new relatives, the Carsons, when their mother Sarah's will revealed how their dear old dad had not only fathered two bastards by another woman, but had secretly adopted one of them into his family, with the full knowledge of his wife. Aunt Jenny had been raised with Robert's legitimate son, Sam, in ignorance of her true parentage.

Given that Uncle Sam had provoked Adam's second stroke, and Joe and his father were emotionally estranged, Joe saw no point in mentioning "family support."

Which was why he'd concentrated his energies on the one variable he could influence—the quality of rehab.

Adam still hadn't responded, and Joe clenched his hands in frustration. For this apathy he'd sublet his apartment and moved into a hotel to minimize expenses? For this, he'd undertaken a crippling bank loan?

Even the unexpected legacy of one-third share in the Carson family home when it sold would disappear to a long-standing debt on some rusty old tub of a crab boat that had sunk thirteen years earlier—uninsured. Some

men, Joe thought sourly, would have learned the impor-
tance of insurance from that. Not Adam.

The silence lengthened, broken only by the hum of the
air conditioner and the faint sound of voices at Reception.

"He's depressed," the case manager had confided.
"Talk to him."

But what did you say to a near stranger?

Where the hell were you when I was growing up?

Why didn't you send money to Nana Jo more often?

Did you ever give a damn about anybody but yourself?

All the old questions smoldered, ready to ignite.
With an effort, Joe unclenched his fists. Why give
Adam power to hurt him now? Even anger was a concession that the past mattered. And it didn't. He no
longer loved his father, but as he looked at the
immobile body under the pale blue sheet, he could
muster pity.

Joe sighed. "Listen, I've got to go early today." Kaitlin
was waiting. "I'll see you tomorrow." At the door he
lifted his hand in a perfunctory wave, then froze.

Tears seeped out from under Adam's lids. For a moment, Joe stood helplessly, then pulled a handkerchief out
of his pocket. Returning to the bed, he wiped them away
with a rough gentleness. "It's okay, Adam. The antide-
pressants will work soon."

"Hate…drugs."

"Yeah."

"Want…die."

Panic gripped him, then anger. Joe said it before he
could stop himself. "This time there's no easy way
out."

Adam's eyes opened. His chest heaved. "Know…
nothing…you!"

"I know I'm almost bankrupting myself trying to return you to some sort of independence, you ungrateful son of a bitch." Joe was suddenly shaking with rage.

His father blinked, then one corner of his mouth lifted. He expelled a choking bark that could have been a laugh. "Stop!"

"No!"

His father's mouth set in a straight line. So did Joe's.

For a moment the two men glared at each other, then Adam closed his eyes. Joe found a chair before his legs collapsed.

Okay, maybe he did care. Or was this revenge? *You wouldn't hang around then, but I'll damn well make you hang around now?* Neither of those. Or maybe both. And his misguided daughter loved the old bastard. He was doing this for Kaitlin. And for his late grandmother.

"I shouldn't have yelled like that. I'm sorry." *Nothing.* Joe tried again. "I'm under a lot of pressure, but that's no excuse."

Still nothing. He needed to go, but Joe couldn't leave it like this.

Talk to him, the doctor had said.

"I spoke to Daniel this morning." Twenty years younger than his half brother, Adam, Daniel Kane was the offspring of Josephine Fraser's brief second marriage and, as it turned out, her only legitimate child. "One of his financiers pulled out of the El Granada housing project, so he's covering the shortfall with his own money."

Which was unfortunate, as his young uncle was the only person Joe would have asked for financial help. "He sends his regards."

Adam didn't respond; there was no love lost between the two men.

When four-year-old Joe had been dumped with his grandmother, Daniel had been thirteen. He'd seen Joe's pain and shared the economic hardship when Adam's promised checks failed to arrive. Yet he'd never complained, never once made Joe feel unwanted. Men now, they were closer than brothers, their loyalty to each other no less fierce for being unspoken.

But then a lot went unspoken in the Fraser family, including how they felt about their late mother and grandmother's exposure as a married man's mistress.

"I can't stay long, because Kaitlin's waiting outside," Joe admitted. "She got into some trouble at school and I had to pick her up. Nothing serious."

Adam opened his eyes. "See Kait…"

Not like this. Joe couldn't subject his baby girl to this. All her life he'd protected her from gritty reality. He remained bitter that Nadia had gone against his wishes and let their daughter spend time with the old scoundrel. "Kaitlin wants to see you, but I don't think she should right now. Let's get you stabilized first."

"Black…mail."

It had never crossed his mind; now Joe steeled himself to be cruel to be kind. "It's up to you, Adam. Make some improvement and I'll bring her in, but she's not seeing you like this."

"What…if…can't?"

But he couldn't allow either of them to think like that.

"Studies show that starting rehabilitation early correlates with a better outcome," he said, and saw a flicker of interest in his father's eyes.

Joe fished for other optimistic statistics from among

the mass of reading he'd done on strokes, bypassing the two keeping him awake at night.

Stroke survivors who don't undergo rehabilitation are more likely to be institutionalized.

The longer there's no movement, the poorer the prognosis.

"The majority of those affected by hemiparesis—one-sided paralysis—make a full recovery." It was actually fifty percent, but he wasn't going to say that to a man who always saw a glass as half-empty.

The speech therapist came in, a young redhead. Joe remembered something else. "A significant number of those suffering aphasia recover completely." The speech therapist opened her mouth to say it was only eighteen percent, glanced at Adam and shut it.

"And Frasers aren't quitters. Think of Cousin Joe."

It was another of his grandmother's sayings. "No matter what happens to us, we brush ourselves off and get up again," she'd say. "Think of Cousin Joe."

Except for the little matter of the boxer's name being spelled Frazier and Smokin' Joe being black. A reference to Cousin Joe in the bad times always elicited a smile.

"Bull…shit." But the corner of Adam's mouth twitched.

"That's better." Joe patted his father's arm, surprising them both, then covered his confusion by digging in his jacket pocket for Kaitlin's homemade greeting card.

"Your granddaughter sends her love," he said gruffly, placing it on the side table where Adam could see it. He hadn't intended giving it to him because it was a picture of a gamboling bear with the message "You'll soon be up and dancing."

Adam stared at it and Joe knew he'd made a mistake. "I'm sorry, it's inappropriate."

He was reaching for the card when Adam grunted. "I...try."

Joe nodded in acknowledgment, his relief too great to articulate. Finally, the universe was giving him a break.

"GOD KNOWS THE OFFICE complex is cheap, Joe, but I'm wondering if it'll get cheaper."

Vaughan Martin was a slow-speaking, fast-thinking septuagenarian who'd made his fortune in winemaking and, upon his retirement, reinvested in office space. "I want a better return on my life's work than the bank can give me," he'd said five years earlier when he'd engaged Fraser & Dunn's services.

Sitting behind his desk, Joe tried to hide his disquiet.

"You're taking me by surprise here, Vaughan. You dismissed that recommendation a couple of weeks ago and told me you were committed to signing the contract today. In fact, I've got it here now." He held up the document.

Vaughan shifted uncomfortably in his leather chair, giving Joe a view of Kaitlin through the glass wall separating his office from his secretary's. His daughter was using a corner of Thea's desk to finish another get well card for Adam. Joe glimpsed a misshapen kangaroo bumping his head on a speech bubble. That likely read: "You'll soon have a spring in your step!"

Head bent over her colored pencils, Kaitlin couldn't stop smiling.

Joe refocused on Vaughan's weather-beaten face. *Don't do this to me,* he pleaded silently. A delay in this major deal would make it impossible to take four days off from work to attend camp. Forget camp, he wouldn't see Kaitlin for weeks because he'd be slaving seven days to meet his financial commitments. Adam's open-ended rehab care, alimony and child support, his own living expenses. This deal would have carried him for six months. "Why second thoughts now?"

Vaughan finally got his bulk comfortable in the chair. "My wife reminded me that you're the expert," he admitted sheepishly.

"You could lose the property by waiting, Vaughan," Joe warned. "Wasn't that why you insisted we close the deal?"

The old man shrugged. "Easy come, easy go."

Not for me, Joe wanted to yell. *Why the hell didn't you tell me you had doubts before I made a promise to my daughter? Factored the commission into my budget?* With an immense effort he kept his face impassive, his tone neutral. "What do you want to do?"

"Whatever you think best." Vaughan gestured to the numerous framed awards on Joe's wall. *Top Producer* eight years running. *Number-One Commercial Real Estate Branch, San Francisco* six years running. "Like I said, you're the expert."

Behind Vaughan's back, Kaitlin dug in her schoolbag, then held up a brochure. *Camp Redwood. Where Nature meets Nurture.*

Joe shoved the contract across the desk. "Sign." Vaughan patted his breast pocket for a pen. "Here." He slid over his Montblanc.

The older man signed with a flourish, then returned the pen and contract. "I trust your judgment, Joe. You've never steered me wrong."

Joe stared at the densely typed document and the zeros standing out like salvation. *Deal honestly with people and people will deal honestly with you.* Except his grandmother's code of honor had been discredited by her disreputable past, he thought bitterly.

For another few seconds he wrestled with his conscience. Then, grasping the corners of the contract, Joe ripped it in half and dropped the remains in the trash. "We'll sit out another couple of months and see what interest rates do."

Nana Jo hadn't lived up to her values, but he could.

"Sure, Joe. Say, I've got some early bottles of this year's zinfandel from my old vineyard. Drop by for a tasting. I'd like your opinion." Oblivious of his broker's sacrifice, Vaughan stood up to leave.

Joe forced a smile. "I'll do that."

Picking up his coat, the older man caught sight of Kaitlin. "That your little girl? She's a real cutie."

A cutie about to get her heart broken unless Joe came up with a plan B. As Vaughan left his office, Joe even contemplated telling his ex-wife his dilemma. He'd insisted on giving her nearly everything after the divorce. But keeping his difficulties from Nadia was so engrained he instantly dismissed the thought. Daniel had no spare cash; the only person who did was Uncle Sam Carson, and Joe would crawl over broken glass before giving that SOB the pleasure of turning him down.

He was on his own.

Kaitlin flew into his office the moment the elevator doors closed on Vaughan. "Do you have a sleeping bag, Dad? Because I have a spare as long as you don't mind pink…. Look, I'll write you a list and you tell me what you have. I'll organize the rest."

His daughter plunked herself on his lap and started to write, brow furrowed in concentration. She was left-handed, like him…. His throat was tight, Joe couldn't trust himself to speak, to confess, "Baby, I can't come."

Her teacher had made it plain that this was his chance

to make things right with his daughter. Oddly, he wished Miss Browne was here to advise him.

Yeah, you just want another look at those legs.

He'd told her that his daughter might be better off without him, but on the verge of losing Kaitlin, Joe knew he could never give her up. Which meant he couldn't quit.

Something might happen between now and camp—an idea, a deal, a lottery win. A miracle. *Think of Cousin Joe,* he told himself, though this time the corny family joke couldn't raise a smile. Still, he wouldn't cancel until he absolutely had to.

CHAPTER FOUR

PIP'S FELLOW TEACHER Anita tapped her on the shoulder as she mustered her high-spirited class. "Joe Fraser called the school office to say he's been delayed. He'll meet us there."

Across the heads of chattering ten-year-olds, Pip met Nadia Fraser's I-told-you-so glance. "Not to worry," Pip said briskly, then clapped her hands. "Okay, kids, everyone on the bus, it's time to roll. Chop-chop, Kaitlin." The girl stood frozen in the midst of seething children. "We want to beat your dad there, don't we?"

Kaitlin's expression was tragic. "You think he's even coming?"

"Sure, he is. Now give your mom a hug goodbye."

She watched Nadia enfold her daughter in a fierce embrace and whisper something in her ear. Then Pip was caught up in the flurry of trying to get seventy-five kids and their luggage on two coaches.

Fortunately, she had the help of several other dads, none of whom had trouble making the rendezvous.

The last to embark, she hesitated, then forced herself to approach Kaitlin's mother. "I still think he'll show, but if he doesn't I accept full responsibility."

"Good," said Nadia tightly, "because I'll be *holding* you fully responsible." As Pip turned toward the bus steps, Nadia caught her by the sleeve. "Look after her, won't you?" The plea shook Pip's confidence. She could take the woman's anger better.

"Don't worry," she said, to reassure them both. "It'll be fine."

Standing at the front of the second bus as the vehicle lumbered north, Pip caught one last view of Nadia's anxious face. The same expression she'd worn a week earlier when she'd asked Pip to drop Joe from the trip.

"I don't want either of us having to deal with the aftermath when Joe cancels at the last minute," Nadia had told her.

"But he knows how important it is to Kaitlin."

"Oh, he'll be sorry," said Nadia, "but he'll do it all the same. Success is a compulsion with Joe, and there's always some million-dollar deal hanging on a knife's edge. He's only ever managed to get to a couple of events important to Kaitlin. In the end I stopped asking him."

Pip had immediately picked up her parents list and dialed Joe's cell phone. "Mr. Fraser, it's Philippa Browne, Kaitlin's—"

"I know who you are, Miss Browne."

"I'm confirming parent helpers." She'd looked at Nadia. "If for any reason—"

"Nadia's been talking to you, hasn't she?"

"I'm ringing all the parents," Pip had said calmly.

"I'm committed."

The coach hit a pothole, jolting her back to the present. Taking her seat across from the driver, Pip turned to the kids. "Who wants a song?"

"Yeahhhh!"

Leading the singing should have taken her mind off Joe Fraser, but after three rousing choruses the only thing coming round the mountain was a dark cloud of foreboding. She broke off midverse. "Anita, can you take over?"

Pip staggered down the aisle of the moving bus, nodding and smiling to kids and dads. Kaitlin sat apart from her friends. "Are you feeling bus-sick, sweetie? I have some pills."

"Dad's not coming," Kaitlin said in a small voice. "Mom said not to get my hopes up."

Pip felt a flash of anger at Nadia. "Of course he's coming." She took the empty seat beside the girl. "In fact, I reconfirmed with your father last night."

Prompted by a lingering doubt, she'd rung him. He'd spoken first, obviously recognizing her number from caller ID.

"I said I'll *be* there, Miss Browne."

Pip had feigned surprise. "Is that you, Mr. Fraser? I must have dialed your number by mistake."

"Are you standing in front of anything, Miss Browne?"

"I'm writing equations on the blackboard."

"Step back, Pinocchio, before your nose hits it."

She'd chuckled. "Looking forward to seeing you tomorrow, Mr. Fraser."

"I repeat. Step back."

Pip had hung up, reflecting how odd it was that this grim man could make her smile so easily.

But she couldn't smile now, seeing Kaitlin's unhappiness. Why was he putting his daughter through this uncertainty? "Let's give him a quick call," she suggested, pulling her cell phone out of her hoodie and punching in his number. It went straight to Message.

She didn't leave one. *If you don't show, I'll hunt you down and kill you* wouldn't reassure his daughter. Besides, Pip didn't want the trail to lead back to her that easily. "No answer," she said lightly. "He's probably trying to concentrate on driving."

She had to believe he'd keep his word. But as she returned to her own seat, she reminded herself that he'd disappointed his ex-wife and his daughter before. Was Pip being naive? Stupid?

She tried to recall what it was about the man that made her trust him instinctively, and decided it was his aura of integrity. At least she hoped it was that, and not the wide shoulders and great butt.

By the time the bus reached its destination in a forested canyon in western Sonoma two hours later, she had a headache and was ready to plunge a stake into his black heart.

The vehicle eased to a halt in the parking lot of the recreation center, and the doors opened with a whoosh. And there stood Joe Fraser. Ruggedly handsome in faded jeans and denim jacket, with an army-style backpack slung over one broad shoulder, he raised an eyebrow. "What took you so long?"

Her relief was so great, Pip smiled at him, when she should have got mad because he'd caused her so much needless anxiety. Instantly, his expression softened. She became aware of a slight heady sensation—no doubt caused by the fresh, redwood-scented air.

Kaitlin squealed and hurled herself down the aisle and into his arms. The other kids bounced out of the bus like fleas off a wet dog, and the next fifteen minutes were a madhouse of organized chaos as the bus was unloaded and cabins allocated. Finally, the camp director made his welcome speech.

Pip took the opportunity to draw Joe aside on the pretext of showing him where to put his gear. The other dads had already unpacked, but Kaitlin had been dragging Joe around with her since their arrival, too thrilled to let him out of her sight.

"You have no idea how glad I am to see you," Pip said when they were out of earshot of the group. On closer inspection, he looked exhausted. "Did you have to sell your soul to get here?"

He looked at her sharply. "Something like that. I have to say I'm surprised by your enthusiasm."

"Are you kidding? I could kiss you." Realizing how fervent that sounded she added hastily, "This means so much to Kaitlin."

A shadow passed over his face, so quickly Pip might have imagined it if she hadn't seen it before, at their school interview. He might look and act the tough guy, but where his daughter was concerned he was a marshmallow.

They'd reached the boys' cabin, a barn-size log edifice more Disney than Daniel Boone. "You'll be fine," she reassured him. "Remember, I'm here to help."

"*That's* the part I'm afraid of."

"I'll be gentle."

"Uh-huh." His tone was skeptical. "Kaitlin said you used to beat up your older brothers."

Pip laughed. "Let me guess… 'Know thine enemy'?"

"I figured I needed any ammunition I could get, but don't worry…" A glint lit his dark blue eyes. For the first time since they'd met, he smiled. "*I'll* be gentle."

Something caught in her throat. His smile wasn't light-hearted—never that from this harsh man—but it warmed her. She even, Pip realized with dismay, felt hot. "When you've dropped your gear, Mr. Fraser, come back to the clearing and I'll introduce you to everyone."

"Call me Joe."

"Our next activity is a nature hike through the red-woods, so wear good walking shoes." With a professional nod, she turned away.

"And I guess I'll call you sir," he said behind her and Pip's, lips curved in an involuntary smile.

Good God, she couldn't find Joe Fraser attractive. He was way too much hard work.

JOE WATCHED MISS BROWNE walk away, her back as erect as a drill sergeant's and her hips rotating with a swing that was entirely feminine.

He hadn't expected to like her.

Work had swallowed his life since the divorce, but this woman captured his attention. Bossy, compassion-ate, aggravating and astute… He had to admit that even with sweatpants hiding those great legs, Philippa Browne was sexy.

Joe believed in forewarned being forearmed, but his information had been filtered through the lens of an adoring ten-year-old.

The only intriguing snippet in the red's-her-favorite-color, Mulan's-her-favorite-princess trivia was that Miss Browne had been a tomboy because it was the only way her three older brothers would let her play with them.

"And even then," Kaitlin had confided earnestly, "she could never, ever cry and she always had to be the person rescued when she wanted to be the person rescuing…un-less they needed an alien to kill."

It explained a lot.

Walking into the cabin to dump his stuff, Joe winced. The dads had a room adjacent to the kids' area, but the flimsy curtain wouldn't keep out the noise of two dozen overexcited insomniacs. He unpacked Kaitlin's pink sleeping bag, eyed the thin pillow supplied and gave up any hope of catching up on missed sleep.

As he was changing his shoes for hiking boots, his cell phone rang. Hooking it out of his back pocket, Joe frowned as he recognized his cousin's number.

"Belle? Something happen?" She and her mom, Emily, were responsible for Adam in Joe's absence. It was the first big favor he'd asked of his new Carson relatives, and he still felt uncomfortable about it.

But Aunt Emily had made herself quietly indispensable through Adam's first stroke, and Belle...well...she'd bulldozed her way into his life after Adam's second stroke using loving kindness. Fresh flowers in Adam's hospital room, pizza delivered to Joe's apartment from her work, Diamante Pizza. Like Belle knew he was too damn tired to think about cooking. And of course they shared the bond of having difficult fathers.

"Everything's fine, at least with your dad," she assured him. "But Sue just visited with her parents." Joe winced at the mention of his other cousin. He already knew that he was in trouble.

He hedged anyway. "What are the Bookmans doing back in town?" Jenny Bookman was his father's new sister—and Sue's mother. She and her husband, Luke, lived in Florida.

"Aunt Jenny's been worrying about Adam and decided she wanted to...well...I'll let her tell you. The thing is, Sue's a teeny bit annoyed that you didn't enlist her help as well as ours." Belle hesitated. "Actually, seriously pissed would be more accurate."

Joe could tell his cousin was dying to know why he *hadn't* asked Sue. Fortunately, their relationship was too new, their rapport too recent for Belle to pry. He had a feeling the barriers wouldn't last long. Jamming the phone between chin and shoulder, he finished tying his bootlaces and stood, ready to rejoin the group.

"I'll give Sue a call. And if I haven't said thanks before—"

"You have," Belle interrupted, "a thousand times. Mom and I are happy to help. We're family now, right?"

Joe changed the subject. "So how's your mom doing?" Emily had left Sam Carson after Adam's second stroke, a stroke Joe privately held his uncle accountable for. Adam had been with Sam when he'd had the attack, though neither man would say what had passed between them.

But Sam's track record suggested culpability. He'd gone a little crazy when the family scandal broke, refusing to acknowledge the Frasers, and insisting his father left him the heirloom diamond necklace bequeathed to Jenny by her adoptive mother, Sarah Carson.

In the intervening months Sam had fallen out with everybody, and caused such uproar at the hospital when he caught Emily and Belle supporting the "enemy," that his long-suffering wife had finally left him.

"Oh, Mom's taken out a new lease on life," said Belle. "It's Dad I'm worried—" She broke off with a self-conscious laugh. "I guess you don't want to hear about my father."

He didn't, but Joe cared about Belle. "It can't be any fun being the go-between for your parents."

"Now that I've got Matt adding more buff to the buffer zone, I'm in a remarkably happy place." Belle had recently become engaged to a guy who gave her the unconditional love her father seemed incapable of.

Kaitlin burst into the cabin, braids flying. "Dad, we're

all waiting for you. Hurry!" Without waiting for a reply, she rushed out.

"I'm glad, Belle." Leisurely, Joe followed in his daughter's wake. "Listen, I've gotta go." In the clearing outside the canteen, Miss Browne, barely a head higher than the tallest of her charges, mustered her class with a piercing whistle. Joe grinned. "I hear the call of the wild."

"I'll give Uncle Adam your love."

His grin faded. "Regards is fine."

"You know, cuz, you're damn lucky I'm too tied up with Mom and Dad to interfere. But I do expect to see more of Kaitlin after camp."

The barriers hadn't lasted long. Joe sighed. "Deal."

"And call Sue."

"I will." Later. Because catching sight of him, Miss Browne gave the imperious John Wayne arm sweep that indicated her wagons were ready to roll out.

One unsettling, opinionated woman at a time.

CHAPTER FIVE

TWO HOURS INTO the slow hike from hell, Joe signaled a reluctant halt to the towheaded tomboy forging ahead. "Grace, wait here while I round up the stragglers."

The little girl gave an anguished groan. "Aww, what? Not again!"

"Tell me about it," he muttered, turning back along the shady trail winding through the woods. He knew nothing about ten-year-old girls, and yet he was in charge of a gaggle of them, because the lovely Miss Browne had assigned him Kaitlin's team.

At the time he'd been grateful.

The trail followed Prospector Creek, a benign trickle after an Indian summer, with its water stained amber and choked in places with leaves. Ferns and mosses thrived in the shade of the towering redwoods. The camp was situated on the edge of two hundred acres of forest, an ecowonderland. Grimly, Joe bent to pick up the discarded wrapping of a Twinkie bar. His prey was close.

Freckle-faced Britney came into sight first. She was taking a photo of Amanda, who was balanced one-legged on a stump with arms outstretched, her smile close-mouthed to hide her braces.

"Who dropped this?" Joe demanded.

Britney swung the camera around and took a picture

of his scowling face. "It must have fallen out of my back pocket."

He tossed it to her. "Plenty of time for photos after we win the orienteering challenge. Now check your compass."

Britney patted the pockets of her shorts. "Uh-oh."

Joe stared at her. To think he was selling the last thing he owned in order to be here. Because despite his best efforts, he'd been forced to make his own miracle.

Only through ruthless self-control was he able to restrain his temper and focus on the immediate task, but it was still five minutes before they found the lost compass on a log.

With short, jerky movements, Joe double-knotted the cord around Britney's wrist. "Okay, are we still heading west?"

"Which way is west again?"

He closed his eyes briefly, then repeated the information. "So, how many feet west have we come along this trail?"

Amanda and Britney exchanged sheepish looks.

"Um, we kinda forgot when we stopped for the photo," Amanda said.

Joe gave up. "Follow the creek until you catch up to Grace, and start looking for a tall red fir with lichen growing on its north side. The next clue is at the base."

Amanda tapped her braces thoughtfully. "What's north again?"

Through gritted teeth he said, "Look at your compass."

"Oh, yeah." They giggled.

He was getting to hate that sound. "Have you seen Kaitlin and Melissa?"

Almost before he'd finished the sentence he heard Melissa's panicked, "Wwwwait for us!"

The two girls looked at each other and got moving. Joe didn't blame them.

"They're leaving us behind!" Melissa wailed again.

If it weren't for Kaitlin, Joe would have been seriously tempted to do so. His daughter's infuriating best friend outwhined the mosquitoes, and needed her homeopathic Rescue Remedy drops every five minutes. "Mom says I live on my nerves," she'd confided, before cannibalizing his.

So far, he'd had to lift Melissa over a log that might contain spiders, hold her hand while she skirted a slippery mud puddle that might dirty her pretty, spangled sneakers, and talk her down from the hysterical conviction that she'd heard a wild animal approaching.

Like one would come near her....

And the hell of it was that Kaitlin adored her, hanging back to offer encouragement, while Joe fought the growing impulse to strangle Melissa with the cord of her American Girl–branded hoodie.

The two girls came into sight. Seeing him, Melissa immediately grimaced and sat on the ground, cradling one plump, bare foot. Her toenails were painted a sparkly pink. It figured.

Kaitlin looked up anxiously at Joe's approach. "Melissa's got a blister."

"Yeah, well, I heard Miss Browne tell her to change her shoes, so I guess it's her own fault." Too late, he heard the snarl in his voice—and Melissa didn't respond well to snarling.

The watering pot immediately started to cry. "But I didn't think it would be so faaar."

"Daaad, don't snap at Melissa. She's very sensitive."

"I wasn't snapping, I was…" Joe met his daughter's

stormy eyes. "Look, I'm sorry, okay?" Pulling the first-aid kit out of his day pack, Joe crouched down and checked the blister. As he'd expected, teeny-tiny.

As he applied a Band-Aid, Melissa stopped crying and sucked in her breath. Anyone would think he was pouring on battery acid. "All better." He dropped the damp little foot. "Now put your shoes back on and let's get going."

Melissa said faintly, "I don't think I can walk any farther."

Joe sat back on his haunches and stared at her. "You're kidding me." Her lower lip started to quiver, and reining in his irritation, he adopted a cajoling tone. "You don't want to let your teammates down, do you? Remember, there's points awarded for every activity." This would shock her into action. "We'll come last."

"Oh, that's okay." Melissa relaxed and repositioned the butterfly clip in her long, blond hair. "Any team with me on it comes last. Everyone's used to it." She caught his eye and her lower lip started to tremble again. "What?"

"Dad!" Kaitlin tugged on his arm. "Stop staring at Melissa like that, you're making her nervous. And winning's not everything."

Incredulous, Joe stared at his daughter. Even Kaitlin was spouting this heresy?

He'd always been driven to win. A job, a deal, a better life. Using Daniel as his role model, Joe had been the youngest kid on his block with a paper route, the youngest player on the high school football team. He'd pushed himself mercilessly in training, knowing the only way into university was through a scholarship.

When his dream of studying viticulture imploded with Nadia's pregnancy, he'd simply changed focus, working multiple jobs to support his new family.

"You mean you're not even going to try?" he demanded.

Melissa started to blubber again.

"Daaad!" Kaitlin put her arm around her friend's shoulders and glared at him, but there were tears in her eyes, too. "You're ruining *everything*."

Joe took a deep, deep breath and let winning—today—go. What the hell, there was no way they'd catch up now, anyway. "I'll try harder," he promised Kaitlin. "Melissa, how about I carry your day pack?" Through her snuffles, she nodded. "Okay then, put on your sneakers…good girl. We'll take our time and catch up to the others."

"Thanks, Dad," Kaitlin whispered.

He took Melissa's backpack, which was surprisingly heavy. "What have you got in here?"

"My diary, some candy, a camera, a book in case we stop, my iPod, a change of clothes if I get dirty—"

"Never mind." Stony-faced, Joe shouldered the bag.

"Wait," squealed Melissa. "I need something."

Kaitlin looked anxious. "Your Rescue Remedy?"

"No, more important than that."

Joe shifted from foot to foot while the girl fumbled through the bag on his shoulder. "Let's catch up to the others first." Assuming they'd waited. He managed a team of fifteen people at the office and he couldn't keep five tweens together?

"No, it's very important." She flicked back her hair. "I need my bag on the ground."

Reluctantly, Joe relinquished it, watched while she laid out all the contents. "It had better be an asthma inhaler."

"Da-ad!"

Melissa pulled something out and waved it triumphantly. "We can go now, I've found Sanderella."

For a moment Joe stared at the stuffed toy—a white Scottish terrier with a jeweled collar—then lost his temper.

"MR. FRASER SENT ME ahead to tell you we're okay," Grace said behind Pip. "Melissa ruined *everything*," she added bitterly.

Oh, dear.

Pip put down the highlighter she was using to write team scores on the notice board outside the main camp office. A leaf was tangled in Grace's white-blond hair and Pip removed it. "Tell me."

"First, I was the *only* one who took it seriously. Second, Melissa got a blister and decided she was *crippled*. And when Mr. Fraser got mad at her, she got all hysterical and decided she couldn't even *walk* anymore." Grace was becoming more and more agitated, so Pip gave her the leaf to shred. "Then Amanda and Britney had a fight over who lost the compass, so *they're* not talking, and Kaitlin's not speaking to her dad because *he* yelled at Melissa and can you get rid of Melissa? Please, Miss Browne?"

"Oh, dear." Pip said it aloud this time.

Beyond Grace, the others emerged from the woods. The Inseparables, as Pip called Britney and Amanda, were using Kaitlin as a human shield while Joe trailed behind, piggybacking Melissa.

If the girls reminded her of Grumpy after a hard day at the coal mine, then Joe was channeling Thor, the god of thunder. He would have looked intimidating if Sanderella hadn't been squished against his neck under Melissa's stranglehold. Catching sight of Pip, she freed an arm and waved as graciously as a homecoming queen.

Though she knew she shouldn't, Pip smiled.

Joe's expression grew even grimmer.

"I was about to send out a search party," she called, only half-joking. The other groups were already showering and getting ready for dinner. "So what happened?"

Britney and Amanda put a spurt on, each trying to reach her first.

"Amanda blamed me for losing the compass."

"You had it last."

"No, I didn't."

"Did." In her indignation, Amanda forgot to hide her braces.

"Well, if I did it was 'cause Mr. Fraser told us to go faster," said Britney. Her freckles were indistinguishable in her dirty face. "He's no fun." Out of the corner of her eye, Pip saw Kaitlin wince as she joined them.

"Give him a chance," Pip said, but mentally she was reviewing her options. Maybe Joe would be better overseeing a boys team.

"I don't like him," complained Amanda. "Can I move to another group?"

"But you can't go to a team without me," protested Britney, obviously forgetting they hated each other. "Miss Browne, I want to move, too."

"Go get showered and changed," Pip instructed. "We'll talk about this later." Nothing was going to get resolved when everyone was tired and hungry.

Kaitlin lingered behind. "Are you mad at Dad?"

"No, it's probably my fault for not thinking about this more."

"You know," said Joe, coming up behind her, "the last straw, Miss Browne, would be for you to start making excuses for me."

"Did Grace tell you I was injured, Miss Browne?" Melissa inquired eagerly, sliding off Joe's back.

Pip put her hands on her hips. "Where are the trainers I asked you to wear?"

"I didn't want…I mean, I didn't know these sneakers would give me a blister." Big fat tears started rolling down her round cheeks.

Pip was unmoved. "I know your tricks, remember?" Immediately Melissa looked sheepish. "Next time you do what you're told or stay behind. Now apologize to Mr. Fraser."

The girl bowed her head. "Sorry, Mr. Fraser."

"Are you telling me you *faked* all those tears?" Joe rasped. He smelled of fresh sweat and Melissa's novelty raspberry perfume, and there were partial footprints of dried mud on the pockets of his jeans. Pip resisted the impulse to brush his rear. Better not to draw attention to the dirt.

Mistaking Joe's inflecion as admiration, Melissa brightened. "Yeah, I just think of something sad and—"

"Go get cleaned up with the others," Pip interrupted, watching Joe. Following Pip's gaze, Melissa realized her error and left at a fast trot, unconsciously adding insult to injury.

Kaitlin ran to catch up to her. "That's a mean, mean thing to do. I carried your day pack and everything."

Both adults waited until the girls disappeared from sight and the sound of childish arguing faded. "Maybe this *is* your fault," Joe stated. "Why didn't you tell me?"

"I thought she'd behave with someone she didn't know," admitted Pip. "She must feel comfortable with you."

"Is that supposed to make me feel better?"

"It was a big task giving you girls," she soothed. "I've got boys. How about we swap?"

He glanced at the chart with the team placements and his eyes narrowed. "You know, I'm kinda tired of being your pity case, Miss Browne."

"It's not pity, it's sympathy. There's a difference."

"If I change teams I won't be with Kaitlin, though, will I?"

"No, but on the upside you won't be with Melissa."

Joe's jaw set as he went through an internal struggle, then he sighed. "I'll stay where I am."

There was no easy way of doing this. "Mr. Fraser, let me be blunt."

"You mean you have another style of communication?"

Pip ignored that. "Amanda and Britney aren't sure they like you."

"Really? I'm damn sure I don't like them."

She was startled into a laugh, and quickly smothered it. "I can't let you lead a team you can't manage."

"I was on a learning curve today, but I'm a quick study. Give me one more group activity. If the girls want to change teams after that, I'll swap."

"Except your next group activity is doing the dishes," she said ruefully. "I'm afraid the last ones home get a penalty."

"There you go feeling sorry for me again. Did I suggest that was a problem?"

"No, but—"

He gestured to the chart. "Your team's at the top and yet you're prepared to take on my losers."

"They're not losers. All they need is the right…" Realizing she was on the verge of being undiplomatic, Pip changed tack. "I am quite good at this, you know."

He finished her original sentence. "The right leader? Okay, Miss Browne, I'm challenging you to a duel. If I can convince those girls to stick with me, we'll take you on. Regardless of how the other groups perform, my team's going to beat yours."

"Let me get this straight." Pip folded her arms. "You've yet to convince your team to keep you, you've come in last tonight, and yet you're still arrogant enough to challenge me? I have to tell you, Mr. Fraser—"

"I wish you'd call me Joe."

"I have to tell you, Joe—you're dreaming, mate."

He grinned. It made him dangerously accessible and way too attractive. "Now who's being arrogant?"

Pip shrugged. "Okay, you're on. On the proviso that the losing team leader takes the punishment for their whole crew. We'll work out terms when you've convinced Britney and Amanda to stay."

"Miss Browne, you have a deal." He held out a hand and she shook it with a strange sense of exhilaration. He hadn't a hope in hell of winning this, but something in his reckless self-belief appealed to her.

"Call me Pip."

CHAPTER SIX

"I GAVE YOU GIRLS a hard time today," Joe said. "I'm sorry."

Kaitlin blinked. Dad never apologized if he didn't mean it. And she knew he didn't mean it because he was smiling. Dad never smiled when he apologized.

She looked at the others to see if they realized something was wrong, but they were nodding as if they'd been in the right, when they'd kinda all been brats. Except Grace.

Kaitlin was a little jealous of Grace for keeping up with Dad longest. And it turned out that Melissa had been pretending. Right now, Kaitlin wasn't talking to her best friend.

"Here's an idea." Dad leaned back against the stainless-steel bench—stacked high with dirty plates and enormous pots—that ran the length of the camp kitchen. "I'll do the dishes for those prepared to give me another chance." He tossed dish towels to Amanda and Britney. "But you two are definitely transferring to another team, right?"

They glanced from him to the mountain of dishes and back again. "No," they chorused.

"In that case, relax." Dad tied an apron around his hips as if he did the washing up all the time. But he'd never used the kitchen when he lived at home. Mom always said it was her domain. "Not you, Melissa. I figure since I carried you most of the way home, you don't qualify as a hiker."

"But that's not fair." Melissa started to cry.

"If you're going to do that," said Dad, "at least stand over the sink and fill it for me." Everyone laughed. Kaitlin's mouth fell open. Dad could tell jokes? "Miss Browne offered to put you on another team," he continued, "but I'm also offering a second chance." No longer smiling, he held out another dish towel. "What's it to be?"

Pouting, Melissa took it.

"Okay, girls, learn from the master." He began handling the plates like a juggler, faster and faster, not dropping one, as he stacked the commercial dishwasher.

"How do you know how to *do* that?" Kaitlin asked.

"I washed dishes through school." Dad moved on to the pots, attacking them with such vigor that Melissa had trouble keeping up with the drying. "Next time, we'll soak the pots in hot, soapy water before we clean anything else. That loosens the gunk so you don't have to scrub as hard."

He grabbed a bottle of vinegar from the pantry and splashed some in the rinse water.

"Yuk," said Britney.

"Adds sparkle to the glasses," Dad said. "And the hotter the water, the quicker they dry." He finished rinsing the glasses, flicked the last one to make it ping, and grinned at them. "Done! How long was that?"

Kaitlin marveled at this strange man who was her father, while Grace checked her Swatch watch. "Twenty-five minutes."

"And that's just with me and Melissa. I reckon with all of us, we can do it in fifteen, maybe less. We're gonna thrash Miss Browne's team."

Everyone looked at him doubtfully. It was left to Kaitlin to explain. "Dad, no one beats Miss Browne. She always wins. And this year she's got the best boys."

The other girls nodded in confirmation.

Her father's gaze swept over them. "Hell, you're right. I forgot you're only girls. What was I thinking?"

Kaitlin stiffened. So did everyone else. "He probably doesn't mean that the way it sounds," she said, wishing that Mom was here. Mom always played the peacemaker when Dad said stuff like this. Kaitlin felt a sharp stab of homesickness.

Dad shook his head. "Boys will always beat girls. They're stronger, faster—"

"I can beat any boy in a running race!" Britney was so white with rage her freckles were 3-D. "I'm the fastest in the school."

"Then how come you walked today?" Dad asked.

There was an embarrassed silence.

"Look, it's okay." He untied his apron and tossed it over the back of a chair. "I get it. Girls just haven't got the mental stamina."

What was he *doing?* Kaitlin shuffled from one foot to the other in an agony of embarrassment. Amanda's braces were bared in a snarl. Everyone was going to hate him again.

"We can do anything boys can do," said Grace, "but they have Miss Browne."

"I know," Dad said humbly. "But I have cunning and I know how boys work."

"How?" Grace asked. All the girls were fascinated.

"Boys," he explained, "have one big weakness. They can't resist a dare. If they start beating us, then we'll make up points by daring them to take part in extra games we know we can win. Like being the fastest to do dishes."

Kaitlin was still confused. By the look of it, the others were, too.

"We find out what everyone's skilled at and make up games around those skills," he explained. "Britney's fast, so we'll have running races."

Kaitlin got a squirmy feeling. "I'm not good at games," she muttered. He *knew* that.

Melissa clutched Sanderella. "Me, neither."

"Everyone's an expert at something," said Dad. "Kaitlin, you're a math whizz. I'll ask one of the other teachers to put together a quiz."

"I'm not good at math or sports," said Melissa. The tears in her eyes were real, Kaitlin could tell. She took her best friend's hand and squeezed it.

"We'll find something," Dad promised. "What about skinning a bear?"

Smiling through her tears, Melissa shook her head.

"I can scale and fillet a fish," said Grace. The other girls laughed and she blushed and mumbled, "Daddy taught me."

"Great," said Dad. "They'll never see that dare coming."

Everyone giggled except Kaitlin, who regarded her father with a mix of awe and concern. Did he honestly have that faith in them after today? Or was he just being crazy?

Miss Browne came into the kitchen. "You guys are taking ages. You need extra help?"

"That's because we didn't—" Kaitlin began to explain, but Dad cut her off.

"We were talking about additional games for our little competition. Gives both teams the chance to win extra points."

"So they're keeping you, then?" Miss Browne waited for everyone's nods. Most teachers sucked up to parents, but she always put the kids first. Kaitlin loved that about her.

"For example," continued Dad, "seeing which team

gets the dishes done first." Behind Miss Browne's back, he winked. This time Kaitlin giggled with the others.

"Bring it on," said Miss Browne.

Later, when Kaitlin was hugging him good-night, Dad whispered, "Katie, I don't know anything about girls, so I'm relying on you to help me learn."

"Truly?"

"Yeah, babe, truly."

She hugged him again. "Dad, why do you want to beat Miss Browne so much?"

"I guess I've got something to prove."

Kaitlin nodded wisely. There was only one reason boys showed off in front of girls.

He really liked her.

IT WASN'T UNTIL AFTER the kids had been sent to bed that Joe finally found time to make his difficult phone call. He walked a couple hundred yards away from the lit camp buildings toward the dark woods. When she answered, he began with a studied cheerfulness, "Hi, Sue, I hear you and your folks stopped by the rehab—"

"Why didn't you ask me for help with Uncle Adam?" she demanded.

Joe had his answer prepared. "Because you've already got your hands full with the kids, not to mention a new husband." His cousin fostered babies and had recently married the uncle of one of them.

"You hurt my feelings, Joe, you know that?"

He blinked, taken aback. Sue was like him—self-contained. But she'd changed after her grandmother Sarah's death, changed more when she'd met Rick.

"Sue," he said helplessly, walking past the sparse trees on the outskirts of camp into deeper woods. The full moon was only a glimpse of silver through the redwood canopy. He'd known her since high school, where they'd been best friends until Joe had made the mistake of falling in love with her.

Her rejection had been unintentionally savage—a guy nervous about losing his virginity didn't want his first love getting cold feet after he'd stripped to his boxers.

Of course, the recent discovery that they were cousins gave them a whole new perspective on that episode. Thank God they'd never done more than kiss.

But the fallout of Sue's earlier rebuff had impacted their lives—and friendship—for years, though the bond had never broken.

Which was precisely why he hadn't involved her in his current troubles. She'd see right through him, then insist on giving him money that she and Rick didn't have.

"I'm sorry," he said finally. "I won't leave you out again."

"Well, you'd better not. Remember, you and I were family before it became official."

"Yes, ma'am." Resigned to a lecture, Joe leaned against a tree. The bark under his palm was cool and gnarled.

But Sue had always been too smart to labor a point. "Did Belle tell you Mom and Dad are staying?"

"Yeah, something to do with Adam?" Aunt Jenny had spent a lot of time with her new brother after his second stroke. Seemed like she and her husband had only recently returned to Florida.

"Mom said he's deteriorated even since they were last here. I guess we don't notice it, seeing him regular—"

"Adam's getting better!" He heard his panic and smothered it. "So what's this latest visit about?"

There was a moment's silence. Somewhere close by, an owl hooted, prompting a flurry of scampering in the undergrowth. "Mom's brooding over the way Uncle Sam's been treating your father like a pariah since we discovered he was related to us. She wants to make a big gesture, one that will show Uncle Adam that he's loved and accepted by the rest of the Carson clan."

Joe frowned. "What kind of big gesture?"

"Mom and Uncle Adam may have been brought up separately," Sue continued doggedly, "but they're still full brother and sister, and Mom treasures that connection. And technically, as the oldest Carson, Uncle Adam has rights—"

"Oh, no!" Joe suddenly saw where this was going. "No way! That bloody necklace has caused enough tension in your family. It's not coming into mine."

Sue sighed. "Mom's already asked Uncle Adam, and he said yes."

"Of course he said yes." Joe realized he was stripping the bark off the tree, and pushed himself away, to walk off his frustration. "Doesn't your mother realize he'll sell the thing off as soon as he's on his feet?"

"Uncle Adam knows it can't be sold, only passed down." The necklace had been in the Carson family for generations.

"It doesn't matter." He sounded dictatorial, but Joe didn't care. "It's Sarah Carson's legacy to her adopted daughter. Aunt Jenny has to keep it." There wasn't enough room to pace among the trees, so he stomped back toward the clearing.

"It's a *love* legacy," Sue said with equal stubbornness. "Used by Grandma Sarah to show Mom how much she loved her. Mom's given it to Uncle Adam in the same spirit. When it comes right down to it, your father's a Carson and so are you."

"Yeah?" He prowled across the clearing and back again. "Well, maybe I'm as ashamed of that as good ol' Uncle Sam is. I have zero respect for my real grandfather and very little for Nana Jo."

"But you adored her."

"I used to." Joe's footsteps slowed. His grandmother's extraordinary secret had tarnished his memory of her. How could she give up a child she could have kept? And hide paternity from the one she *did* keep? He stopped in the middle of the clearing. "But that's beside the point. Sam's been driving your mother crazy trying to get her to hand over that necklace. Giving it to Adam will make him madder than a hornet."

"Yeah, well, maybe he should have thought about that before he played his 'I'm still Sarah's only child by blood' card."

"The son of a bitch." For a moment Joe was tempted to let things stand just to see his uncle's face, but he had bigger things to worry about than Sam's pathetic obsession. "I don't want to give that lunatic any further reason to harass Adam. I can barely refrain from wringing Sam's neck as it is. Your mom has to withdraw her offer."

"Okay, okay, no need to shout. I'm on *your* side, remember? I'll sort it out with Mom and Uncle Adam. Mom's so desperate to do the right thing that she's talked herself into believing that Uncle Sam wouldn't dare harass a sick man. But you're right, we can't take that risk."

The outside light of the girls' cabin flicked on. Pip came out on the porch, dressed in a striped flannel night-shirt and thick woolen socks, and holding a flashlight.

The beam swept the grounds until she spotted Joe. Then she put a finger to her lips.

Despite his annoyance, Joe had to smile. She only needed a nightcap and a candle to look like Wee Willie Winkie out of the nursery rhyme Kaitlin used to love. *Are the children all in bed? It's past eight o'clock!*

Raising his hand in a conciliatory wave, Joe walked back into the woods. "I know you're on my side," he said to Sue more quietly, "but you don't need to do my dirty work. I'll tell both of them when I get back."

"Actually, I don't think you'll get a protest from your father," she commented. "I got the feeling he only said yes to take the heat off Mom."

Joe snorted. "Yeah, he's got such a great track record of caring about his relatives."

"We can't seem to strike common ground tonight, can we?" she said lightly. "So tell me how it's going at camp and I'll leave you in peace."

He hated hurting Sue, so he made an effort. "I feel like Kaitlin's dad again," he confessed. At bedtime his daughter had whispered, "I'm so glad you're here" and the fierceness of her hug had brought unexpected tears to his eyes.

"That's great, Joe," she said softly.

He hid his self-consciousness under a laugh. "Yeah, well, let's see if she still loves me at the end of camp."

He filled his cousin in on the day's events and she started to chuckle. "It's like Rambo meets Middle School Musical."

"And to make it interesting," he replied, "I've got a little competition going with the female teacher of one of the boys' teams."

"Oh, God," Sue said in an awed voice. "Does she have

any idea what she's got herself into?" In high school football circles he'd been nicknamed Killer.

In the dark, Joe grinned. "Not yet."

CHAPTER SEVEN

HE WAS BEATING HER. Not winning—that Pip could handle. But rubbing her nose in the dirt...

Because whenever Fraser's Fillies won their crazy challenges—skinning a fish, what was *that* about?—there was none of the "oh, it's nothing, really" diffidence of New Zealanders. Joe and his gang of formerly sweet little girls celebrated every victory American-style with big, brash, shoot-'em-in-the-air, eat-my-shorts glee.

"A prime number is..." In the center of the small stage, Kaitlin paused.

Sitting cross-legged with her team at the other end of the stage, Pip held her breath. Even the bulbs illuminating the small-windowed, barracks-type hall that constituted home base seemed to flicker. Kaitlin's thin chest swelled in triumph. "A number that can only be divided by itself and one."

Dang it, they'd just won again.

Anita adjusted her glasses and looked at the answer. Pip's best friend among the faculty, the young brunette had been dragged in as quiz adjudicator. "Fraser's Fillies stretches their lead—" The rest of what she said was drowned out by squeals of delight and howls of despair, as the other teams and their adult leaders—mostly dads with a sprinkling of teachers—rooted for their favorite.

Pip put her hands over her ears. Seventy-five kids made a lot of noise, especially when reenergized by a lunch break.

Squeezed around the official program, the competition-within-an-official-competition had proved a lot of fun over the past twenty-four hours, with vociferous supporters on either side.

Among the kids it came down to gender. The girls championed Joe's team and the boys cheered for Pip's.

Among the adults it got more complicated. She frowned at Anita, who was exchanging grins with Joe. "You're on my side, remember?" Pip mouthed. *And you're married, missy.*

At least Pip was popular among the dads, though some had been sucked into Joe's testosterone-charged jet stream. And the half dozen camp professionals who managed the program were definitely on the side of authority—with the exception of the cook, who said Joe's team left the kitchen the cleanest it had ever been.

Kaitlin and the other girls fell into formation and did their familiar hip-swiveling victory dance. "Who's the best? Fraser's Fil-lies…Fraser's Fil-lies."

Pip leaped to her feet. "It's not over till it's over!" she hollered. "Right, Pip's Phantoms?"

"Right!" Her boys adopted the stance of the Maori warriors she'd taught them, all fierce eyes and poking tongues. Because of course she had to respond to the dare.

Across the stage, Joe puffed out his chest and clenched his fists to pump up his biceps. *Oh, dear God, those biceps.* "Want some tips on kicking butt, Ms. Browne?"

Pip cupped her hands to her mouth. "Quick, somebody call a paramedic! Mr. Fraser's ego needs an emergency deflation."

All the kids dissolved into laughter. How she and Joe Fraser had fallen into this ridiculous wrestler-style posturing, Pip had no idea.

Joe grinned at her. They were frequent now, his smiles, which meant she was forever stripping down to her T-shirt and saying, "Gosh, haven't we been lucky with the weather?" Though it was the last days of a sunny September in Sonoma County, the inland forest had its own microclimate. Permanently shady, always cool, with enough chill at night to warrant a campfire.

"You wanna piece of me, Ms. Browne?" The line always had the kids rolling around the floor as though it was the funniest thing anyone had ever said. Little Ms. Browne and big Mr. Fraser.

Unfortunately, Pip's thoughts always turned in a different direction, one completely inappropriate for a kids' camp. *Just a small piece, please. I'm on a man diet.*

She'd discounted romance during her fifteen months in the States. Why make it harder to leave? And she certainly hadn't spent twelve of them resisting the lures of charming, easygoing Californians to fall for this hard nut, as close as she was to going home.

Even if Joe *was* interested—which at times she thought he might be—now was the time to be cutting ties, not forging new ones.

As the kids filed out of the hall, Kaitlin lingered behind. "Sorry I beat you, Miss Browne."

Affectionately, Pip patted the girl's shoulder. Existing ties were hard enough to cut. "It's only a game, sweetie."

The fight to the death is between me and your dad.

Joe fell into step beside them. "Still happy for the leader to take the rap for their losing team?"

"Don't get ahead of yourself, mate," Pip advised kindly. The last two activities of the day were archery and table tennis, both events at which her boys excelled. "We'll be kicking butt within the hour."

He laughed and moved on, leaving her staring at the portion of anatomy she intended kicking. *Inappropriate,* she reminded herself.

Kaitlin misread her frown. "Don't worry," she reassured her, "we've already told Dad you're *not* going in the mud wallow."

Over his shoulder, Joe flashed Pip a wicked grin. She returned a basilisk stare, but her lips twitched. Little did he know she'd talked the boys into choosing that punishment for him.

How could she possibly be attracted to a man with such a sad lack of gallantry?

But later, after the kids had been sent to bed and the adults were relaxing on the canteen's deck in the moonlight with mugs of hot chocolate, her gaze drifted to Joe again. Tilted back in a chair, his long legs balanced on the porch rail, he was talking football with another dad. The darkness seemed to accentuate the husky timbre of his voice, making it deeper and sexier.

Pip shivered. Without interrupting his conversation, Joe shrugged off his jacket and handed it to her.

"That's kind, but…" It was warm, scented with wood smoke from tonight's campfire.

"No fraternizing with the enemy?"

Reluctantly, she handed it back. "Something like that."

ON THE THIRD MORNING, as he strode to the canteen for breakfast, hair damp from a recent shower, and the woods adding a resinous spice to the tantalizing aromas of bacon and eggs, Joe tried to remember the last time he'd had this much fun.

With a rare surge of happiness, he stopped and raised his face to the sun. The deal he'd reluctantly had to initiate to get here didn't matter. He had his daughter back.

At the sound of voices, Joe sheepishly lowered his face. But the two adults approaching were too deep in conversation to notice him.

"Ten bucks says he'll do it," Anita said.

Joe grinned. All the grown-ups were laying surreptitious bets on the outcome of his and Pip's little contest. "I mean, Joe's obviously attracted," she continued, "and he mentioned he's not seeing any—"

Anita caught sight of Joe at precisely the moment he realized what this particular wager was about. "Yeah," he said sternly, "you *should* look guilty." As with Pip, appearances were deceptive with Anita. Tall, thin and bespectacled, she looked like Miss Prim, but had as much mischief in her as any of her charges.

Joe nodded hello to the dad with her. "At least Vince has the sense to bet against me asking Pip for a date." In the real world, Vince was an insurer, erring on the side of caution. At camp, the big man was a commando, always instigating impromptu games of tag.

Vince found something interesting to look at up in the trees. "Actually," he confessed to a squirrel, "I said Pip would do the asking."

"So you think—?" Joe stopped before he made a fool of himself.

"Yes," said Anita. "We *do* think she's interested. So what are you going to do about it?"

"Quit trying to skew the bet your way," Vince warned.

Joe looked incredulously from one to the other. "Have you two forgotten we're at school camp?"

"Yes, but when we go home there's nothing to stop you asking her for a date," Anita pointed out.

"It's not going to happen." Even back in San Francisco Pip would still be Kaitlin's teacher. And given his financial constraints, the only place Joe could afford to show her a good time was in bed. He blocked transmission before his imagination got him into trouble.

"She could still ask him," Vince reminded Anita.

"You two need to stop eating mushrooms you find in the woods," Joe said. "Now if you'll excuse me, I'm hungry."

In the canteen, he lined up for a plate of bacon, eggs and hash browns, served by two dads in aprons. Then he threaded his way among the tables to where his daughter sat with the rest of his pink-clad brigade.

"Good morning, Fraser's Fillies." Dropping a kiss on the top of Kaitlin's head, Joe took a seat opposite so he could stare at her. No wonder he was half in love with Pip. She'd helped him win back his daughter.

Appalled, he immediately corrected himself. He was only dazzled because he'd been living in a dark cave for two years. Across the room, Joe heard Pip laugh and resisted the urge to turn around. He was nowhere ready to leave the cave yet. His soul was still too bruised by the divorce.

"Have you thought of a task for me yet?" demanded Melissa, who was pretending to feed Sanderella from the sugar bowl. With sugar crystals clinging to her furry nylon snout, the stuffed Scottish terrier looked like a coke addict. "We've only got two more challenges."

Joe met Kaitlin's anxious gaze. Despite constant brainstorming, neither of them could think of a single thing Melissa could win. "We're working on it."

Melissa slumped back in her seat. "You mean it's hopeless."

Kaitlin patted her friend's arm. "Don't worry, Dad will think of something."

But hey, no pressure. He'd gone from zero to hero in three days. Now Joe realized that meant he had so much further to fall. "Anyone want some of this bacon? I'm not as hungry as I thought I was."

All five girls clamored for it. Pushing his plate into the middle, Joe sat back with his coffee, trying to think of something for Melissa.

Talking with her mouth full? He looked around the table; nope, they all did that. "So, have you guys decided what Miss Browne's penalty will be when her team loses?"

"Yeah." One by one they got the giggles.

"Are you going to tell me?"

Kaitlin beamed at him. "We're going to make her go on a date with you."

Joe choked on his coffee. They were all looking at him with such childish excitement that he bit back his first reaction.

Amanda's braces glinted as she giggled again. "Kaitlin told us how you like her."

"Kaitlin Josephine Fraser." He glared at his daughter. "I never said any such thing."

"No, but you laugh with her a lot and you're showing off and you—"

"Pull her pigtails?" Joe was momentarily diverted.

"Silly!" Grace tugged at her own cropped blond mop. "You can't braid short hair."

"I told you we should have left it a surprise," Melissa admonished the others.

He shuddered. Thank God they hadn't. At least now he had the opportunity to fix this. "Listen very carefully." He leaned forward and waited until they'd put their heads together. "No."

The girls groaned and sat back. "But she hasn't got a boyfriend," said Amanda. "I asked her."

"And you haven't got a girlfriend," argued Kaitlin.

"And she's so pretty," breathed Melissa, "and you're sort of handsome."

Britney cupped her freckled chin, her gaze dreamy. "And we could all be flower girls when you get married."

"Except me," said Kaitlin. "I get to be a bridesmaid because I'm the daughter."

Joe understood the magnitude of his task. Little girls who saw nothing mismatched about Beauty and the Beast wouldn't understand that a loner had no business with a woman who made family of everyone she met. Only a sledgehammer approach would work now. "Girls, I *forbid* you to do this. I do not want to date Ms. Browne."

Shocked silence met his announcement. "Don't you like her, Dad?"

"Yes, but only as a friend," he said firmly. "You have friends who are boys, don't you?"

The girls exchanged blank looks and he realized he was talking to the wrong demographic. Britney's freckles merged as she wrinkled her nose. "Only if there are no other girls to play with."

Joe racked his brains for a comparison. "What about Scooter? You all like him." Scooter was a large, friendly boy, a little short on personal hygiene, but long on a dim cheerfulness that gave him a free pass among his peers.

Kaitlin looked at him doubtfully. "Are you saying you think of Miss Browne like we think of Scooter?"

Joe bit back a "God, no!" and ran with what he'd been given. "I'm saying Miss Browne's not my type," he lied. "Like Scooter isn't yours."

Opposite him, three pairs of eyes widened. Good, he'd got the message across…. Uh-oh. Joe turned his head. Pip stood behind him, her smile faltering as his words sank in.

Oh. Shit.

Immediately, she recovered her composure and gave everyone a big, big smile that only made Joe feel much, much worse. "I just came to remind you that it's time for the ecology field trip, girls…. Joe, a quick word?"

Out of earshot, she didn't quite meet his eyes. "Listen, I know you're struggling to find something for Melissa, and thought I should mention the obvious."

Wondering how to clarify his position without embarrassing them both, Joe took a second to really hear her. "Wait a minute. This is the last challenge. If you tell me, we'll beat you."

"And if I don't tell you," she said tartly, "Melissa's going to believe she's hopeless, possibly for the rest of her life."

Pip *was* mad at him. About to explain, Joe hesitated. Maybe it was better this way. She was too damn good for him, and her altruism only proved it.

"Okay, tell me what it is."

"She can cry at will," said Pip.

Way too good for him. "Thanks."

"Hey, no problem." But all the warmth had gone out of her smile.

He let her walk away. But later, when Melissa was bawling sincerely because she'd won her challenge *and* the competition for Fraser's Fillies, Joe gave a prearranged signal to Anita.

"And for bonus points," she yelled over the applause, "who's showered since they've been at camp?" The girls shot up their hands. "And who hasn't?" Without much hope, the disconsolate Phantoms stuck their hands in the air.

"Five bonus points to the boys for water conservation," trumpeted Anita. "The competition's a draw!"

CHAPTER EIGHT

"EVERYONE WAS *VERY* thirsty," intoned the narrator. The floodlights bounced off Anita's spectacles as she glanced up from the podium to check the action.

Six parent helpers sat in a row of chairs on stage with a trestle table of props in front of them and their arms hidden under their sweaters. Concealed behind each of them sat a teacher or camp staffer.

Reaching past Joe's body, Pip fumbled for the glass of water on the props table. She'd performed the "phony arms" skit many times, but never when fighting a sexual attraction to the fall guy.

Who this morning had made it excruciatingly clear that he wasn't interested.

She couldn't quite reach the prop. Reluctantly, Pip laid her cheek against Joe's shoulder blade trying to gain an extra few inches.

It was too intimate; why hadn't she noticed it before with previous male partners? Maybe they'd been smaller.... With Joe she had to press close to get around all that muscle. Her breasts came into contact with his broad back and he straightened in his chair, obviously disliking the contact.

Pip's embarrassment became anger. Well, tough. Her fingertips nudged the glass. Grabbing it before it toppled, she raised it to where she thought Joe's lips would be. The juvenile audience's shouts of laughter suggested she was nowhere near target.

"You're making me drink water through my d'ose," he murmured thickly.

"Sorry." Pip reminded herself she had no right to be mad that he didn't want her. Attraction was random and uncontrollable. Good heavens, wasn't her desire for him a patent example of that? As she adjusted the glass she decided that if Joe's pheromones lacked good taste, well, that wasn't his fault.

On the other hand, she was a good-looking woman who'd had guys beating down her door all year. And to compare her to Scooter…

"Oww," Joe muttered as the glass chinked against his teeth. Then he spluttered as she tilted it much faster than he could swallow. The kids roared. "Can you be more care—"

His request became a watery gurgle as she tipped the glass at a sharper angle. Pip smiled as cold water ran down her arm and presumably, Joe's face. "Oops," she said sweetly. "Sorry."

"Liar." His voice rumbled in his chest and vibrated through hers, still pressed against his back. His breath was warm on the back of her hand. "How come the other parents aren't getting this wet?"

Okay, maybe she was taking the spurned woman thing a bit far. "I'll dry you off," she whispered grudgingly, and groped for the towel on his lap. Her fingers made contact with his hard warm thigh.

There was a moment's shocked stillness, then Joe said hoarsely, "Remember, this is a kid's show."

Pip jerked her hand away. Thank God he couldn't see her blush. Then she realized her burning cheek was still plastered against his left shoulder blade—he'd feel the heat—and hauled herself upright.

Anita picked up the narration. "It was scorching outside so they put on their sunscreen and sunglasses."

It's scorching inside.

Gritting her teeth, Pip pressed forward again, reaching past Joe for the suntan lotion. Silly to get nervous just because she had her arms around him.

Squirting the lotion into her hand, she was intensely conscious of every rise and fall of his ribs as she threaded her arms under his armpits to smear sunscreen over his face.

Just because he smells dizzyingly, knee-tremblingly good.

She shivered as the light stubble on his jaw abraded her palm and sent a burning tingle down her forearm. Her fingers brushed his lips and Pip recoiled as if she'd touched an electric eel.

Just because I've never had this reaction to any other man.

Joe's back tensed, became a living wall of resistance, and Pip started to sweat microscopic beads of shame and indignity. *Just because he isn't interested.*

Gripping the sunglasses tightly in one hand, she slid her hands over his face to get her bearings, brushing the slightly crooked nose and warm cheekbones. Long lashes tickled her questing fingers.

She wondered, amid the audience's laughter, if he could feel her heart thumping against his back. Prayed he didn't.

Then Joe shifted forward slightly in his chair, setting the seal on her humiliation. He wasn't remotely interested, but now he knew for sure that she'd been.

Fumbling awkwardly with the sunglasses, Pip finally managed to put them on him. "They're crooked!" yelled her delighted spectators.

The rest of the performance passed as slowly as a nightmare. With every intimate task she performed for him—feeding him bread, cleaning his teeth—Joe got tenser and tighter until revulsion rolled off him in waves. The audience cried with laughter; Pip prayed for the floor to open up and swallow her.

At last the show was over, and the performers stood to take a bow. Then it was the turn of the fall guys to get payback. Around them, parent helpers wiped the glop, a mix of sunscreen and food, off their faces and smeared it on their cringing tormentors.

Joe's fingers were perfunctory on Pip's face; he avoided eye contact. She winced and grinned like she was supposed to, while the kids cheered and stomped. Actually, she wanted to be covered in glop; it would hide her mortification.

At last everyone filed offstage, exclaiming and laughing. Head down, her smile plastered on her face along with the glop, Pip murmured, "Cleanup," and escaped into the dark.

She was halfway to the shower block when Joe called her name. And even though it would blow her cover once and for all as a disinterested party, Pip ran.

Dispatching one of the girls for a towel and change of clothes, she ignored the chill drafts and stood under the dribble of lukewarm water for ten minutes, trying to scrub off her humiliation.

Then she dressed, spent another five minutes silently practicing her "Hey, that was fun, wasn't it?" line, and finally ventured outside.

Joe stood on the porch of the boys' cabin with the light behind him, a towering silhouette. Waiting for her.

Losing her courage, she pivoted in the opposite direction. She heard a thud behind her as he jumped off the deck. Pip walked faster.

"Pip, wait up."

Steeling herself to apologize, she turned around, standing her ground as he loomed in the dark. Joe spoke first. "I embarrassed you in there with my reaction. I'm sorry."

She'd been the one to make a fool of herself and *he* was apologizing? Oh, pity made this *so* much better. "Forget it."

His deep voice was rueful. "At least that clears up any misunderstanding about what you overheard this morning."

Yep, Joe recoiling every time she'd touched him, plus the "she's not my type" comment, added up to a very clear picture. Was he deliberately being cruel? Pip strained to make out his features in the dark, but couldn't. "Please," she repeated more desperately, "let's forget it."

There was a brief silence. "If that's what you want."

Was he serious?

"No, you're right," he added, "it's for the best."

Pip felt like a worm squirming to get off a hook while the fisherman kept finding another wiggly bit to pierce. She started to hate Joe Fraser.

"Listen, I just had a phone call," he said. "Something urgent has come up and I have to leave now."

Her pent-up feelings found a legitimate focus. "You made a commitment, Joe." As though having him disappear wasn't her greatest wish.

He hesitated. "If I could get out of it, I would."

Pip hauled him into a puddle of light from the hall window. He'd showered and changed into jeans and a shirt. His wet hair gleamed and he smelled of pine soap. "Answer me one question, is it personal or business?"

Another hesitation, then he met her eyes. "My business."

"You bastard."

Joe blinked. "Excuse me?"

Pip embraced the rage. "All the progress you've made with Kaitlin and you're going to blow it for some stupid deal."

His jaw tightened. "It's not just any deal, Pip, and I don't have to explain myself to you."

She planted her hands on her hips. "Have you explained yourself to your daughter?"

"I've told her I wouldn't go unless it was really important."

Pip's anger was so great she shook with it. "Have you told her *why?*"

"She doesn't need to know every detail."

Pip stared at his impassive face, cold as granite under the reflected light. How could she ever have thought this man attractive? Her laugh was scornful, intense with the heat of her aversion. "You're just going to default back to the same old Joe Fraser, loser dad, aren't you?"

His gaze locked with hers. "I don't know what authority you think you have because you've helped me, but you're grossly exceeding it." His voice was icy calm. "Or is this really because you're still pissed about what happened earlier? I've already apologized for that."

Pip didn't like being told she was overreacting any more than any other angry person and the grain of truth in his question only aggravated her.

"Go away," she ordered. "I can't bear the sight of you a minute longer."

Without another word he turned on his heel. She heard the slam of a car door, then the gunning of an engine. Headlights swept the woods as the car accelerated out of the clearing, then there was nothing but the occasional rustle of leaves and the distant murmur from the buildings.

Pip used her towel, still damp from the shower, to wipe her eyes. She was crying because she was mad and no other damn reason. Stalking to the girls' cabin, she dumped her gear and sat on her bunk until she regained her composure. When her anger finally passed, a strange desolation took its place. *For Kaitlin*, she told herself.

The thought galvanized her into returning to the hall. She finally tracked Kaitlin to the canteen where she was drinking hot chocolate with the rest of Pip's class, under Anita's supervision.

"At last," her friend called.

She looked like a cross between a scarecrow and a scurvy victim, and Pip gazed at her blankly, then gasped. "Oh, God, I'm sorry, I forgot you still needed a shower. Off you go."

"In a minute." Anita drew her aside. "Did Joe find you?"

She frowned. "Yes."

"And?"

"And what?" Kaitlin saw Pip and waved. The poor kid was obviously putting on a brave face.

"Did he ask you for a date before he left, stupid!"

That caught her attention. "Why would he do that?"

"C'mon, Pip," Anita said impatiently. "The two of you all but spontaneously combusted on stage. And with him having to leave suddenly...I felt sure I was going to win my bet."

Pip let that pass, too busy replaying Joe's apology. Had she misconstrued his comments? Her distracted gaze followed the other teacher as Anita left to get cleaned up.

What if he'd felt the same way Pip had? Embarrassed at betraying an attraction he didn't think she returned? But that didn't explain his comment to Fraser's Fillies. *She's not my type.*

Pip shook her head to clear it. It didn't matter. He was still a louse for leaving camp early for a business deal when he knew it would devastate his daughter.

Picking up a mug of hot chocolate from the serving counter, she watched Kaitlin surreptitiously between sips. Laughing, chatting as she was, no one would guess the little girl was hiding heartbreak. Pip ached for her. The bell rang, signaling bed, and the kids shoved their chairs back and returned their mugs.

"Kaitlin, can you stay behind a minute?"

When the others had left, she laid a comforting arm around the girl's shoulders. "You feeling okay about your dad leaving?"

"Mostly." Kaitlin pulled a face. "Of course I'm sad, but I can't be selfish."

Pip wanted to kill Joe Fraser. "That's a great way to look at it, honey."

"'Specially since this deal means Grandpa can stay in the special hospital.... Um, Miss Browne, you're kind of squeezing my shoulder too hard."

Pip dropped her arm.

"Oops!" Kaitlin put her hand over her mouth. "I forgot, it's a secret. Dad doesn't want the rest of the family involved."

Pip's fleeting "Why?" was washed away by waves of shame as she recalled the things she'd said to him.

Kaitlin prattled on. "Dad told me so I'd know only something *really* important would make him leave early." She looked at Pip anxiously. "You won't tell him I said anything, will you?"

Too mortified to speak, she shook her head. Pip was pretty sure she'd never see Joe again. Certainly not by his choice.

JOE SPENT THE TWO-HOUR drive back to San Francisco cursing himself for his stupidity in ever letting his guard down with Pip Browne.

He thought of the worst thing he could accuse her of: being overly emotional. Jumping to illogical conclusions, making unjustified accusations, adding two and two and getting five. Being female. He clenched the steering wheel. And he'd been a complete fool.

The skit had been agony. As soon as Pip wrapped her slim arms around him, Joe knew he was in trouble. It was one thing ignoring a sexual attraction at a distance, another to ignore it when the object of your lust was plastered against your back, sliding her fingers over your face.

From the first press of her rounded breasts he'd felt like a pervert, sexualizing a completely innocent pursuit. Even staring at laughing children couldn't stop him fantasizing about getting their teacher naked.

Then her hand groped his lap… Joe opened the car window, breathed in the rush of chill air.

The trouble was, he'd forgotten the touch of a woman, the scent and softness of one. He'd forgotten what it was like to want someone with a fierce, primal hunger, not the perfunctory lust of two people who should never have gotten married.

He'd forgotten the pangs of unrequited love. No—Joe shook his head to clear it—his unreciprocated desire for Pip was baser, more carnal, than what he'd once felt for Sue. Which made him feel even worse.

Pip had helped him win back his daughter. He owed her gratitude, respect…as much respect as you could give a friendly adversary you intended to roll in mud when your team kicked ass.

Just thinking about her ass and mud rolling made Joe groan.

The traffic got worse as he joined the freeway, two lanes becoming four, then six.

So he'd gone to apologize. And okay, maybe to find out if some of her embarrassment could be pinpointed to a similar sexual charge. Her tight-lipped response had made him feel like a testosterone-driven brute.

And when he was feeling lower than the beasts of the field, she'd double-whammied him with a lecture about leaving Kaitlin that made it very clear she didn't even *like* him.

In fact, Miss Browne despised him.

The sharp knife twisting in his gut was anger. "Right back at you, sweetheart!"

To think when he'd first got the phone call to leave, he'd toyed with telling her everything. Because despite the chest thumping and mock fist shaking, he'd come to regard her as a friend, a confidante. Someone he could trust.

Yes, he was a complete fool.

He drove over the Golden Gate Bridge, oblivious to the city lights, and took the first right on Lincoln. Ten minutes later he pulled up outside an apartment building and got out of the car.

Down a side alley, two cats spat and hissed at each other in a territorial dispute by the bins. He hadn't been back to this neighborhood since he'd sublet his apartment.

When he'd bought the place two years ago, it had looked shabby to him. Compared to the family home he'd left on Russian Hill with its views of the bay, a one-bedroom apartment in an aging seven-story building close to the airport was a major comedown.

Now, as he stood on the street corner, counting the

windows up to the sixth floor and the glow of light behind the drapes, Joe felt a pang of homesickness. Funny how living in a hotel gave a guy perspective.

The cats collided in a flurry of yowling, rolling fur, then one disengaged itself and tore past Joe, so close it brushed the toes of his hiking boots. Of course it was black.

"Too late," he said, then squared his shoulders and went to sign the sales contract on the last thing he owned.

CHAPTER NINE

THE NURSING STAFF WERE in the middle of a shift change when Joe walked into the rehab center at noon the next day. They welcomed him like a long-lost relative before returning to their clipboards. It made him realize how much time he spent here.

His father was watching CBS news on the big-screen TV, the curtains partially pulled to reduce the glare from another bright, hot October morning. Fall in other parts of the country was summer in San Francisco.

"Hey, Adam." Joe went to the coffee machine he'd installed on a side table next to the couch, and made himself a strong cup. "I just caught up with your, uh, sister, Jenny, and her husband."

"Coffee...smells...good." There was longing in his father's restlessness.

"I'll make you one."

When the coffee was ready he adjusted the bed so his father was sitting up, then supported him while he drank through a straw.

"Why...back...early?"

He couldn't tell him the tenants who'd snapped up his apartment had wanted to sign papers before flying to Saint Thomas for a month's holiday. "I missed you."

"Cut...crap."

Joe put the cup on the bedside table and resettled his father on the pillows. "Fine. I know Aunt Jenny offered you the Carson diamond. I want you to turn her down."

An angry flush mottled Adam's cheeks. "Not...your... business!"

"What the hell are you going to do with a necklace, anyway?" Joe said more mildly. "It's not like it can be sold."

"Only...temporary." His father paused to rest. His color began to return to its normal pallor. "Teach... Sam...lesson."

Certainly Joe's new uncle deserved one. The man was a tyrant and a bully, and the only enigma was why his gentle wife had put up with him for so long. Even Belle, who had more gumption, still showed enormous forbearance when dealing with her father.

Joe didn't understand that kind of forgiveness and he didn't want to.

Standing by the bed, he stared down at Adam. "What happened at the country club?" It bugged him that his father wouldn't divulge details of his meeting with Sam.

Adam hesitated. "Tell...stop...hassle...Jenny," he admitted, confounding Joe. So his father did feel protective of his long-lost sister.

"I bet that went down well." Sam didn't take kindly to criticism. "Wait a minute...did he hit you?"

"No." There was a glint in his father's eyes. "I...hit... him."

Joe stared at the feeble man in the bed and then slowly started to laugh. "God, what I would have given to see that." He sobered abruptly. "Except it triggered a second stroke. Which brings me back to my point. You're in no shape to play the white knight."

Adam looked at him expectantly.

"Oh, I get it." Joe walked back to the side table where he'd left his own coffee. "Uncle Sam has to come through me first."

"You…broad…shoulders," Adam said reasonably.

Joe resisted the urge to tell his father exactly what those broad shoulders had been carrying lately. With the sale of his apartment finalized, the short-term pressure was off. But he couldn't live in a hotel for the rest of his life. And he certainly hadn't divested himself of one problem only to take on another.

"Want…heat…off…Jen…." Adam was clearly exhausted. "Tease…Sam."

"You're fifty-eight," Joe responded irritably. Didn't his father know he needed to conserve his energy for recuperation? "That's too old to play childish games with your half brother. Take the high ground."

"No."

"Yes!"

The door swung open with a great deal of force and— speak of the devil—Sam Carson stormed in. Ignoring Adam, he eyeballed Joe. "This is your doing, isn't it? You blame me for your father's second stroke and this is payback."

"Hello, Sam." Wearily Joe put down his coffee cup. "Finally come to inquire after your brother?"

"Half brother." His uncle faced the bed and flinched, then dug his hands in the pockets of his rain-splotched Burberry raincoat, unbuttoned over a gray suit. "I thought this was a rehab unit," Sam said gruffly. He was so obviously shocked by Adam's infirmity that Joe excused his tactlessness.

"Adam's got a way to go but he's making good progress." Joe moved to stand by his father's bedside. "No thanks to you."

Sam addressed Adam in a tone that was half bluster, half apology. "You can't hold me accountable for putting you here. The hospital said you discharged yourself after the first stroke against medical advice."

Because he had no insurance, something his son hadn't known at the time. When Adam snorted, Sam turned back to Joe. "I had absolutely nothing to do with him showing up at my country club."

"Now that I do believe," he drawled. "Introducing your illegitimate half brother to your cronies would be anathema to a pillar of the community such as yourself." Though it was pathetic, he could never resist using big words with his uncle.

Sam eyed him with active dislike. Only a few months younger than Adam, he was still a handsome son of a bitch—no doubt through a deal with Satan—with a full head of blond hair, piercing blue eyes and an infuriating air of entitlement. "The Frasers might not have a reputation to uphold, but the Carsons have." Sam looked down his nose. "Your father instigated the argument, not me."

"And finished it, too, I hear?" With grim satisfaction Joe watched his uncle Sam shuffle his feet. "Kinda sad that he felt the need to defend a sister he barely knows from the brother she'd grown up with, don't you think?"

Recovering his composure, Sam glared at him. "You young whelp. Do you honestly think I'm going to stand by and see the Carson diamond given to my father's bastard? I'd sooner let my half-blood sister keep it."

Adam grew agitated; Joe laid a hand on his father's arm. They were *not* getting involved. "Good idea," he said coldly. "Let's sign something now to that effect."

For a moment his uncle appeared nonplussed. "Don't be ridiculous," he snapped. "That necklace was promised to me by my father. Jenny only got it because my mother was bewildered." The older man's lip curled. "And Jenny knows she's in the wrong, which is why she's avoiding my calls."

Joe stared at him. "She's avoiding your calls because you're being obsessive, obnoxious and unreasonable." Not to mention self-delusional. "Sue told me her grandmother was as sharp as a tack right up to her death." Maybe the Carson women did need protection. With an effort, he reminded himself that his cousins' husband and fiancé were more than capable of providing backup. "For God's sake, man," he added in exasperation, "haven't you lost enough?"

"Yes." Sam jutted out his jaw like an old bulldog. "Which is why I won't give up what's left. Now that I've seen Adam's condition, it's clear who instigated this con. He doesn't want the family heirloom, *you* do."

Joe felt his temper rise. "That's insane."

"You're thinking that your old man's on his way out," Sam persisted, "and see an opportunity to get your hands on the Carson diamond. You've played on Jenny's sympathies and—"

"That's enough," Joe snarled. "Now get the hell out of here before I continue the new Fraser tradition of kicking Carson butt."

"Not without the necklace." Sam stepped toward the bedside table, obviously with the intention of searching the drawers.

Folding his arms, Joe blocked the way. Any rational man would have run for cover, but his uncle stood his ground, breathing hard, his hands curling into fists and his eyes glassy.

This close, Joe could smell whiskey on Sam's breath and see a faint food stain on his uncle's usually impeccable clothing. He wished he'd noticed these things earlier, when pity still had the power to stir him.

"Back off," he warned.

For another moment Sam, his breath hot and sour, held Joe's gaze, before he broke eye contact. "You'll be hearing from my lawyer," he barked over his shoulder as he left.

Fighting to regain his equilibrium, Joe picked up his cup with slow deliberation.

"He…was…drunk."

"You'd know." The acid comment slipped out before he could stop it. Swallowing the cold coffee in three gulps, Joe slammed the cup down. "Sorry. That was petty."

A choking sound came from the bed and Joe quickly turned. One side of Adam's face was contorted in laughter. "High…ground…?"

Joe's mouth twitched. "Shut up."

WHEN PIP FIELDED A THIRD come-on from yet another intoxicated guy partying in the bar adjacent to the lobby, the hotel manager gave her a key card for Joe's room.

"Honestly, we're a respectable establishment," he told her with a wry grin. "But there's a Teamsters convention in town and the boys are celebrating some contract breakthrough. You're getting caught in the crossfire."

Relieved, Pip took the key card. "Thank you." She had no idea how Joe was going to react to this visit, and the thought of inebriated witnesses was decimating the little courage she had left. It had been bad enough watching reception ring Joe's room, and waiting to be told politely to go to hell. But he wasn't back from work yet and she'd decided to wait.

Standing up, she tucked the key into the pocket of her poppy-red swing coat.

The manager gestured toward the elevators. "Suite 415. Right at the elevator, end of the corridor. Incidentally, I wouldn't do this if Joe wasn't a buddy of mine. But I recognized your name. Kaitlin's teacher, right?"

"Yes. Has Joe… Did he mention me?"

"Before camp. I haven't had a chance to talk to him since. How'd it go?"

"Great," she said, suddenly eager to be gone before Joe walked in and called her a liar. "Well, thanks—" she looked at his name tag "—Michael."

"Anytime." He gave her one of those charming Californian grins that suggested he'd be happy to flirt with her. Right now, however, Pip was only interested in winning one of Joe's grim smiles.

Upstairs, she shoved the card into the key slot and pushed open the door. The first thing she saw was a big bed. *Maybe this is a bad idea.*

The suite was decorated in soft sage and cream, from the rugs to the wallpaper and the plump-cushioned couches and chairs. Heavy embossed fabrics and ornate patterns lent the room lushness, but it was saved from femininity by the dark wood and square, simple design of the desk, tables and armoire.

Pip's footsteps made no sound on the thick carpet as she crossed the room and closed the sliding door separating the bedroom from the rest of the suite so she couldn't see the bed. Then she turned on all the lights to make the suite seem less…intimate, and pulled the velvet drapes, more to block out the sight of her nervous reflection than keep the chill out of the room.

She'd timed her visit for eight, figuring even Joe

wouldn't work that late, substantiated by a covert phone call to his office. It also gave her plenty of time to wash off the camp dirt, change into a simple gray shift dress and high-heeled boots, and apply some light makeup, the first she'd worn in four days. She figured she needed whatever confidence boost she could get.

Dry cleaning in a plastic wrapper lay over the back of the couch; Pip hung it on a lamp shade and sat down. She picked up a winegrowers periodical from the pile of wine industry magazines on the coffee table, then replaced it and nervously tidied the stack. She probably shouldn't touch anything.

It was warm in the room, but she didn't take off her coat, though she undid the single button under the bustline.

Trying to relax, she sank back into the couch cushions, then yawned. She'd spent a sleepless night and was completely exhausted. It galled her to admit it, but she'd come out of her corner swinging only because Joe had hurt her feminine pride.

And even though her inner coward suggested she make reparation through a card, e-mail or flowers—anything but looking into those blazing eyes again—Pip knew she owed him a personal apology.

The minutes passed, excruciatingly slowly. Her head drooped forward and Pip jerked upright, trying not to fall asleep. Maybe he'd gone somewhere after work? She stood up. Then she sat down again. Traffic could be bad; she owed him another ten minutes.

She became aware of a tap dripping and followed the sound to a tiny kitchenette behind a marble-topped bar. She turned the tap off. Now she needed to use the bathroom.

Pip opened the hotel room door and glanced up and

down the long corridor, before shutting it again and hurrying to the bathroom.

After flushing the toilet, she quickly washed and dried her hands. The faint, lingering scent of Joe's after-shave made her mouth go dry and stole the last of her nerve. She opened the bathroom door, intending to grab her bag and run.

In gym clothes, with a towel around his neck, Joe leaned against the opposite wall. His arms were folded, his mouth set in a stern line. For a moment, the only sound was the last gurgle of the cistern refilling.

"Do you mind telling me what the hell you're doing in my room? Other than using my facilities?"

Pip managed a weak smile. "Goldilocks had it easy. She was only caught sleeping in Poppa Bear's bed."

Joe's expression didn't change by so much as a muscle twitch. She lost her bravado.

"I needed to talk to you."

He hurled the towel onto the couch. "And I need to talk to Michael about security."

"I picked the lock," she lied.

"Let me make it easier for you on the way out." He opened the door.

She walked back into the living room on shaky legs, moved the damp towel and sat down. "In a minute."

Joe didn't budge. "If you've come to deliver another loser-dad lecture you can—"

"I apologize unreservedly. I had no right to talk to you as I did."

He hadn't anticipated that. For a moment he said nothing, then shut the door. "Then why did you?"

She was well aware that nothing but the brutal truth would fix this. "I...I let hurt feelings goad me into believing the worst of you." Pip focused on the topiary plant on the coffee table. "I thought I'd given away the fact that I found you attractive, and you were apologizing because it wasn't mutual."

"You thought…" Joe trailed off. The plant was pruned and trained into the shape of four green disks. Pip counted them. Twice.

"That's the dumbest thing I've ever heard."

Pip forgot the tortured plant.

"Considering I all but got a hard-on on stage," he continued bluntly, "where did you get such a ridiculous idea?"

Pip blinked, but made a quick recovery. "Gee, I don't know. Maybe it was the Scooter analogy. Or when you got really cryptic and said, 'she's not my type.'"

He started to laugh and, infuriated, she stood up. "I think I should leave before I take back that apology."

"I only said that because the girls were going to make you go out with me as your punishment for losing the team challenge."

She blanched, imagining *that* public announcement. "Oh." Pip concentrated on rebuttoning her coat. "Where did they get that idea?"

"From my daughter. She's quite a fan of yours."

Pip adjusted the straps of her bag on her shoulder. "That would have been embarrassing."

"You think?"

It was time for a dignified exit. "Well, I've said what I needed to say—"

"I haven't." Joe frowned at the closed sliding door, shoved it open and disappeared inside the bedroom. Pip waited. He returned with fresh clothes. "There's a bottle of Reverie Roussanne in the fridge. I won't be long."

"But—"

The bathroom door closed behind him.

"I'm not going to grovel," she called.

A laugh was her only answer. She poured herself a half glass of white wine and sipped it nervously, wondering if Joe would notice if she closed the sliding door again. Probably. Through the wall she heard the muted sound of the shower, and tried not to imagine him naked.

Her admission had given him the upper hand, and she had only Anita's word for it that he fancied her back. And if he did? Pip took another sip, savoring the honey and pineapple accents. She hadn't thought past the apology. Now she wished she had.

Did she want to date Joe Fraser? A hot, sexy fling with the guy she was salivating over, knowing she had a safety net in place. She was going home soon, so no strings. She finished the half glass and poured herself a little more. He certainly had good taste in wine.

The phone rang, loud and discordant, and she spilled her drink. "Damn." Distractedly dabbing at the mark with Joe's discarded gym towel, she automatically picked up the receiver, then paused. What if it was Kaitlin or Nadia? Poised to hang up, Pip grunted in what she hoped passed for a deep male grunt.

"Joe? Paul. I can transfer the money from the sale of your condo into your account tomorrow if you give me your num—"

"It's not Joe," Pip interrupted. "One moment please."

She knocked on the bathroom door and it opened, releasing a billow of steam and the spicy scent of male toiletries. Joe wore a pair of jeans and nothing else. Shaving cream covered half his face and he held a razor.

Averting her eyes, Pip held out the cordless phone and

said apologetically, "It sounds important or I would have taken a message."

Shrugging on a shirt, he came out, holding the receiver to the clean side of his face. "Hello? Paul... What can I do for you?"

He listened, then his gaze lifted to Pip's, intent and searching. "Let me get those details for you."

She perched on the arm of the couch and tried not to listen as Joe relayed his account details. It wasn't hard; she was acutely conscious of his muscled torso under the unbuttoned shirt. The gym was obviously a regular hangout for him.

Joe hung up and gave her an inscrutable look. "Come talk to me while I finish shaving."

She leaned against the doorjamb, reluctant to enter what was suddenly a dangerously small space.

Unbuttoned sleeves fell back from his strong forearms as Joe lifted the razor and resumed shaving, seemingly absorbed in the task, but watching her in the mirror. "What exactly did Paul tell you when he thought you were me?"

Something about his studied nonchalance triggered a memory for her. He'd reacted like this when she'd asked him whether he'd had to sell his soul to get to camp. Then there was Kaitlin's comment that Joe was doing a deal to help Grandpa stay in hospital. The recent telephone call became invested with new meaning. Pip blurted, "My God, you sold your apartment to be able to come to camp."

She read the answer in his eyes before the shutters came down. "You've got a vivid imagination." Seconds passed before he added, "But not a word to my ex-wife or daughter."

"Of course not." Still stunned, Pip could only stare at him.

"And it wasn't only about keeping my promise about

camp. A major deal I was relying on fell through last week, which would tie me to working longer hours. I sold my apartment to free up weekends for Kaitlin and to meet my father's medical bills—he's in private rehab after a stroke."

He'd honored his commitment to his daughter…and his dad. Pip's throat tightened.

In the mirror he frowned at her. "And it was minimum fuss, minimum effort. My tenants had once expressed an interest in buying it—all I had to do was call them. Only the sale moved more quickly than I expected."

She nodded, still unable to speak.

Joe rinsed the razor under the faucet. "For the record, I can't stand my father," he said harshly. "So quit looking at me like I'm some kind of saint."

If anything, that made his sacrifice more laudable, but Pip got the message. "No fear of that. The girls told me all about your underhanded tactics, Mr. Pro Dishwasher. So I'm onto you."

He grinned despite himself, she could tell. "We'll still beat you next year."

"I won't be here, next year. I'm going back to New Zealand at Christmas."

Joe paused in his shaving. "Damn, I'd hoped to be in a better financial position by then. To ask you for a date."

Her pulse leaped. "For the record, I'm not interested in your money." Their eyes met in the mirror, and Pip marveled that it didn't crack with the heat. "You could ask me now."

Joe wiped away the last remnants of shaving cream with a hand towel. When he looked up, his expression was detached again. "If I don't have anything to offer a woman, I don't offer."

"Then why even tell me you're interested?"

His mouth twisted. "I'm human."

"Don't you know it's not a man's troubles that define him," she said softly, "it's the way he handles them."

"Yes, I do, which is precisely why I'm not embroiling you in my messy life." As he spoke he did up the buttons of his shirt, then stepped past her to open the entry door. Gently he knuckled her cheek. "Next lifetime, Miss Browne."

"If that's what you want."

A muscle tightened in his jaw and he dropped his hand. "Yes."

"Then goodbye, Joe."

Pip walked down the hall toward the elevator with dragging steps. Why was she so loath to let him go?

He was the kind of man—arrogant, wounded, stubborn—who never attracted her. Why work that hard? She pushed the elevator button, conscious of his gaze still on her. There was so much more to him, depths she wanted to plumb. Integrity. Hurt she could soothe. Pip was instinctive in her emotional choices; her family said impulsive. But she trusted the big insights.

The elevator doors opened, she turned and strode back to Joe. She refused to spend the rest of her life regretting the what-if. "I have to do this, at least once." Grabbing his open shirt, she tugged until he lowered his head. Then kissed him.

His lips parted under hers in surprise, then Joe caught her hands and broke contact. "You shouldn't have done that."

Pip blushed and dropped her gaze in confusion. Of course, a girl could also regret the things she *did* do. She tried to pull her hands free, but his grip tightened. "I've told you before about patting tigers through the bars."

Her heart started to beat faster in a queer tattoo. She raised her eyes back up to his. "But they're so cute," she managed to say before his mouth captured hers, firm, demanding. It was a kiss that left her without a shred of lipstick or common sense. At last Joe lifted his head.

"Now go home," he ordered roughly, and released her.

Pip held up a shaky finger. "One more," she said, and with a groan he complied.

Kissing him was like playing with matches. One led to another, then another, and before Pip knew it her body was on fire, Joe's shirt was unbuttoned and she was sliding her palms up and over all that muscle, heedless of being burned.

His skin was smooth and hot, taut over flesh and sinew. He lifted her so they were chest to chest, his fingers splayed across her rib cage, just under her breasts. She wrapped her arms around his neck, losing herself in sensation.

"So I said to Harry—"

Still holding Pip, Joe spun so his back blocked the open doorway, sliding her down his body and out of view of the passing couple.

"Evening," said a man beyond Joe's shoulder.

"Evening," he croaked back.

They went on, the two voices, down the hall and into the elevator.

"Shut the door," said Pip in a voice she barely recognized, when he turned back to her.

Joe left it open and started doing up the buttons of his shirt. His fingers shook. She laid her hand on them, a question in her eyes. He lifted her hand and kissed it.

"Pip, until I brokered my next big deal, I don't even have a home. But that's not what's stopping me. Kaitlin's the only part of my personal life that's going well and that's entirely thanks to you. I'm not ready for another relationship and I don't want to hurt you."

The yearning in his eyes contradicted every word he said. She smiled at him tenderly. "You think I'd let you?"

A ghost of a grin touched that harsh mouth. Joe shook his head.

"Remember, you're the one who's going to be left," she reminded him. "I'm returning to New Zealand in eleven weeks. The only reason I'm still here is to cover another teacher's maternity leave until Christmas."

His hand tightened on hers. "Last chance to run."

She was already half in love with him. But did any woman walk away from the lure, the temptation of a dangerous attraction? Pip never invested more than she could afford to lose. And she figured she could handle a little heartbreak—if she had to. She lifted her chin. "Hey, I'm the woman who pats tigers, remember?"

"Then you're in trouble." Joe kicked the door shut. "Because this one's out of the cage."

CHAPTER TEN

TAKING PIP INTO HIS ARMS, Joe bent his head and gently nipped her full lower lip. She drew a sharp breath and he smiled into her eyes, the clearest lagoon-blue, flecked with green and a little uncertainty.

"Not so fearless now?"

Smiling, she grabbed a handful of his shirt and tugged him into a deep, no-holds-barred kiss that set his heart pounding and his blood roaring. He felt himself go mindless and hard. She didn't wear any perfume and her fresh, natural scent was incredibly sexy.

Her hands scrambled with the buttons of his shirt; he shoved the coat off her shoulders and unzipped her gray shift dress. Between kisses, they stumbled backward toward the bedroom, littering clothes behind them until they were both down to their underwear.

By the bed, Pip reached for the zip on her knee-high boots and he saw with satisfaction that her hands trembled. "Let me." He sat her on the bed, knelt down in front of her and took over the job. Her body was shaped like an hourglass with full curves and a tiny waist that Joe could almost span with his big hands. She was so fine-boned it gave him pause. "I don't want to hurt you."

Smiling, Pip leaned forward and smoothed out his

frown with her thumb. "I might have sore shoulder muscles from rock climbing, but I won't break."

His chest tightened at that smile, the gold and cream perfection of her. *No, but I might.* "I had no idea you were so beautiful," he said honestly.

"Except for the sports bra," she murmured, and it struck him that she always turned aside compliments. "I didn't come prepared for this."

A thought hit Joe like a bucket of cold water. "Then I guess you haven't got condoms?" She shook her head. "Damn." He rezipped the boots. "Neither have I."

"I'm on the pill," Pip reassured him, then colored. "Unless you mean we need to do blood tests and things? I'm healthy... Are you..." Her color deepened. "I mean, do you do this often? I don't." She blushed with her whole body. Fascinated, Joe's gaze followed the glow.

"I haven't had sex for two years and only ever with one woman."

He'd come close a couple of times, but both women would have expected a more meaningful relationship, which had cooled his libido.

"Seriously, I'm the first since your divorce?" She regained her composure and an impish smile curved her lips. "I've had two lovers, so I guess I'm twice as experienced. In fact—" she lounged back on the pillows, and struck a provocative pose "—I'm almost a femme fatale." She seemed so delighted Joe had to laugh.

"Bet I've had sex more."

She pouted. "Not everything's a competition, Joe."

"Hey, you started it." Her playfulness was a joy. He leaned forward to kiss her smiling mouth, and felt all his troubles slide away. "It's only pregnancy that I'm paranoid about," he reiterated.

"That's why I'm still on the pill after nearly a year's celibacy," she said. Her smile faded as she sat up, unconsciously massaging one shoulder. "But we could go out and buy condoms if it will make you more comfortable."

Her pragmatism reassured him. This woman wouldn't be careless about birth control. Silently, he unzipped her boots again and pulled them off. Her shins were covered in bruises. Lightly, he touched one. "From camp?"

Pip looked and winced. "My femme fatal status didn't last long."

He saw she was embarrassed, and sat next to her on the bed, lifting her fingers to kiss them. "I like *real* better."

She snatched her hand away. "Oh, Lord, I still have dirt under my fingernails."

Joe captured her hands and kissed them again. "And I *really* like dirty girls."

"How about recovering tomboys?" she joked, but he heard the undertone of mortification. It was oddly endearing that a woman who looked the way she did would have hang-ups about her femininity.

"What else could you be, growing up with three older brothers?" He could imagine her as a spitfire kid, hiding all her feelings under the veneer of a tough. It aroused a strange tenderness in him. "Pip, you could chew tobacco, kick tires and belt your jeans with frayed rope, but you'll never be anything but a sexy, utterly feminine woman."

She dropped her gaze. "Hey, Fraser, you've already got me into bed."

"Yeah, so it must be true. Now turn over." When she blinked, he chuckled. "Let me work on those sore shoulders before I get to the rest of you."

"You don't have to—"

He trailed a finger gently from the dip in her collarbone down, over her bra to her navel, stopping on the white bikini briefs. "Tonight, Miss Pip, I'm in charge." He pressed lightly on the briefs, in exactly the right place, and her eyes darkened. His own control started to go and he had to remind himself they had all night.

Swallowing hard, Pip turned and lay on her stomach. Joe straddled her, unhooking her bra and massaging the nape of her neck and her shoulders. She squirmed in pleasure. "Oh, that's so good, don't stop."

He kneaded his way down her back, hauling off her panties and barely resisting the temptation to slide a hand between her legs. Instead, he traced her spine with his lips, kissing a bruise on her left buttock, another on the back of her thigh. "Call yourself a toughie, Miss Browne?"

She turned over, distracting him with her pink-tipped breasts, firm and high, and a golden triangle of curls. Then she punished him with a teasing kiss that nearly decimated his self-control.

"Joe," she pleaded, but he was nowhere ready to let her off the hook yet. He lowered his head to her breasts, teasing a nipple, sucking and pulling, his hand finally moving between her legs. Separating the curls, he found her so slick the ache in his groin went from pain to agony. Her questing fingers closed on him, not helping at all.

"Two can play at that game," she whispered, her slightly prim New Zealand inflection at odds with the way she stroked him and the sensuality in her heavy-lidded gaze.

He'd suffered through a relationship that never overcame its rocky beginning. In the bedroom, Nadia was always desperate to please, while Joe had been equally desperate to feign the love she needed from him. All that pretending hadn't made for good sex.

He'd never known what it was like to make love to a woman whose feelings he couldn't hurt. Who had no shadows in her eyes. A woman who played with him, and drove him crazy—for her pleasure as much as his.

But tonight was all about giving to the giver. Trapping her exploring hands, he took back control.

JOE APPROACHED THEIR lovemaking with the same intent focus he'd brought to the camp challenges.

Pip's breath hitched as he explored her body, so good, so very good at giving her what she wanted. She realized he was using her breathing as a guide to what she liked— a swirl of tongue in her belly button, a teasing brush of his fingers, a graze of teeth on a sensitive nipple.

Closing her eyes, Pip surrendered to sensation.

With my body I thee worship.

The line came into her head, so perfect a description of what he was doing. Making her feel beautiful, desirable, female in a way she'd never experienced.

"Philippa." The deep timbre of his voice, husky with desire, burned through her like a lick of flame. She shivered as he brought her to the brink of orgasm, only to pull back. Again and again.

They had all night.

Making love in a hotel room, with the occasional sound of muffled voices passing down the corridor, lent a delicious illicitness to their passion, freeing Pip to indulge every seductive fantasy.

They kicked off the covers and lay naked on top of the bed. Under her fingertips, Joe's skin gave off a wonderful radiant heat that made her want to burrow into his body.

"Enough," she finally gasped, and straddled him. As she began easing herself onto him, Joe's expression, predatory and tender, made her stomach swoop. Emotions pulled at her and, confused, she closed her eyes.

A finger gently stroked her lashes. Instinctively, Pip opened her eyes again, only to fall into the shimmering intimacy of Joe's gaze as he thrust upward and filled her.

Something fragile, tentative, came to life, a wonder.

No! She read a similar consternation in Joe's eyes and moved on him, distracting them both.

He gripped her hips, lifting her up, drawing her down, and she got lost in the feel of him, his hands guiding her, his body driving her in the slow, sweet building of an orgasm, followed by the dark rush into nothing but sensation.

Afterward, they lay for a long time, fingers linked, not speaking, in that quiescent peace that followed sex. Finally, hunger drove Joe to order room service. Pip had shared an early Chinese takeout with Anita, and settled for peppermint tea to settle a slight indigestion.

Wearing Joe's bathrobe, she curled up on the sofa, sipping her drink, and watched him demolish a steak. Dressed in jeans, and with his hair ruffled, he looked good enough to eat.

Pip yawned. "I should go home." She picked up her clothes from the floor.

"Stay," Joe invited, pushing his plate aside. "I'll take you out to breakfast in lieu of dinner."

"My brother Ben usually calls on Friday night."

With a wicked grin, Joe stood and ditched his jeans. The bedside lamp shadowed the indents in the long planes of hard male muscle.

The carpet was soft under Pip's bare feet as she padded

back to bed. "But I guess he can ring back. Do you have any siblings?"

"No." Joe loped across the room and joined her under the sheets, tugging at the tie of the robe she still wore. "I have an uncle only nine years older who's more like a brother, but work commitments mean we don't spend much time together."

Pip relinquished the robe. "I'm sensing a pattern here."

He shrugged. "All the males in our family are loners. It's in our genes. Seems we're not cut out for matrimony—on both sides of the family tree." At camp he'd made brief mention of his grandparents' clandestine affair. "Though thanks to you, I'm improving our legacy as fathers."

The robe was a tight bundle in his hands. Gently, Pip took it from him. "If you keep tensing your shoulders every time you mention your relatives you'll end up with a bull neck, which would be tragic." Joe looked at her blankly. "I mean," she continued, "you've already got the tough guy look going on. Don't overplay it."

The next second she was lying under him, while he supported his weight on his forearms. "Don't tease a tiger, Miss Browne."

Having achieved her aim of making him smile, Pip turned her mind to other matters. "How did you break your nose…a fight? A football injury?"

Joe started to laugh. "I stepped on a rake when I was six."

Pip caught her breath. Laughing, he was irresistible.

She would stay tonight, she told herself, only tonight. First thing after breakfast she'd leave, before this guy got any more addictive than he was already.

But for now…Pip slid down his magnificent body. "Maybe I am still hungry," she said.

JOE WOKE IN THE NIGHT to the sound of Pip retching in the bathroom. It took him a while to come alert after the first deep sleep he'd had since he could remember.

He heard her again. Instantly, he rolled out of bed and reached for his jeans. Looking at the bedside clock's luminous numbers in the dark, he saw it was only 1:00 a.m.

"Pip?" The bathroom door was locked.

"I'm okay." More retching; it sounded as though very little was left in her stomach.

Joe rattled the handle. "Open the door."

"Noooo!" It was a moan of self-conscious anguish.

"Now," he ordered.

The toilet flushed; there was the sound of running water, then the bathroom door opened a crack. "Please," she whispered hoarsely. "Go back to bed. This is embarrassing enough...oh!"

He heard her scramble back to the toilet, then more gagging. Joe pushed open the door to see Pip embracing the porcelain bowl. He held her shoulders until she'd finished throwing up and sank weakly onto the floor, then saturated a hand towel under the faucet and bathed her face with warm water.

"What did you have for dinner again?"

Sweat beaded on her forehead. "Don't mention the fried—" She grabbed the toilet bowl again.

"You really have a thing for my bathroom, don't you?" Joe said three hours later. Fully dressed, he sat on the floor with his back against the tub and Pip, a ball of bathrobe-clad misery, cradled in his arms. He'd coaxed her back into bed once—a mistake.

Housekeeping had taken away one bundle of ruined sheets at 2:00 a.m. and delivered a new set, which Joe had made up.

"No jokes," she moaned. Both of them had dozed between Pip's bouts of nausea, and he'd forced her to drink a little boiled water. It gave her something to hurl, but he figured enough stayed down to prevent dehydration.

The rest of the hot water had gone into a plastic water bottle, which she clutched against her cramping stomach.

Somewhere in the long night, Joe had stolen ten minutes to do an Internet search. Given what she'd eaten and the symptoms, it seemed likely she had Bacillus Cereus food poisoning, which would last around twelve to twenty-four hours. In all probability, Anita was suffering similar symptoms.

Pip was an uncomplaining patient, wan and so pathetic it was no hardship to look after her. Though she was too exhausted to apologize anymore, he knew she was mortified.

"It's been thirty minutes since you last threw up. Think maybe you can risk bed again?"

She roused from a half doze and struggled to her feet. "I'll go home."

"You're not going anywhere like this." With one arm around her shoulders, Joe opened the bathroom door and firmly steered her toward the bed. She didn't argue with him, crawling between the sheets and hauling them over her head like a child.

Joe tucked her in and positioned the champagne bucket where she liked it, in the crook of her arm. Pip opened her eyes. "Thank you," she rasped.

He kissed her brow and smoothed the blond curls. Even with hair like a rag doll, she was appealing. It seemed extraordinary that he'd known this woman only two weeks, biblically less than eight hours, and here he was, solicitously tucking her into bed.

But they'd met under circumstances that stripped away a conventional relationship, and everything since had fast-tracked them to intimacy. In some ways, he felt closer to her than he did to the woman he'd been married to for almost nine years. The thought gave Joe pause.

How had Pip insinuated herself into his life and thoughts so quickly? If she wasn't leaving the States he might worry about it, but her departure date, like a warning beacon, showed him where the rocks were. And with an end implicit from the beginning, he could relax his guard, enjoy the voyage.

Even weather the seasickness.

CHAPTER ELEVEN

IN THE END, Pip stayed the whole weekend, cocooned in muted luxury, a temperature-modulated climate and crisp sheets. She passed the intervals between attacks of nausea with sleeping, standing under the needle-sharp hot shower and drinking packets of electrolytes mixed in ice water.

After a while, she even managed to keep some down.

Anita, who'd developed symptoms earlier and already visited a doctor, confirmed Joe's Internet diagnosis. That saved Pip the humiliation of going out in public carrying a bucket—the same persuasive argument Joe had used to make her stay. Frankly, she was too ill to argue.

She'd given him the key to her apartment and he'd picked up toiletries and clothes. If she'd been well she would have asked what he thought of the candy-pink building and the over-the-top interior decorating she'd inherited. Instead she was simply grateful he didn't mention the camp laundry still piled in the living room.

More often than not when she woke from some half-fevered doze, through that interminable Saturday, her gaze fell on Joe, sitting at the desk with his laptop or pacing the living room with a phone pressed to his ear, talking contracts in a deep-voiced murmur.

Their eyes would meet, he'd give her an encouraging smile and she'd either stumble to the bathroom to continue her worship of the porcelain bowl or, as her symptoms subsided, close her eyes and drift back into sleep.

He made no unnecessary fuss, simply made sure she had everything she needed.

That night she woke to find him sleeping beside her. On Sunday morning, she opened her eyes to the steamy scent of a recent shower and a note.

"Taking Kaitlin to the zoo, then visiting Adam with Daniel. Expect you here when I get back. Joe."

His dictatorial tone annoyed her. She must be getting well. With a weak chuckle, Pip showered, donned a fresh nightgown he'd brought from her place, then made peppermint tea and called Anita.

"I've finally recovered enough to realize you've gone through this alone," said her mortified coworker. "You want me to send my hubby over with chicken broth?"

"No, I'm staying with a friend." Fluffing up her pillows, Pip leaned back against the headboard. She and Joe had decided to keep their romance secret; they'd been subjected to enough virulent interest at camp.

"On the bright side, we're lucky it was the emetic toxin," said Anita, "and not the other one. Personally, I think throwing up is better than diarrhea."

Pip's sense of the ridiculous reasserted itself and she laughed until she cried. Diarrhea would have been the ultimate indignity for Joe's poor bathroom. And no doubt the end of the affair. So much for femme fatale.

"Pip, you're obviously still delirious," said a puzzled Anita. "Go back to sleep."

Instead, she got up and packed, until a wave of dizziness sent her back to bed. She'd have a quick nap, then catch a cab home before Joe returned. The poor man had done enough.

"HEY, ADAM." Joe led the way into his father's room. "Look who's back from El Granada." Because he was expecting it, Joe saw the flare of shock in Daniel's gray eyes as he took in Adam's condition. The wasted limbs under the pale blue blanket, the gaunt cheekbones and saggy jowls that made Adam so hard for the nurses to shave and explained the tiny cut on his jawbone. The scent of allspice warred with the tang of disinfectant.

Joe swallowed. He could discount Aunt Jenny's opinion, dismiss Sam's reaction as insensitive, but he couldn't ignore Daniel's response. Guess he should stop avoiding that "talk" the specialist wanted to have.

"Listen, there's someone I need to catch up with," he said. "I won't be long."

The late-afternoon sun was painting the far wall when Joe returned, walking against the flow of the departing Sunday visitors. Daniel was standing beside Adam's bed, holding up sketch plans and outlining details of his latest construction project. Saving Adam the effort of having to talk.

"Sounds like you're about to hit the big time," Joe commented.

"Either that or go bust," said Daniel. "I've pretty much put everything I have into it." He might be joking or he might not. His deadpan expression gave nothing away.

Both of them were good at hiding things.

"Coffee?" said Joe. He needed it. As he measured the ground coffee into the dispenser he went over the specialist's report in his head.

"How strong are you making that stuff?" his uncle asked, amused.

Joe looked at the mound of coffee, then spooned most

of it back into the jar. "So what sort of return are you looking for?"

Telling himself it was the specialist's job to err on the side of caution, Joe lost himself in the technical details of Daniel's residential subdivision. His very first job had been with Kane Construction before he switched to commercial real estate, where sales were driven more by intellect and less by emotion. Joe preferred to stay away from people's dreams.

Handing Daniel his coffee, he picked up an album from Adam's bedside table. "These photos of the project?"

"No...Emily...brought," his father answered.

Joe opened it at random and saw a picture of Sam and Jenny as skinny-legged children. Arms folded over a knitted vest, Sam already had his bluster. Jenny stood beside him with a shy smile.

Frowning, Joe turned more pages. Robert Carson in his serviceman's uniform, a wedding photo of Robert and Sarah. "What the hell was Emily thinking?"

"I...asked...."

He came across a photograph of his grandfather as a young man. Except for Robert's blond hair, Joe could have been looking in the mirror. He'd been told there was a similarity, but seeing it sickened him. "How can you stand to look at Robert Carson? The bastard didn't even have the decency to offer your mother financial support."

"Jenny...thinks...did."

"She uncovered something in her mother's papers?"

"No...says...good...man."

Joe snorted. "She loved her daddy and doesn't want to think badly of him. The fact is, not a penny made its way into the house that Josephine didn't work for."

"Maybe...turned...down?"

"That would be stupid."

"Or Mom," said Daniel. He'd always had issues with his mother, felt that Adam had been the favorite, then Joe. It was true that Joe had an easy rapport with his grandmother, but she'd loved her youngest son despite their difficulties. Some relationships came easy and some—Joe glanced at Adam—some didn't.

Still, Daniel had a point. Josephine had prided herself on never having gone on welfare to raise her sons and grandson, working long hours rather than surrendering one iota of independence.

She'd been financially comfortable when Joe was sent to live with her—at least that's what she'd told Adam. In reality, she and Daniel had been living hand to mouth, relying on Joe's child support checks.

But Adam's payments had always been erratic, far too dependent on a good catch and far too influenced by his proximity to a bar. Yet Josephine had never suggested Adam quit chasing the big dollar and settle for a regular wage. In his mother's eyes, her oldest son could do no wrong.

Irritably, Joe flipped through the rest of the album. "Robert Carson should have *made* Nana Jo accept money."

"As though anyone could make Josephine Fraser do what she didn't want to," said Daniel with as much bitterness as affection.

"Maybe you're right." Joe hesitated at a shot of Robert Carson and Billy Fraser. That's how his grandmother and her lover had met. Robert had been a close friend of her husband. In the picture, both men were in uniform, their arms slung around each other's shoulders in easy friendship. Billy wore his Medal of Honor. By the condition of the uniforms, the picture had probably been taken after the presentation ceremony. Robert had been one of the men Billy had saved.

How ironic that Billy had survived the war a hero, only to be killed in a car accident. Then his best friend got his widow pregnant.

Joe touched the face of the man he still thought of as his grandfather. Adam had always been so proud of Billy Fraser's Medal of Honor, only letting Joe help polish it when he was old enough to be awed. Their best times as father and son had been discussing Granddad's heroics.

Joe shifted uncomfortably. Now Adam was the illegitimate bastard of a torrid affair, with a father who hadn't cared enough to be part of his life. How must that feel?

Like I felt all my life. Abandoned.

He snapped the album shut and a loose photograph fell onto the carpet. "Care…ful," growled Adam.

"Yeah, yeah." Joe bent and picked up the Polaroid, glanced at it, then froze.

"You okay?" said Daniel.

"Fine." Surreptitiously, Joe pocketed the photograph. "Listen, Sue's putting on a farewell dinner next week before Aunt Jenny and Uncle Luke fly back to Florida. She wants you to come."

"Sorry, I'm tied up."

"I haven't even told you what night yet." It occurred to Joe his uncle had been working today; why else would he carry plans and be dressed for a work site on a Sunday? "The dinner's Thursday."

Adam spoke. "Jen…wants…know…you."

Joe took up the argument. "She is your sister and Sue's your niece."

"Half sister, half niece."

"Now you sound like Uncle Sam." Joe studied

Daniel's intractable expression and added, "He won't be there, if that's what you're worried about."

Daniel gave him the kind of look a lion might give lunch. "Terrified."

"Kaitlin's coming. You haven't seen her in a while." Good God, he was wheedling. "Don't make me beg," he added, "I need you as my wingman. I'm picking up the Carson necklace." He filled Daniel in on the latest.

"Fine, but this is a once-only. Are we clear?"

Joe nodded.

"Adam?" Daniel turned to his half brother.

Adam gave his noncommittal grunt, but Daniel wasn't practiced in interpretation and read it as a yes.

Joe glanced at his watch, wondering if Pip had followed instructions and stayed. Given her independence, probably not. Still, the possibility lured him, as irresistible as a worm to a hungry fish.

The fish knew there was a hook in there, but he just couldn't help himself.

WHEN PIP WOKE UP it was night. The sliding door had been closed and only a sliver of light suggested Joe had returned. Disorientated, she glanced at the clock: 7:00 p.m. She'd slept for eight uninterrupted hours. Sitting up, she felt no nausea, no dizziness. She drank some water from a glass on the bedside table and her stomach rumbled, not in protest, but in hunger.

Turning on the lamp, she opened the slider. The other room was empty, with only one light on, in the entry. Joe wasn't there.

Yawning, she padded to the bathroom and stopped in the doorway. Joe sat in the three-corner hot tub, arms resting on the rim, head back, eyes closed. For a moment Pip thought he was crying, then realized his face was beaded with water from a recent dunking that had also flattened his hair against his head. But the water wasn't what misled her; his expression was the saddest she'd ever seen.

Something about him evoked her favorite childhood fairy tale, "The Happy Prince," about a beautiful statue that cried real tears when he saw the misery of the city at his feet. So he commissioned a sparrow to pluck out his jeweled eyes and strip him of his gold leaf and give it away to the needy. But it would never be enough.

"What's wrong?" she asked, then remembered he'd visited his father after dropping off Kaitlin. "Is it your dad?"

The water sloshed in the tub as he opened his eyes and sat up, forcing a smile. "You're awake." Unlike the Happy Prince, this man gave everything away *but* himself.

"What is it, Joe?" she asked again. "You look so sad."

"I had a meeting with Adam's specialist about his slow progress. His prognosis for a full recovery isn't good." She'd noticed before that he called his father by his first name.

Joe picked up the washcloth and started soaping his shoulders. "I figured you'd be hungry when you woke up so I ordered some food. Bananas, toast and applesauce seem to be the invalid diet of choice. Incidentally, Michael the hotel manager sends his best wishes. You made quite a hit with him."

Pip took off her nightgown. His running commentary stopped. She stepped into the tub and sank into the hot water. "Come on in," said Joe drily, but she'd startled some of the desolation out of his eyes.

"Turn around," said Pip. "I'll wash your back."

With the washcloth and soap she worked on the tense muscles of his shoulders, felt them gradually relax.

"How's Kaitlin handling it?"

"She doesn't know. Hell, Adam's been working so damn hard at therapy, too." Joe gave a shuddering laugh. "I used the promise of a visit from Kaitlin as an incentive, and now it's come back to bite me."

Surprised, Pip stopped the massage. "She doesn't visit?"

"His speech is impaired, he's paralyzed down one side. I don't want her to see him like that. It will frighten her."

"If you prepared her—"

"Pip…"

Leaning forward, she touched her lips briefly to his wet spine. "Butt out?"

"Yes…no!" He returned to his end of the spa bath and shot her an exasperated look. "You've got two minutes to give me your best advice, Counselor, but I reserve the right to ignore it. Go."

"You're trying to protect her, but sometimes kids feel more secure by being included at difficult times." Pip cupped a handful of soap bubbles and watched them pop, rainbow colors under the ceiling light. "My grandmother lived with us in her last years. It taught me that illness and death are a part of life, and being family means supporting each other through good times and bad."

When only a couple of bubbles remained, she fisted her hand. "If they're close, Kaitlin will want to be involved, and it may aid your father's recovery. And if he dies, well, then she'll have more memories."

He frowned. "He's not going to die. But I'll think about it."

Leaning forward she smoothed Joe's brow, the lines of fatigue around his mouth. "You need rest."

He shook his head, and tiny droplets of water fell from his wet hair to his broad shoulders. "Do you ever," he said, sounding frustrated and amused, "stop looking after people?"

"Do you?" she countered. "You've sold your home to pay for your dad's care, you've been nursing a sick woman—"

"Money, a bed and a jug of water are easy. But you give time, attention—you give yourself." He hesitated. "I don't do that, Pip."

She wrung out the washcloth, then wiped away the steam on her face. "My oldest brother and his wife had my first niece since I've been away," she reflected. "Dad's had some heart trouble—nothing serious, but enough to remind me I won't have my parents around forever. And I have twenty-six cousins, half of whom I'm close to." Pip smiled. "Even a 'charmer' like you can't compete with the pull of family."

He chuckled, then hauled her around so she rested against his chest. Taking the washcloth, he began a slow, soapy sponge down. "How the hell did such a homebody end up living more than six thousand miles away?"

Pip surrendered herself to the sensual roughness of the washcloth on her upper arms and shoulders. "I'd been burning the candle at both ends, slotting counselor courses around a full-time teaching job, when one of my mentors suggested the teacher exchange program as a working holiday.

"The clincher was my breakup with Rob. He was a good friend of my brothers and I got tired of seeing hurt expressions every way I turned—and that was just Ben and Chris." Behind her, Joe chuckled again. "Leaving the country was the only way I could make a clean break."

He ran the washcloth across her collarbone. "And has absence made the heart grow fonder?"

"Of Rob?" Pip turned her head so she could look up at him. "Do you think I'd be in this tub if it had?"

He paused in his work. "No," he conceded, "but I'm trying to stay neutral. Isn't that a rule in holiday romances? Or in our case, working holiday romances?"

"I don't know. You're my first, too. We'll just have to wing it." He dipped the cloth in the bath, then trickled hot water over her breasts. It felt wonderful.

"So is Rob still pining?"

"God, no! It took him only three months to meet someone else and get engaged." She was finding it hard to concentrate as Joe ran slow circles over her breasts, the washcloth a delicious abrasion on her nipples. "I wasn't that special, after all."

He nuzzled the side of her neck, his erection nudging her bottom. "Quit fishing for compliments."

"I am special?" Pip said innocently.

"You're here, aren't you?" There was laughter in his voice.

She pulled the washcloth out of his hand and dumped it over his head. "Of all the arrogant—"

He put his mouth on hers and Pip punished him through the kiss instead, capturing his exploring tongue between her teeth, before acquiescing. Their bodies slid together, unbearably erotic. Until the alarm on her sports watch beeped, and they broke apart.

"What's that?" said Joe.

"A timely reminder to take contraception."

"You do take it seriously."

She reached into her cosmetics bag, sitting on the vanity, then popped the pill. "No kids until I'm in my thirties and the most sought-after family therapist in Auckland, with at least fifteen staff under me."

"Always wanting to be on top." He pulled her back into the tub, reversed their positions and entered her in one thrust.

"Oh," said Pip.

"Wrap your legs around me," he said huskily.

"Way ahead of you," she whispered back. And then they didn't talk for a long, long time.

CHAPTER TWELVE

"IT'S SO PRETTY," Kaitlin breathed, holding the ornate necklace against her purple T-shirt.

The gold chain was a bit old-fashioned, but she loved the heart-shaped diamond and all the blue stones around it. She gave the highest compliment she could pay. "It's exactly what a princess would wear."

She sat in her second cousin Sue's bedroom, surrounded by the four Carson women and thrilled to her toes to have long-lost relatives who were both beautiful and kind. She wasn't quite clear on *how* she'd got them—Dad was vague on the details—but if it was good enough for *The Princess Diaries,* it was good enough for Kaitlin.

And the story behind the necklace was *so* romantic. About a poor English boy, Kaitlin's great-great-great-great—she kinda got lost with the greats, but there were a lot—grandfather, and the rich man's daughter who gave him the necklace to help him escape to America when their affair was discovered. He was supposed to sell it, but instead he worked hard and kept it, and gave it to his wife when he eventually got married. Kaitlin thought it would have been even *more* romantic if he'd died of a broken heart, but then *she* wouldn't be here so she forgave him for falling in love again.

"I'll lend it to you for your wedding," promised Great-

Aunt Jenny, replacing the jewel carefully in its black velvet box. "Now let's take it to your father."

Dad was going to be looking after the necklace for a while. It had something to do with keeping it away from Great-Uncle Sam, who was the only one of her new relatives Kaitlin hadn't met yet. It seemed odd that a man would want a necklace, but the grown-ups had noticed she was there before she could hear the whole story.

"Can we wake up the babies so I can play with them?" Kaitlin asked Sue, who only laughed and shook her head.

"Honey, we've just got them to sleep." Sue had the best job in the world—looking after foster babies, though baby Carrie was hers and Uncle Rick's by adoption.

"Come and eat pizza instead," suggested her other second cousin, Belle, who had the next best job in the world; working for a pizza company. She'd brought a Hawaiian one especially for Kaitlin, since the grown-ups were all eating shrimp. Yuk.

"First we'll go give this necklace to your daddy," said Great-Aunt Jenny.

Kaitlin skipped ahead to where the men had gathered around the barbecue in the yard. The horizon sucked the last heat from the setting sun like a kid with a lollipop. This family needed more babies, she decided, so there'd always be one awake to play with.

It was just after five-thirty on a Thursday evening in early October and she was thrilled to be seeing Dad on a school night. Thrilled to be spending time with her new relatives.

Dad and Uncle Daniel had moved away from the barbecue to make room for the cooks to serve up the food. "You have the look of a guy that's getting la—" Uncle Daniel caught sight of her. "Laid pipe," he continued. "Gas pipes, electrical conduits."

"Uncle Daniel," Kaitlin interrupted impatiently. "Do you want a baby?"

His eyes crinkled as he smiled. "No, thanks, honey, I've got a beer."

Following a half dozen steps behind her, Great-Aunt Jenny paused at the open sliding doors to exchange a word with her husband, who carried a plate of grilled corn inside.

"No, I mean do you want to get married and have babies. Since you're so old?"

"I'm only thirty-seven and three quarters," he said solemnly. "And you're my favorite baby."

She pulled a face; he pulled one right back. "So Great-Aunt Jenny's your sister, right?"

Hearing her name, Great-Aunt Jenny started walking over.

"Half sister. Your great-grandmother was our mom but we had different dads."

"And Sue's your niece." Kaitlin grinned. She loved that you could be someone's uncle even when you were only nine years older. She knew that Uncle Daniel was really her great-uncle, too, but he seemed way too young to call him that. "Are you related to anyone else here?"

"Only you, pumpkin, and your dad. You're my real family."

Great-Aunt Jenny's smile faltered. She stopped just short of their group.

"Jenny, I'm sorry," Uncle Daniel said awkwardly. "I only meant that I've always known these guys."

"That's fine, Daniel." She smiled again, but you could tell she was still kinda hurt. "Joe, thanks for doing this." She held out the black velvet box. "I appreciate it."

Dad took the necklace, but he didn't look happy about it. "I'm thinking a month max," he said.

"Let's hope Sam's given up by then," Great-Aunt Jenny replied. She looked at Kaitlin and said brightly, "Who wants to eat? Sweetie, go tell Belle and Sue we're ready."

En route, Kaitlin stopped to listen by the babies' door just in case they were awake. Not a peep.

"Have you noticed anything different about Joe?" she heard Sue say to Belle, down the short hall in the kitchen.

"I have, but I can't put my finger on it. I mean, he's always been a good-looking guy...but granite, you know? He's softer somehow."

"He's got the glow," said Sue softly.

"The love glow?" Belle sounded in awe. "You think there's a woman brave enough to slash through those thorns?"

"He's not *that* bad," protested Sue, but she was laughing. "Well, okay maybe he is, but he wasn't always." There was a moment of silence. "I so hope I'm right." She sounded like a kid wishing for a very, very special Christmas present.

"We could ask him," Belle suggested.

"Go ahead," said Sue.

"Are you crazy?"

"Aunt Jenny says the barbecue's all ready," Kaitlin announced, stepping into the kitchen. Both women started guiltily. She thought about telling them that Dad wouldn't go out with Miss Browne, then decided against it. Sue would only be disappointed.

Still, Kaitlin had a question for her dad when they began the drive home a few hours later. "Love doesn't make you glow, does it, Dad?" she asked sleepily.

"No, honey, not as far as I know."

Kaitlin yawned, snuggled down into the leather seat and closed her eyes. "Don't forget your seat belt, Dad."

"TELL ME HOW YOU MET Nadia," said Pip a month later.

Considering they were sitting in a downtown restaurant, celebrating Halloween by eating Creepy Crawler pasta and Monster Mash salad, it was fitting, Joe thought wryly, she'd ask a question that raised specters.

By now he knew his girlfriend well enough not to flinch at her fearless inquiries or suspect a sinister female agenda. For all her frankness Pip respected his right to privacy and took no offense if he shook his head on a subject. Which meant he rarely did.

As he weighed his answer, a group of young hobbits and goblins at the next table started singing along to "Monster Mash." The ghosts on Pip's head-bopper bounced as she swayed to the music. They'd been given the damn things at the door and Joe had chosen the smallest—devil's horns. "Remind me how we ended up here?"

"Because I wanted a Halloween experience." She passed her scissored fingers across her eyes, imitating Uma Thurman in *Pulp Fiction,* and Joe grinned. "And Anita said this was the place all the kids recommended," she finished.

"It is," agreed Joe. "Nadia and I used to bring Kaitlin here before she went trick-or-treating."

Pip stopped swaying and the ghosts trembled to a halt. "Oh, Joe, I'm sorry. Would you prefer to go somewhere else?"

"No, it's okay." He'd got used to the ache around events like this. "It's fun watching you have fun." Her enjoyment of everything, from the jack-o'-lanterns and cobweb place mats to the costumes worn by the junior patrons, gave him a new appreciation of the holiday.

Just then a body walked past their booth, carrying his

head under his arm. Pip stared after it in fascination. "You want me to tell you how the costume works?" he offered.

She shook her head and the ghosts danced. "No, I prefer the magic."

Joe picked up his Bloodthirsty Mary. "To magic," he toasted, and their eyes met. Lately he couldn't tear his gaze away from hers.

"Monster Mash" faded into Screamin' Jay Hawkins, who sang "I put a spell on you."

Joe blinked, then raised his glass and drank, welcoming the grounding burn of Tabasco in the tomato juice.

Pip picked up her fork, then put it down again.

"Something wrong?" he asked.

"I still get the occasional wave of nausea.... It's gone now." She picked up her fork again. "That food poisoning sure is persistent."

"Did you ever get checked out by a doctor?"

"I've made an appointment for next week." Spearing a shrunken-head baked potato, she began eating. "So, you were going to tell me how you met Nadia."

"She was my college roommate and I was on the rebound. We got drunk together one night and ended up in bed."

Brokenhearted and gut lonely after Nana Jo's death, he'd taken advantage of Nadia's feelings for him. He still despised himself for that.

Pip added sour cream to her potato. "You must have been in a lot of pain to be that irresponsible."

"It was self-indulgent teen angst," he said, stabbing at his bloodbath lasagna. "I'd been rejected by my high school crush and thought a bruised ego entitled me to cut loose."

"Except Nadia got pregnant and you got married."

"It was the right thing to do."

To his astonishment Pip slid around in the booth and kissed him, all soft lips and sour cream. "What was that for?" he asked as she slid back and resumed eating.

"You're a good person."

"The marriage failed, Pip," he reminded her.

"It lasted almost nine years," she answered. "Given its beginning, that was some effort you two made. Did you ever love her, Joe?"

Only Pip would have the nerve to ask that question. "Yes," he said. "But never the way she needed me to, never fervently. For the most part we worked hard, and we did a lot of pretending."

In contrast, his relationship with Pip over the last month had been effortless, probably because they had no expectations of each other. Actually, that wasn't true. Last week when he'd called to say he'd be forty minutes late to pick her up because he wanted to clear some paperwork, she'd said, "I'm not Nadia."

"What's that supposed to mean?"

"Either you arrive at the time we arranged or we postpone." No threat, simply a statement, delivered in a cheerful and reasonable tone.

"Okay, let's postpone." Joe didn't respond well to ultimatums, no matter how cheerfully delivered. "How about tomorrow?"

She lost none of her friendliness. "I'm going to the movies with Anita."

"Thursday?"

"Having dinner with my neighbor."

"Friday?"

"Remember I'm spending the weekend in Tahoe?"

Unwilling to back down, Joe made a date for the following week. They had a wonderful evening being scrupulously nice to each other, followed by raw makeup sex. And he'd learned his lesson.

"Let's make a deal," Pip said now. "Honesty between us no matter what. And if it gets too difficult with me leaving, we part with no hard feelings."

So damn earnest, so endearingly a stickler for fair play. They still had seven weeks before she returned to New Zealand for Christmas. Plenty of time to start reining in this infatuation.

Joe tapped his horns. "You shouldn't be making deals with the devil."

"Ah, but I know his weakness," said Pip, peeling back the lapel of her silk shirt to reveal a scarlet bra strap.

He stopped smiling. "Let's skip dessert."

While they waited for their check, he nuzzled her neck, making her shiver as he whispered huskily what he was going to do to her when he got her back to the hotel. "Joe, we're in public," Pip said breathlessly.

"Let 'em look," he growled, and kissed her, because he badly needed to. When they finally broke apart her eyes were heavy-lidded. Then she glanced beyond him and her eyes widened. "What, another headless body?" he teased, turning with his arm still around her shoulder.

Staring back were Nadia, Doug and two princesses.

"WELL," SAID PIP BRIGHTLY, as they all sat in the booth watching the girls eat dessert. "Isn't this nice?" The adults had settled for coffee.

Eyes shining, Kaitlin and Melissa both nodded vigorously. Delirious with joy that their matchmaking had worked. "If you marry my dad," said Kaitlin, "we'll be related. Won't that be cool?"

Dressed in a yellow satin ball gown—"I'm Belle from

Beauty and the Beast"—Kaitlin squished her hoop skirt under the table to reach her dessert, and her tiara fell into the ice cream. Retrieving it, she licked it clean.

"Not very princesslike," said Nadia, her face set in a smile. At any minute Pip expected writhing snakes to break through.

"We're not getting married," Pip assured Nadia. She nudged Joe for confirmation, but he'd taken refuge in a conversation with Doug about sports, the male equivalent of a panic room. The two men were getting on better now that Kaitlin's relationship with Joe had been sorted out.

"Besides," said Melissa authoritatively, "if she married your dad she'd turn into a wicked stepmother. They all do." Melissa was dressed as Ariel from *The Little Mermaid,* and appropriately blue because she refused to wear anything warm over her puffed short sleeves. In a long red wig she looked more like Pippi Longstocking on a bad hair day. "You'll just have to stay in love." She sighed theatrically and the tight skirt that made up her tail strained at its chiffon seams. "It's so romantic."

Pip said, "Excuse me while I go to the bathroom."

Joe paused in his conversation to give her an "I think this is going well," look as she squeezed past him. *Men.*

When Pip left the toilet stall, Nadia was standing at the vanity repairing her perfect makeup. *Uh-oh.* With a smile of acknowledgment, Pip went to the basin and washed her hands. In the mirror, the little ghosts quivered on her head and she took them off. They were far too frivolous for the conversation she suspected was coming.

"Well, this explains why you were such a champion of Joe's cause leading up to camp," Nadia said, powdering her nose with short, sharp dabs.

"We didn't start dating until after camp." Pip activated the hand dryer to discourage further conversation.

Nadia's lips tightened, which made it difficult for her to reapply the vermilion lipstick. "To tell the truth," she called over the dryer, "I'm feeling a teensy bit betrayed, Pip." She smiled to take the sting out of the words, but her eyes told Pip she was furious. "I revealed things I would never have divulged if I'd known you were sleeping with my ex-husband."

Resigned, Pip turned away from the dryer, rubbing her still-damp hands together. "You and I had those conversations prior to camp, but regardless, I would never betray a professional confidence. I understand that seeing your ex with another woman for the first time must be upsetting, but—"

"Upset? Of course I'm not upset…damn, my lipstick's smeared!" Retrieving a tissue from her bag, Nadia scrubbed fiercely at her lip. "I look such a mess."

"No, you don't." Pip was confused by the other woman's self-disgust. As always, Nadia was impeccably groomed, tonight in a cream sweater and fine wool pants. Her glossy tan boots were exactly the same shade as her handbag, and strands of fine gold gleamed at her ears, neck and wrist. After dinner she and Doug were trudging the streets, supervising a gaggle of trick-or-treaters, but as far as Pip could see, the other woman's only nod to casual was a chic ponytail.

Glancing at her own reflection, Pip grimaced, then self-consciously finger-combed her short hair, disheveled from the head-bopper, and reapplied the lip gloss that Joe had kissed off. *This is not a competition,* she told herself.

Just as well, 'cause you'd lose.

Nadia dropped the tissue into the bin. "And I'm only

upset for Kaitlin. It was a huge shock seeing her father playing tonsil hockey with her teacher."

As Pip opened her mouth to point out that traumatized children rarely yelled, "Yay!" before celebrating with a double helping of witches' pudding, the other woman added vehemently, "*Why* did I wear my hair this way?"

Pulling off the scrunchie, Nadia ransacked her bag for a comb and dragged it through her hair with shaking fingers.

And Pip finally got it. Despite Nadia's painstaking efforts with her appearance, she'd never been able to make her former husband fall in love with her. Because he'd been in love with someone else.

"I'm going back to New Zealand at Christmas, so the relationship's not serious for either of us." She wanted to reassure Nadia, but the reminder steadied Pip, as well. "And the only reason we kept it secret was because we didn't want to give anyone the wrong idea."

Nadia bit her lip, then met Pip's eyes in the mirror. "I'm sorry, I don't know why I'm reacting like this. It's not like I still love him."

"You were married a long time. It's natural to feel a little territorial, under the circumstances."

"I assure you it's only a reflex." Dropping the comb into her bag, Nadia pulled her hair back into a ponytail. "Doug thinks I look gorgeous like this," she said awkwardly. "God knows why."

"You always look gorgeous," Pip assured her. "And I can see why Kaitlin raves about Doug." Though he wasn't what she'd expected. Pleasant-looking and affable, he was the polar opposite of Joe.

"Does she?" Nadia's face lit up. "I'm so glad. Things were tense for a while." She hesitated. "Thanks for your help with Kaitlin and Joe."

"You're welcome."

Turning from the mirror, Nadia squared her shoulders. "You're a good person, so let me give you some advice. Don't fall in love with Joe. He doesn't cope with that at all well. He shut down his emotions after he had his heart broken in high school."

Pip had two opposing impulses—to defend Joe and to try to learn more. "He dismissed it as a crush."

The brunette shook her head. "Su…she was more than that. As Princess Diana once famously said, 'there were three of us in this marriage, so it was a bit crowded.'" Nadia opened the ladies' room door and gestured for Pip to exit first. "I sometimes wonder, if we'd known the truth about her then…" She paused, and the two women looked at each other.

Nadia was obviously waiting for her to ask about Joe's disreputable first love. Heroically, Pip bit her lip and walked on. Out of loyalty to Joe or self-protection? Both, she decided.

Shrugging, Nadia closed the door behind them. "Well, it's water under the bridge now. Still, be careful."

"Like I said, we're keeping it light…. So Kaitlin mentioned you're going to Hawaii for your honeymoon?"

Much to Pip's relief, Nadia accepted the change of subject and they chatted about tropical destinations as they returned to the table. "Even though Doug's so mellow, he makes every day feel like a holiday," Nadia finished.

Joe glanced up as they approached, his charisma potent even at this distance. He was a holiday, too, Pip thought, but adrenaline-fueled, thrilling…dangerous. And while she might be open to adventure, she had a safety harness firmly in place.

In a couple of months she'd be celebrating a summer

Christmas and picking the red brush blooms of the pohutukawa tree for the festive table.

Besides, she wasn't stupid; she'd already taken his measure.

When they'd met he'd been too battle-weary to hide his vulnerability. Now the only time Pip glimpsed the inner man was in bed, where Joe's lovemaking was so tender it would have broken her heart if she'd let it.

So Pip wouldn't let it.

CHAPTER THIRTEEN

"TELL ME AGAIN," said Daniel. "It's the best Halloween story I ever heard. Ex-wife springs you with secret girl-friend, a real horror."

"Yeah, well, I'm not here just to be your entertainment," Joe said. They were drinking beers at Murphy's Bar, watching football on the big screen and talking idly between plays.

Daniel sipped his drink. "So how'd it end?"

"Pip lectured me walking home from the restaurant. Apparently, I should have tried harder to love my ex-wife." When Daniel spluttered, Joe grinned. "Turned out she felt bad for hurting Nadia's feelings by keeping our relationship secret."

"Your girlfriend sounds kind," said Daniel. His mouth twisted at some private joke. Or it could have been the slaughter on-screen. "Did you tell her that love can't fix everything that's broken?"

"Pip knows I don't want long-term." Seizing his courage, Joe pulled a photograph out of his jacket pocket and pushed it along the bar toward Daniel. "Recognize this guy?"

His uncle tore his eyes from the frenzied celebrations on-screen. The Washington Redskins had just killed the Oakland Raiders' Super Bowl hopes with a touchdown in extra time. "There's something familiar about him."

"Remember he was at Josephine's funeral?"

"Vaguely." Daniel studied the photograph more closely. "He wore one of those old-fashioned soft-brimmed hats. But you were the one who talked to him."

Sue hadn't come to the funeral; Joe had asked her not to. Her rejection of him as a boyfriend had still been too raw, too painful.

The old man had arrived near the end of the service and taken a seat in the last row, laying his hat respectfully across his knees. Though he'd carried himself with dignity, sorrow rolled off him, thick as fog. That's why Joe had noticed him.

At the cemetery it had started to rain, a gusty shower that swept under umbrellas and sent everyone running for cover. Avoiding the crowds, Joe had sought shelter under a mottled oak on a small rise where the old man stood apart from the other mourners.

He'd stiffened at Joe's approach, but other than nodding an acknowledgment, Joe hadn't initiated conversation. For perhaps ten minutes the two had stood side by side in silence, listening to the rain patter on the overhead canopy, and dodging the soft splashes of water that made it through the leaves.

Joe had stared down at the coffin, abandoned by the open grave and worried that Nana Jo would get wet inside it. Even though he was seventeen, logic couldn't shake the childish fear. The raindrops were liquid welts on the varnished mahogany, blisters on the gold handles. He told himself it didn't matter—as soon as the shower passed, the coffin would be lowered in the earth and covered with wet dirt anyway. But still he watched in silent agony.

"Good thing she liked the rain," said the old man, and Joe was reassured by that simple truth.

"Into every life…" he murmured, then stopped because tears burned his eyes. It had been one of his grandmother's sayings.

"A little rain must fall," whispered the old man.

Eventually the shower spluttered to a stop and mourners started making their way back to the grave.

"I wonder," said the old man, "if you could point out Adam Fraser for me."

"You know my father?"

The old man started at that. "You are…?"

"Joe Fraser, his son. Adam couldn't make it back in time." Again.

"So you're doing this alone?"

"No. Daniel…Josephine's son by her second marriage is here."

He'd pointed out his young uncle, but the old man gave Daniel only a cursory glance. "You were named for her."

"Yes. When did you know my grandmother?"

"A lifetime ago." The brim of the hat hid his face as the old man bowed his head. "She was an incredible woman."

Below, Daniel beckoned, his face stony with repressed grief. Twenty-six years old was too young to be burying your mother. "We need to go back down," said Joe.

"I wonder if you'd put these on her coffin for me," the old man said hoarsely, pulling a slightly crushed posy from under his coat. "I find myself unable to say goodbye."

Joe had accepted the flowers, the palest lilac roses. They smelled exactly like Nana's favorite perfume and for a poignant moment it felt as if she was there with them.

"God bless you, son." The old man's farewell handshake had a faint tremor and he'd taken a while to let go.

"You know," Joe said awkwardly, "some of Nana's friends are hosting an afternoon tea back at the house."

"Thank you, but I'm due home."

"It was your grandfather Robert Carson, wasn't it?" Daniel's touch brought Joe back to the present. On-screen, the Redskins fans were still leaping around in a frenzy of burgundy and gold. The glass in front of Joe was empty.

"Yeah." He gestured to the bartender for another round. Ironically, Joe had visited the old man's house after Sarah Carson's funeral six months ago, when he'd given Sue a ride to the Twin Peaks home and been talked into staying for a drink. At that point he'd simply been her old friend, plain Joe Fraser, son of Adam, grandson of Billy, exchanging polite condolences with strangers.

Strangers who'd proved to be his aunts, uncle and cousins.

If only he'd known, he would have examined his surroundings, searched out the family portraits, hunted for clues in the minutiae of his real grandfather's life. For decades Robert Carson lived in that house. He'd built it. Surely Joe would have found some echo of the man.

It was too late now. Sam had cleared out the place for sale, stripped it of its character. But Joe did remember one thing. The wine collection. His grandfather had been a connoisseur. Like him.

The bartender delivered the beers. Joe picked up the glass, icy to the touch. "You know what really gets me now?"

"What's that?" His uncle's gaze was compassionate.

"I liked the son of a bitch."

"BUT I CAN'T BE PREGNANT," Pip told Dr. Giles at her after-school appointment. Despite telling Joe at Halloween she'd get checked out, it had taken another two weeks to find time in her busy schedule. "I'm on the pill," she insisted. "I'm fanatical about taking it at the same time every day."

Sitting in his consulting room, she locked her hands in her lap and waited for the physician to admit he was wrong.

Dr. Giles was a thin, beak-nosed man with enough experience to know when to meet his patient's eyes and when to look away. He doodled a tiny line of spirals at the bottom of his notes. "If you had food poisoning and were throwing up, it's likely your protection was compromised, even if you had taken it during that time."

He ran out of doodle space and dropped to a new line. Pip's gaze followed the pen. "And women who get pregnant on the pill may have intermittent bleeding, which would explain the spotting you thought was a period."

"No." Instinctively, she shook her head, and Dr. Giles's eyes darted to hers before returning to his spiral doodle. She decided he was drawing her brain wave, chaotic, whirling.

"How long did the food poisoning last, Miss Browne?"

Realizing she had slid down in the chair, Pip struggled upright. "Only twenty-four hours…give or take." Thinking about it, she realized she'd compromised two doses, maybe three. Why had it never occurred to her?

Too sick, too infatuated, too—

Nausea came in a rush and Pip leaped to her feet, trying to swallow the bile. "Excuse me," she managed to say. Yanking open his office door, she ran to the bathroom and frantically jiggled the handle, clamping a palm to her mouth.

The door was locked.

"Key," Dr. Giles called sharply behind her. The receptionist came flying. Sweat on her forehead, Pip stopped heaving through sheer force of will as the woman fumbled with the key. Finally, Pip shoved the door open, slammed it behind her and threw up lunch, closing her eyes against the sight of regurgitated corn chowder.

Not residual food poisoning, but a baby.

Trembling, she flushed the toilet, rinsed out her mouth at the sink, then tidied her hair in the mirror. All small, methodical actions designed to reassure the terrified face looking back at her. A woman nowhere near ready to be a mother.

With a paper towel she dabbed her forehead, clammy with sweat, then crouched under the dryer and lifted her face, needing the hard blast of air. *Soon,* she thought, *I'll wake up.*

"Miss Browne?" The receptionist knocked on the door. "Are you okay?"

"I'm fine." Pip hauled herself upright on shaky legs. "I'll be out in a minute." *Pregnant.* She touched her flat stomach, but all she felt was a flutter of panic. In a daze, she returned to the consulting room, where she listened carefully to Dr. Giles's advice and accepted all his pamphlets.

Then, with no recollection of anything he'd said, she walked out of the doctor's office and straight into a drugstore, where she bought a pregnancy kit.

Back in her North Beach apartment, Pip did the test twice, in between drinking mugs of hot, sweet tea. The result was the same both times. Positive.

Despairingly, she tossed the second tube into the bin. How could a negative be a positive? Once again she tried to think of the baby as real—and failed.

Dear God, she wasn't ready to be pregnant. She wasn't married, she wasn't in New Zealand, she wasn't thirty-something and, most importantly, she wasn't with a man who loved her.

No, Joe loves you. He just doesn't know it yet. Except Nadia had held that hope for almost nine years. Pip groaned as the implications sank in.

Now, when she could least cope with it, "I left my heart in San Francisco" stopped being a cutesy sound bite and took on a sinister, ripped-out-of-your-chest, blood-and-guts menace.

The possibility that she loved Joe Fraser hit harder than her pregnancy, because this one she found easier to believe.

She recalled, all too clearly, how paranoid Joe had been about risking conception, and how breezy *she'd* been about being fully protected. Her stomach swooped in a way that had nothing to do with morning sickness. This pregnancy would kill whatever feelings he had for her. Destroy his trust.

In a panic, Pip crawled into bed and burrowed under the covers. Okay, she wouldn't tell him. She'd simply go home, back to New Zealand as planned. But even as the notion rose, her conscience quashed it.

Joe had the right to know he was going to be a father again. In the warm, dark womb of her blankets Pip practiced saying it aloud. "I'm pregnant." Her breathing came faster, she started to hyperventilate, and kicked off the blankets in a panic. Swinging her legs to the floor, she bent her head forward until the dizziness subsided.

She'd always been so intolerant of women who got themselves into this situation, and now she was one of them. But she had *used* birth control, so wasn't she innocent? A laugh escaped her, like the valve release on a pressure cooker. Could you get pregnant innocently?

Oh, God, how am I going to tell my family? She laughed again, a pained, hysterical sound that ended in a sob. Pip stripped off her clothes and stood in the shower, letting the jets pummel heat into her body, which was chilled with delayed shock. She tried to empty her mind of everything but the steam catching in her lungs as she forced herself to breathe. In, two, three. Out, two, three.

I will get through this. Somehow.

The intercom buzzed as she finished dressing, and Pip stood there blankly. The buzz came again, as impatient as an angry bee. Oh, hell! She was supposed to be going on a night tour of Alcatraz with Joe, Kaitlin and Melissa.

Scrabbling for an excuse, she stepped onto her tiny first-floor balcony with its fanciful wrought-iron railings. Three faces looked up, two wreathed in excited smiles. Joe gave her a crooked, sexy grin and she resisted the urge to cry.

"We haven't got time to come up today," Kaitlin began, then frowned as she eyed Pip's hair, still damp from the shower. "Are you nearly ready? We don't want to miss the ferry."

Belatedly, Pip remembered Kaitlin had organized the whole outing herself.

Avoiding Joe's gaze, she began, "I can't…"

Kaitlin's face fell.

"…wait," Pip finished weakly, then put on her happy face. "I can't wait."

KAITLIN HAD BEEN to Alcatraz heaps of times, but never at night. She spent the twilight ferry ride to the island arguing with Melissa over whether it was dark enough yet to be truly scary, and fussing because Pip couldn't see anything through the squall of rain that had hit the minute they'd boarded.

"It's okay, Kaitlin," her teacher soothed, "I've seen the city from the harbor before."

"And you're not getting seasick?" Because Pip did look kind of washed out, and she wasn't eating any of the sugar doughnuts they'd bought on the wharf.

"I think I can cope for fifteen minutes."

"Pip," said Melissa, "there's the lighthouse. Do you see it, Pip?"

Kaitlin looked at Dad and rolled her eyes. Melissa was making the most of calling Pip by her first name, which she had said they could do outside school. Kaitlin shared the thrill, but at least she managed to act cool about it.

"Shush," she told Melissa, "Pip needs to listen to the captain." As tour officiator, she didn't want her to miss a minute.

And she certainly seemed to listen pretty intently, because she didn't say much, except "Wow," whenever Kaitlin looked at her to make sure she was having a good time. It did mean that Melissa got most of the doughnuts, though she claimed Sanderella ate a couple, which didn't deserve an answer.

Dad was watching Pip, too, Kaitlin noticed, and she started watching him instead. Lately he looked at Pip like it kinda hurt, when he used to smile.

He and Pip never hugged or anything when Kaitlin was around, but when they sat together they liked to have their legs touching. Except today, Pip sat with her legs crossed and her arms folded.

"You okay?" Dad asked at one point, and she nodded and smiled at Kaitlin.

"Fine!"

"I was hoping they'd kiss or something," Melissa said

as she and Kaitlin went to use the bathroom on the ferry, in case it was fun to pee on a boat.

"They never do," said Kaitlin, opening the restroom door.

Wrinkling her nose, Melissa closed it again. "Gross," she said. "So do you think they've changed their mind about getting married?"

"Miss Br…Pip's going home in four weeks, remember?"

"So? She could stay, or come back when she's seen her folks…or your dad could go with her."

"He can't do that, he's got me. And I can't go because of Mom."

"Let's go stare at them again," said Melissa, "just in case they kiss."

AT THE ALCATRAZ DOCK, when Kaitlin put her hand in his and whispered, "You're going to miss her, aren't you?" Joe felt like the emperor caught in public with no clothes on.

It took a kid to state the obvious and explain his growing sense of foreboding.

Swept forward by the surging crowd, Pip and Melissa stepped to one side and waited for them to catch up. The rain had stopped, but the dusk was chill with sea fog. Pip was hugging herself again, something she'd been doing intermittently through the ferry ride, although she'd refused Joe's jacket. "I'm not cold, just impressed by the spookiness of it all," she'd insisted, which tickled Kaitlin.

She'd been distracted ever since they'd picked her up, and right now, thinking herself unobserved, she reminded him of a prisoner on her way to incarceration. She caught his eye, smiled and turned away.

Kaitlin tugged on his hand again. "Make her stay, Dad."

"How am I supposed to do that, honey?"

His daughter looked up at him like a dog begging for a bone. "Marry her?"

"Kaitlin, men and women who like to spend time together aren't always planning marriage." *But the guy you eventually date better be.* "Pip and I always knew she'd be going home."

"I don't see why she can't stay," said Kaitlin.

"She wants to be with her family. You can understand that, can't you?" He'd realized in the weeks they'd been together that Pip felt about her whole family the way he did about Kaitlin. As if something was missing if they weren't around.

The way—as his daughter had pointed out—Joe was starting to feel about Pip.

Kaitlin pulled a face. "I guess."

"Look, there's Melissa waving." His daughter dropped his hand and ran ahead, leaving Joe with a truth he could no longer ignore. And a question. What was he going to do about it?

As he came up behind Pip, Joe took off his jacket and laid it around her shoulders.

She acted as though he was trying to put a straitjacket on her. "I can take care of myself, Joe."

"I know you can," he said quietly.

"Sorry." For a moment she leaned into him. "Wrong side of the bed this morning."

"Premenstrual tension?" Nadia had suffered from it.

Pip didn't answer, rejoining the girls, who were listening to a brief overview of Alcatraz's history before the guide sent everyone up to the cell house. "What did I miss?"

"Al Capone got taken away from Alcatraz when his syphilis got worse," said Kaitlin. "What's syphilis?"

Things went downhill from there. Darkness lent the

prison a menace it didn't have by day, scaring Melissa, who saw ghosts around every corner.

Joe's ghosts walked, too. He might have got over Sue a long time ago, but the experience had taught him a valuable lesson. Love hurts. Hold back.

Pip seemed oblivious to the atmosphere, walking through the multitiered cell block and listening to the audio tour through her headset. "Have you got to the good bit yet?" Kaitlin asked. When Pip didn't respond, she turned to her dad. "You know, when the inmates dug escape routes using spoons?"

He gave his daughter the reassurance she needed. "She's having a great time, sweetheart."

Satisfied, Kaitlin put her own headset back in place and ran to catch up to Pip.

Clutching Sanderella to her chest, Melissa hung back with Joe. Her free hand, sticky with doughnut sugar and fear, stole into his. "This is too creepy," she wailed. She'd refused to listen to the audio commentary, claiming her "imagination was too vivid," and kept glancing around nervously. "An' I don't want to touch anything," she murmured, "in case I catch syphilis."

Deliberately vague, he and Pip had explained to the girls that it was a communicable disease.

"Okay, everybody," the guide called. "We're gonna turn off the lights and reenact prison shutdown."

Melissa's hand tightened on Joe's. The lights went off and they heard a *graunch*ing sound, then the cell doors rattled closed, floor by floor, the groans and clangs echoing through the vast space.

"I need to go out," whimpered Melissa. "Now!"

Joe lifted Pip's headset. "I'm taking Melissa outside," he said. "You and Kaitlin finish the tour."

Outside, the lights of the city shimmered in the darkness while the Golden Gate Bridge glittered like a diamond bracelet. Melissa's spirits made an immediate recovery. "Isn't it pretty? Let's go to the lookout."

Joe remained where he was, contemplating his dilemma. His world was here, Pip's in New Zealand. And even if he could persuade her to stay, he was still a loner with a disastrous relationship history who would never marry again. In his mind, these were absolutes, convictions he'd held for so long they were beyond question.

But if he and Pip separated now—by choice, instead of circumstance—he could retain a sense of control. And the relationship would remain what they'd always intended it to be—a wonderful hiatus.

His decision made, Joe followed Melissa to the lookout. He'd expected to feel lighter. Instead he felt as heavy as lead.

CHAPTER FOURTEEN

"REMEMBER THAT PACT we made?" said Joe. "Honesty, no matter what?"

They were parked on Pip's street after dropping the girls home. She'd made some excuse why Joe couldn't come up, because her smile had worn so thin with pretending nothing was wrong, she felt sure he'd see through it.

Except it seemed he'd already seen through it. Pip tried to read Joe's expression, but passing cars only briefly illuminated his face.

"Honesty no matter what," she echoed. She had every intention of telling him, but not tonight, not until she'd processed the news herself and made some sort of peace with it. Right now, she ached for solitude in the same way a wounded animal needed a cave, somewhere to curl up small and wait for the emotional maelstrom to pass.

"You also said if it gets too difficult with you leaving we can part with no hard feelings." His voice was rough. "It's getting that way, Pip."

This morning her only dilemma had been whether to take an umbrella on her walk to the doctor's. This morning she hadn't known she was pregnant or acknowledged she was in love with him. If Joe had told her this morning, she would have understood.

She sat completely still in the eye of the hurricane.

Don't hate him. He doesn't know and it's not fair. Then a roaring in her ears blocked out reason.

"I'm pregnant, you son of a bitch!"

Scrambling out of the car, she slammed the door behind her. Rage swept her up the steps and into her apartment before he'd had a chance to react. There it left her, a piece of flotsam standing in the dark in her tiny apartment.

The strength suddenly went out of her legs. Pip sank to the floor with a whimper, absolutely determined not to cry. She sat on the rug, arms wrapped around her knees, rocking herself, needing her family with a desperate, painful yearning.

For ten minutes, maybe more, she sat like that before she could stand and go to the window. His car was still parked on the street, Joe motionless inside it. She knew what he was feeling because she was feeling it, too. Pip pulled the mulberry drapes on his suffering because right now she could only cope with her own. Except...that was the coward's way out.

Before she could chicken out, she walked back downstairs. As she approached the car, Joe turned his head. She saw in his eyes the same desolation as when he'd talked about his father's prognosis. The same helpless anger, the same grief.

Opening the passenger door, Pip dropped her spare key on the seat. "When you're ready," she said, and her voice sounded thick even though she hadn't shed a single tear since hearing the news. "Come up and we'll talk."

Joe nodded. Clicking the passenger door shut, she went back upstairs, where she drank a glass of water to moisten her dry throat, then put on pajamas and her velour dressing gown. It was pale blue with lambs marching around the hem and cuffs, a silly farewell present from her brothers, specifically designed, they'd said, to keep foreign wolves at bay.

Blinking back tears, Pip dragged a comb through her hair and brushed her teeth. Then curled up on the couch and waited.

NOT AGAIN. The car seemed to close in on him as the windows fogged up, until it felt as if he were entombed in a chill, damp coffin. He started the engine, set the heat on high until the windows cleared and Pip's princess balcony came into view, the plastic geraniums a ghostly white in their pots. She'd pulled her curtains open again and the French doors were a yellow maw in the tall, dark building, an openmouthed silent scream.

He'd trusted her. Not just with contraception, but at some deep, instinctive level. And he felt bitterly, furiously betrayed. Joe tried to remember his previous feelings for her, but there was only anger and a fear that he'd reached the end of his ability to cope. Already staggering under responsibility, he had no idea how he was going to carry another one.

Briefly, he fantasized about getting on the freeway and driving until the tank ran dry. Starting again, free, somewhere far away from here.

Instead he started the engine and drove to a bar where he downed two whiskeys in quick succession, then sat brooding over a third, barely aware of his surroundings or the abortive attempts of the bartender to engage him in conversation. Alcohol numbed his emotions, but left him with a profound sense of melancholy.

What the hell was he going to do?

He considered calling Daniel, and glanced at his watch, blinking to bring the luminous dial into focus. He stared at the display: 1:00 a.m. It had been two hours since Pip had left him her key and told him to come up when he was ready.

The chair made a harsh, scraping sound as Joe pushed it back and stood up. Except he'd never be ready for this conversation.

Leaving his drink untouched, he walked back to his car, still with no idea what he was going to do. What he was going to say. He could offer marriage, but he'd been down that road before—and failed. Then, he'd been fully confident of loving Nadia; now he knew his limitations. And the painful fallout of good intentions.

And right now, Joe didn't even have those.

PIP WOKE UNDER A BLANKET, sometime around dawn. Joe was sprawled in a chair opposite, staring out the window at the lightening sky, his jaw shadowed with beard. Despite his casual posture, his body vibrated with tension. When she pushed back the blanket and sat up, he glanced over.

"How?" he said. "I saw you take the damn pill I don't know how many times. How is this possible?"

"The food poisoning...all that throwing up...compromised my protection."

He made a sound somewhere between a laugh and a groan. "I want to blame you so bad," he said, "so bad, Pip. But I made you responsible for contraception. Despite everything I knew about the repercussions of an unplanned pregnancy, I still—"

"Trusted me," she said quietly.

"It's not a question of trust, dammit, it's a question of never, *ever* ceding control of what matters to anyone else. I knew that!" Raking a hand through his hair, he stood up. "Could there be a worse time?"

"No," she whispered, "there couldn't."

His expression inscrutable, he looked down at her. "Are you considering an abortion?"

You. Making it plain this wasn't his problem. She'd tried to prepare herself for that, yet it still hurt. "No. If it comes to that, I'll adopt." She needed something to do with her hands other than wringing them, so she straightened the cushions, then picked up the blanket. "At the moment it's not real, so I can't think clearly. I only found out yesterday."

"You're due to go home in four and a half weeks."

Pip stopped folding the blanket. "I'm still going home."

"Carrying my baby?" His voice was flat.

Her anger was a relief after so much guilt. "So an abortion's okay, but you're horrified if I take the baby away?" Dumping the blanket, she stood and retied the sash of her dressing gown in a tight knot. "What difference does it make, if you're not required to have anything to do with it?"

"I never said I was in favor of an abortion, Pip." His gaze remained level on hers. "And I'm not the enemy."

Tears finally prickled her eyes; Pip blinked them back. "What can I say except I'm sorry?" It was cold in the apartment and she switched on the electric space heater, watching the elements warm to bright glowing orange. "I don't want to deal with this, either. I'm not ready for a baby. Not until I'm thirty-five and living in New Zealand with a husband who loves me."

"You forgot to add 'one that can support you,'" Joe said grimly. "Be that as it may, I can offer our child legitimacy, at least."

"What is this, some knee-jerk reaction when you get a woman pregnant?" She faced him. "You just dumped me and now you're suggesting marriage? Yeah, that'll work."

His mouth tightened. "I do learn from my mistakes. We marry to give the child legitimacy and, more importantly, from your point of view, to institutionalize my obligations as its father. Then divorce further down the track."

So clinical, so detached. He was back to the guy he'd been when she met him. And she was another load to carry. Her throat tightened. "I don't need your support or sanction or whatever you think you're offering. Whatever help I need, I'll get from my family…people who love me, not look on me and this baby as another burden."

She sounded petulant and needy, and Pip hated being reduced to that. Somehow she mustered a smile, trying to convey some sort of benevolent autonomy. "I only told you because you have a right to know. I absolve you of any responsibility or obligation." Walking to the front door, she opened it. "Go in peace."

"Peace!" Joe stared at her as though she was crazy. "You really think I'm going to say, 'well, good luck with that,' and walk away? This isn't some damn souvenir you picked up on your visit to the States, it's my child."

"That's why I told you, Joe."

But he'd stopped listening. "We'll need to talk to an immigration expert."

Pip stiffened. "Why?"

"Marriage could also be a prerequisite for dual citizenship for the baby."

"I haven't decided against adoption yet," she reminded him, unconsciously twisting the cord of her dressing gown. He was making this terrifyingly real and she wasn't ready for real yet.

"Oh, you'll keep the baby." For the first time since she'd told him, his expression softened when he looked at her. "First scan…the baby's first kick, and it's not sacrifice anymore, it's devotion. And that's from a tough guy. You'll be Jell-O."

Things were going too fast. She needed solitude to process not only her emotions, but also her options. "Joe, I need some time to think." Pip gripped the open door. "I'll call you in a couple of days."

"Call in sick. We're meeting later today." His expression hardened. "Because whatever you decide about marriage, Pip, let's be very clear. Even if it doesn't carry my name, our child will know its father."

CHAPTER FIFTEEN

"I DID SOME RESEARCH," said Joe. He and Pip sat at a window table at Nordstrom's Café Bistro seven hours after he'd left her apartment. Four floors below, two opposing streams of midweek shoppers struggled against each other, their umbrellas a bright canopy of colors as they clustered at intersections. Christmas was still over five weeks away, but already there was a slightly manic quality to the bustle.

Up here the atmosphere was peaceful, civilized…precisely why he'd chosen this restaurant. "With you being a foreigner—"

"Alien," she interrupted.

She still looked tired, wan. Yesterday he would have leaned over and kissed the slight furrow between her brow. Today Joe kept his hands—and his lips—to himself.

"That's your immigration department's official term for me. And if we marry we apply for something called 'extended parole' on my visa." As she spoke she dipped her sourdough bread into the pale green, creamy asparagus soup, looked at it, then put the bread down. It made a little green puddle on the white plate. "The baby will still be eligible for U.S. citizenship through you as its father if we're not married."

"I don't want my child born outside of marriage." There had been enough of that in his family to last a lifetime.

"Better out of wedlock than having its parents in jail because they're lying to their governments," Pip retorted. "If you've done your research you'll know we have to convince immigration of both countries that our marriage is real."

"I think the baby will help," stated Joe drily.

"When it comes right down to it," she said, "we're only looking for short stints in each other's country, so visitor visas are fine." She picked up the bread but didn't eat it. "We don't need to get married."

"You don't want that, do you?" he asked.

"I thought I did, but now it's here…" She shrugged and took a sip of her Earl Grey tea. "I guess this odd appetite is normal."

Joe heard her uncertainty and gave her the reassurance he'd been unable to last night when he'd been too angry, too devastated, to appreciate Pip's feelings. "It's normal."

He'd told her he wasn't the enemy, but his actions hadn't backed that up. He needed to redress that, to convince her that marriage was their best option. To convince her to stay until the baby was born.

"Try some of this." He handed over the remaining half of his steak-and-blue-cheese sandwich, and she took a tentative bite.

Her eyes closed. "Oh, yeah, that's good."

Her brown eyelashes were gold at the base, like her hair. He brushed the tips gently with his thumb and Pip's eyes opened warily. "I wonder whose coloring our child will have," he said.

Her face relaxed into a tentative smile. "Is now the time to tell you red hair runs in my family?"

"Uncle Daniel has auburn hair. He used to beat up anyone who called it red. He can teach the kid to fight."

Pip stopped smiling, put down the sandwich. "You keep assuming that I'm going to stay."

"Until the baby's born and we've sorted out all the paperwork, yeah." Joe leaned forward to stress his point. "It makes sense. And marriage is the only way you'll get an extension on your visa."

"I think it makes more sense for the baby to be born in the country where it'll be living." Her gaze was level, but there was an angry flush in her cheeks. "It will take a year, even two, to get the marriage recognized as legit, and that would involve living together. I'm not making a life here simply for your convenience, Joe."

Frowning, he sat back. "What about the baby's need for a father?"

"Our child will have grandparents, uncles, aunts and cousins—a loving extended family to compensate for a father living abroad." When he started to protest she overrode him. "Even if I stayed here, once we were able to divorce you'd only be visiting weekly, anyway."

"That's not true. Kaitlin and I see more of each other than that now." *Thanks to you.* But Joe couldn't afford to give her an advantage in these negotiations. "And don't forget Kaitlin when you're toting up relatives. Our baby has a sister, uncles, aunts, cousins and a grandparent in the States, too, remember."

"Oh, so now your family's close, now when it suits you." Pip threw down her napkin. "Here's an idea. Move to New Zealand. Then you can see the baby as much as you like...." He made a gesture of dismissal. "No? Not so easy when the rugby boot's on the gridiron foot, is it?"

Joe kept shaking his head. "Our situations are entirely different," he argued. Surely she could see that? "For a start, you've lived here for nearly fourteen months. The States is already a second home."

When she opened her mouth to speak, he overrode her, but pitched his tone low and reasonable. "You have friends and a transferable job skill. I know nothing about commercial real estate in New Zealand, and even if I did, my industry's built on personal contacts. To start from scratch? No, Pip. Not with two kids to support."

Her set expression was wavering, so he produced his ace in the hole. "And how would living on the other side of the world work with Kaitlin?"

There was a short silence. "It wouldn't," she conceded, "not if you want to see her more than three times a year." They both knew Kaitlin needed more than that from him, at least for the next few years. "But you'll be living on the other side of the world from one of your children, Joe, because I'm going home." Picking up her napkin, Pip laid it over the remains of the sandwich, her appetite obviously gone. "Unlike Nadia, I don't hold any hope of making you love me, you see."

They both realized at the same time what she'd implied. Joe's mouth went dry. "You sound like you want me to."

"You misunderstood me." His gaze followed the blush as it swept across her face, down her neck, into the V of her blouse. "We were never about love."

"Which is exactly why I ended it when I did." Now *he'd* revealed more than he wanted to.

"Are you saying you'd begun to have feelings for me?" There was something disquieting threaded through her skepticism. Alarm kicked in as Joe recognized it. Hope.

He didn't raise hopes, particularly in himself. "What guy wouldn't?" Joe sat back in his chair and folded his arms. "You're beautiful, funny, intelligent, sexy as hell, and your leaving has given our relationship an urgency, even an emotional component it might not otherwise have had."

As he spoke a range of expressions crossed her face, ending in a penetrating look that made him feel exposed. "I suppose I should be grateful you said '*might* not otherwise have had,' rather than *wouldn't* otherwise have had."

"I'm trying to be sensitive to your feelings."

Pip did the last thing Joe expected. She laughed.

At the next table, two elderly women glanced over and smiled. He could read their thoughts. *Young love.*

"It's hard to imagine an admission of affection couched in more unflattering terms, but go ahead." Pip leaned forward and cupped her chin in her hand. "Tell me what you would have said if you weren't being sensitive."

He was at a loss as to why she found this uncomfortable conversation remotely funny. "You've made your point, Pip." It seemed very important suddenly that he make his. "Still on semantics, I'm glad you recognize it as an *admission* of affection and not a declaration."

Deliberately, he adopted the language of commerce. "What I'm proposing is simply a one- to two-year business partnership to facilitate custody access and ensure our child has the citizenship of both countries."

Pip uncovered the steak sandwich, picked it up and bit into it. "So this sham marriage..." Her pink tongue flicked out to catch a crumb at the side of her mouth. "Would we still have sex, Joe?"

As if she knew she'd just given him a hard-on. "I haven't thought—"

"Because your burgeoning feelings might complicate things."

He stared at her through narrowed eyes. "This isn't a joke, Pip."

"I'm sorry, but don't you realize you're denying the one thing that would make me consider staying? That you actually care about me?"

Joe balked. "Let's not muddy the waters by pretending sex is going to carry us through this. We've been living outside the real world, not in it. Would these feelings last when we're renting some dive with a newborn, juggling family issues on both sides, and you're resenting me because I'm making you live permanently away from your home and family? Nadia and I started with better odds than that."

Pip put down the remains of the sandwich yet again, her momentary elation deflated. Having three older brothers made her an expert in translating guyspeak and it was very clear to her—if not to Joe—that he was halfway in love with her and terrified. That was the good part.

The bad part was that she, too, was grappling with feelings she had no experience of. For all she knew, Joe could be right. This might just be sex. And even if it wasn't, love might not be enough to overcome all their other problems. But there was only one way to find out.

"I'm prepared to test a marriage…situation," she said. "You move into my apartment, I meet the rest of your oh-so-close family and in three weeks we'll review." He nodded, triumphant. "But I make no promises, Joe," she warned. "And in the meantime my pregnancy stays a secret. This is something you and I resolve without outside pressure."

"My family knows not to interfere in my life."

"I'm warming to them already," she said. "Unfortunately, mine don't."

Living together might not resolve his feelings, but it would resolve hers. Which was a risky strategy if it turned out she really loved him. But she knew only one thing for sure. If he loved her, nothing would keep them apart. If he didn't, then nothing would keep them together.

ON FRIDAY NIGHT, suitcase in hand, Joe knocked on the door of Pip's tiny apartment.

She opened it with the phone pressed to her ear, face averted. Her smile was brief and unconvincing. "I'm talking to Mum, make yourself at home." Disappearing into the bedroom, she closed the door.

There were tearstains on her cheeks.

Oh, God, what have we done? Joe hardened his heart. So Pip was homesick. Well, so was he—homesick for the way things were before she'd told him she was pregnant.

Walking into the living room, he groaned aloud. They hadn't spent much time at Pip's place, by unspoken agreement sticking to the neutral ground of Joe's hotel room. And in the shock of her pregnancy, he hadn't noticed a damn thing last time he was here.

Now he felt as if he was standing in enemy territory, and not just because he was wary of Pip's uncanny ability to shift the ground under his feet. He'd committed to living in a fairy bower for three weeks.

The one-bedroom, open plan kitchen/dining/living room apartment in western North Beach nudged the base of Russian Hill, a stone's throw from Chinatown. It had come as part of the teacher exchange deal and been furnished by someone misguided enough to think the building's pink exterior was a good idea inside, too.

Kaitlin had adored what she called the pink palace on sight; Joe had got them out of the building as soon as possible. It reminded him too much of the pastel-painted houses of his Sunset District childhood. Girlie cute.

He dropped his suitcase on the salmon-pink floral rug, then gingerly laid his briefcase and Blackberry on the spindle-legged rosewood table. Amazingly, it held. The sooner he could convince Pip to marry him, the sooner they could start searching for another apartment and bring all his stuff out of storage. Though waiting enabled him to pull in a few more deals.

Loosening his tie, he sank onto the fuchsia couch and checked his phone messages.

Two from Sam's lawyer, asking Mr. Fraser to get in touch as a matter of "increasing urgency." Up until this week Sam had been silent, no doubt rebuilding his rightful-ownership case for a different foe and unaware that the necklace would soon be returned to Aunt Jenny.

With a grim smile Joe deleted the lawyer's messages, then rang his cousin Belle to invite her and Matt to a Thanksgiving lunch. Stage one of his campaign to convince Pip to marry him.

Everyone he'd called so far had said yes, but Joe didn't kid himself that his family's universal acceptance was driven by anything other than avid curiosity. Even Nadia and Doug had muscled in on his invitation to Kaitlin.

"Sure, Matt and I will be there," Belle said when he told her the reason for his call. "I'm just glad this business with Dad hasn't affected your willingness to see me."

"You're not responsible for your father's behavior." How many times had Joe told himself that over the years?

Belle was silent for a moment. "I'm worried about him, Joe. Last week when I visited…" She stopped herself. "It's not your problem."

"Talk to me."

"I caught Dad drinking in the middle of the day. That's something he'd never normally do."

Joe recalled the smell of stale alcohol when Sam had visited Adam in hospital. So it hadn't been a one-off. "You want me to stop this charade?" he offered.

"No. It's not over the necklace, it's over Mom. And frankly, the only thing that's going to make a difference is a change in attitude. I told him that. Anyway, let's talk about Thanksgiving lunch. Where is it?"

Joe gave her the restaurant's address and hung up, frowning. This was the only part of his genius idea to backfire. Good restaurants had been booked out for weeks and he'd been forced to settle for a third-class eatery in a suburban mall in Palo Alto. But beggars couldn't be choosers.

Opening his briefcase, Joe unearthed the box of Ghirardelli chocolates. They were Pip's favorite, and a peace offering for arriving at eight when he'd told her he'd be here before six.

As he sat on the girlie couch, clutching the chocolates and waiting for her to reappear, he felt as nervous as a teenager waiting for his prom date. How had it come to this?

His cell phone vibrated; Joe checked caller ID, then picked up with relief. "Daniel."

"I got your message. I thought I made it clear that the last family outing was a once-only."

"The last one was for Adam's sake. This one's for mine."

Daniel swore. "Don't do this to me."

"Thanks, buddy." Joe gave him the pertinent details, leaving out the pregnancy. "You don't have to stay long, just be charming while you're there."

"Are you in love with this woman?"

"Define love," Joe hedged.

"You're asking me?"

Joe grinned, then, catching movement in his peripheral

vision, said in a low voice, "So you'll be there, and you'll be charming?"

"Don't push it," said Daniel, and hung up.

"DEFINE LOVE." Pip entered the living room in time to hear Joe say that and see him grin. Having lied to her mother that yes, everything was fine, Pip was in no mood for whatever sexual spin the caller had put on his response to elicit such a very male grin. Obviously a guy.

I can define love. How I feel about you. "Who was that?" she asked when he ended the call.

"My uncle, Daniel. I've organized a Thanksgiving lunch to introduce you to the rest of my family."

Immediately, Pip cheered up. "Then here's an insider's tip. Coming home late isn't a great start to convincing me that I won't be isolated with a new baby if I marry you."

"You're right, I should have called. I got delayed because the deal I've been relying on finally came back into play."

Pip forgot the lasagna drying out in the oven. "Joe, that's great."

He stood and handed her a box of Ghirardelli chocolates. "If I work hard now, by the time the baby's born I'll be a position to cut back my hours."

"You have nine months to do that, Joe, but I only have three weeks to decide whether I'm marrying you for the baby's sake. You kinda need to be here during that time." Pip tried to keep the comment light, but her new insecurity made the words clunky and cudgel-like.

This was no longer a game. The stakes were high for both of them and she was dealing with two new and frightening experiences—being in love and being pregnant.

His expression hardened. "So if I'm not at your beck and call the decision might not go my way? That sounds like emotional blackmail."

"Only if you want to be paranoid and defensive," she snapped, feeling hormonal and on edge.

"I'm not—" Joe stopped himself. "This pregnancy's tough on both of us."

"I don't see you hanging over the toilet every night or telling your family how great it will be to see them at Christmas, when you might not be—" To Pip's horror, tears came to her eyes. This was the latest side effect of pregnancy. "Excuse me." Head down, she walked past him to the bathroom.

"Come here," Joe said gently, but Pip only shook her head and kept walking. Calling her mum had been a bad idea. As soon as she'd heard Kathleen's chuckle, Pip had started to cry, and then she couldn't stop. "I just miss you, that's all," she'd sobbed.

"Well, not long now and you'll be home."

In the coral-tiled bathroom, Pip rinsed her face with cold water, braced herself and went back out.

Joe was standing in the living room, his shoulders slumped. When he heard her, he straightened up and smiled. "I'm sorry. I'll do better."

Now she didn't know if he really meant it or if he was responding to her so-called emotional blackmail. And she couldn't ask him because the answer might hurt.

"Are you hungry? I made dinner."

"I picked up a burger on the way here. I'm not expecting you to cook for me every night."

"That's good," she said, "because half the time it's your turn."

He blinked.

"Oh, God, you can't cook."

"Nana Jo taught me to cook," he said, "though I'm a little rusty. Nadia considered the kitchen her domain."

Pip knew without asking that Nadia was cordon bleu. *This is not a competition,* she reminded herself, but another thought had already intruded: *And such a great mother.*

"You know, I think I'll get an early night," Pip said, suddenly worn-out. "I put some bed linen next to the couch…it's a pullout."

She couldn't see his face as Joe looked at the couch, but imagining it lifted her spirits. "Like you said, sex only muddies the waters, so let's take it out of the equation."

Pip had planned this tongue in cheek—they could no more keep their hands off each other than breathe. She waited for Joe to laugh, to haul her into his arms and say, "this is ridiculous. We can find a better way."

"Whatever you want, Pip." His tone was completely neutral, his expression unreadable.

I want you. And us, back to the way we were before pregnancy changed everything.

"Good night, Joe." Pip went into her bedroom, closed the door and leaned her forehead against it. The wood was cold. So much for honesty no matter what.

CHAPTER SIXTEEN

PIP HAD NEVER SEEN Joe more nervous. He must have straightened his tie a dozen times and apologized for the restaurant's decor at least two dozen as they stood in the vestibule waiting for his family to arrive.

"It's fine," she reassured him through the gloom. Admittedly, the eatery was small and badly lit, and the carpet had the musty smell of too many beers spilled over the years. But the staff was cheerful and the table beautifully decorated with a Thanksgiving centerpiece of baby pumpkins, green apples and autumn leaves.

Joe had booked the whole place, even bringing in his own wine selection, and she'd had to resist the impulse to ask if he could afford all this. "You done good," she reiterated, "and the menu sounds wonderful."

Except for the marshmallow and yam dish...what was *that* about? But her mouth watered for the rest—turkey breast, cranberry stuffing, green beans and mashed potatoes, with pumpkin and apple pies to follow. Having thrown up breakfast, Pip was starving.

Pregnancy seemed to have a lot of disadvantages with few benefits. Her breasts were sore, she became nauseous at odd times of the day and she couldn't drink.

Which was a shame because she'd been infected by Joe's anxiety. Nervously, Pip sipped her cranberry juice.

There was too much riding on this event, and that was her fault. She was the one who'd insisted on meeting the people who would temporarily replace her family if she decided to stay. And Joe had taken it to heart, which made her feel guilty and agitated and pressured.

Didn't the damn fool realize her decision to stay rested on how *he* felt about her, not on how well his family behaved? After a week of living together, they were still hiding behind a scrupulous politeness. "So is there anything I should know about the people coming?"

"Like what?" He was immediately defensive. Their easy rapport had been lost with the pregnancy, and that hurt.

"Sorry we're late. This place was murder to find," said Doug, as he opened the door for Kaitlin. "Nadia's in the parking lot talking to..." His words trailed off as he followed her into the restaurant and squinted.

"Wow, it's like being in a cave," enthused Kaitlin, very pretty in a purple party dress. Pip wondered if she should have worn a skirt instead of black trousers and an angora knit top. Seemed like people dressed up for Thanksgiving. Then everyone arrived at once and she was struggling to keep up with Joe's staccato introductions. Cousin Belle... Sue's husband, Rick... Aunt Emily, Aunt Jenny, her husband, Luke.

Pip got lost in a confusing deluge of names and handshakes. Overwhelmed, she stepped back and found herself standing next to Doug. "Thank God, a familiar face," she murmured.

"Nadia was nervous about this, too," he confided. "She's still intimidated by Sue."

Pip tried to remember which one Sue was. Oh, yes, Joe's good friend since high school, who'd turned out to be his cousin. Pip studied the woman holding one of the three babies. Willowy, naturally beautiful, self-possessed. "I would have thought they'd be soul sisters," she said. "They seem so alike."

"Exactly." Doug gave her a penetrating look. "You don't know?"

"Don't know wh—?"

"Pip." Joe touched her arm. "I want you to meet my uncle Daniel. Doug, you haven't got a drink—let me sort you out."

Left alone with Daniel, Pip smiled and held out her hand. "Pleased to meet you." Joe's young uncle shared three obvious family traits with his nephew. He was equally muscled, equally tall and equally grim. Keen navy eyes assessed her, then he shook her hand with a grip that made no allowances for wimps.

"And I'm pleased to meet you." He released her hand and Pip wriggled her fingers to get the feeling back. It wasn't hard to imagine his schoolboy reaction to anyone who called his deep auburn hair *red;* she could only marvel that anyone had dared.

"So, Daniel, what do you do?"

Amusement lightened his countenance. "Joe talks about me that much, huh?"

Pip drained her cranberry juice, the ice making her teeth ache. "Actually, I don't know much about anybody here," she confessed.

"That's okay, we don't know anything about you, either," he replied without a trace of irony. Pip spent the next ten minutes trying to get to know him better, but failed. He was polite, happy to do small talk and as close as a clam. Bloody Frasers.

In the end she excused herself on the pretext of going to the bathroom.

"Great guy, isn't he?" said Joe as she passed. He was talking to the maître d' about laying out the buffet.

"Charming," said Pip, but Joe missed the sarcasm.

"He doesn't show that side of himself to many people. He must like you."

Oh, great. "Is there anything I should know about Sue and Nadia?"

Joe's face lost all expression. "Why?"

"Doug mentioned something."

"Nadia was jealous over my friendship with Sue." Joe shrugged as if to say, "Women."

"Your cousin?"

"Remember, we didn't know that then…. What the hell?" Pip followed Joe's astonished gaze to the new arrival standing in the doorway. Somewhere in his late fifties, the man was still handsome in the meticulous way of aging alpha males. His blond hair was immaculately styled, his expensive, pale blue suit buttoned over a slight paunch.

"Excuse me." She watched Joe stride over, reaching the man at the same time his cousin Belle did.

Kaitlin came over, holding a baby. "I think that's my great-uncle Sam," she said excitedly.

"Who's this?" Pip smiled nervously at the infant.

"One of Sue's foster babies. His name is Donnie. Right now she only has two, plus Carrie, but Carrie is hers and Rick's. They adopted her."

Pip was learning more about this family from Kaitlin than Joe had ever told her. She glanced over at Sue, who was soothing a one-year-old while chatting with Nadia and Doug.

Pip could see why Nadia might find her intimidating. The woman obviously took multitasking even beyond Nadia's level. Pip loved kids, but her experience of babies was negligible. And in seven and a half months she'd have one. "Can I hold him?"

"Sure." Kaitlin hefted the baby forward like a pro and Pip awkwardly settled him on her hip.

Donnie stared at her as though she were a monster from the deep. She had this effect on horses, too. It didn't matter how bravely she approached, they knew she was scared of them and would toss their heads, or skitter nervously until she gulped and ran.

The baby's lower lip dropped. Pip gave him a frantic little jiggle. "You're okay, mate."

Crystal tears welled in his big blue eyes; Donnie started to howl.

With sweat breaking out on her forehead, Pip patted his back. The baby howled louder. Conceding defeat, she thrust him at Kaitlin. The crying stopped. Donnie's chubby arms tightened around the girl's neck. Like an owl, he swiveled his head to look back at Pip. His lower lip started to quiver again.

"How weird that he doesn't like you," said Kaitlin and took him away.

Pip stared after the baby. Over Kaitlin's shoulder he stared back. What did Donnie know that he wasn't telling?

"WHAT THE HELL DO you want?" Joe asked.

"Dad," his cousin Belle warned, "if you're here to cause trouble…"

Uncle Sam held up his hands with an expression of aggrieved innocence. "I'm here to spend Thanksgiving with my little girl," he said, "same as I've always done."

He fixed his gaze on Aunt Emily, who remained on the other side of the room with Aunt Jenny and her husband, Luke. Emily seemed conflicted. *Oh, great,* thought Joe, *she still loves this bastard.* He moved to block her from Sam's view. "It would be better if you left."

"That's for my daughter to decide," Sam said coldly. "And why haven't you been returning my lawyer's calls?"

"I'm not talking about the goddamn necklace now." Very aware of Pip somewhere behind him, Joe kept his manner pleasant.

Sam seemed to collect himself. "You're right, this isn't the time or place." He turned to his daughter. "You said I should make more of an effort. I'm making more of an effort."

"This wasn't what I meant, Dad."

"I'm not a skulker, Belle, and Thanksgiving is a Carson family tradition. Are you saying your daddy's no longer welcome at the table?"

"No, Dad, but..." Belle scanned the room for her fiancé, Matt, obviously hoping for moral support, but Matt was making a phone call outside. Joe put an arm around his cousin's shoulders.

"It's not Belle's party, Sam, it's mine. And since your overbearing behavior's the reason you're not hosting Thanksgiving this year, maybe appeasement would work better for you. You can start by leaving quietly."

Sam glanced toward Aunt Emily. When his gaze returned to Joe's it was reptilian cold. "I won't mention the necklace. I will make an effort with you and yours. Outside this restaurant, we still have unfinished business. Inside it, I will be civil for the sake of my wife and daughter."

Under Joe's arm, Belle stirred. In her expression, he saw the hope he'd long extinguished where his own father was concerned. The possibility of change, of healing. A false hope, but he couldn't be the one to extinguish it. "Okay," he said to Belle, "as long as your mother agrees."

All three looked over to Aunt Emily, whose gaze fluttered between her husband and daughter before settling on Belle. She nodded assent. *What we do for our kids,* Joe thought. *At least some of us.*

Then Aunt Emily turned away to talk to Aunt Jenny and Luke, her message clear. *So far and no further.* Sam still had a hell of a lot of work to do.

Transmitting a "happy families" smile to Pip, Joe said to his uncle, "You put one step out of line, and you're out of here. You got that?"

Before Sam could respond, Kaitlin asked, "Are you Sam Carson?" She sounded a little disappointed. "I'm Kaitlin Josephine Fraser and I think we're related."

"If you're Joe's daughter then yes, you're my greatniece," Sam said politely. "Is this one of Sue's foster children?"

Belle pulled Joe aside. "Thank you," she said in a low voice.

"How many chances, Belle?"

"As many as it takes."

Joe didn't get it; he would never get it.

Kaitlin was still talking to Sam. "Did you name Belle after the princess in *Beauty and the Beast?*" Without waiting for an answer, she turned to Joe. "Dad, you and Mom should have called me that."

Joe remembered the scrap of humanity handed to him at the hospital, all squalling, red-faced indignation. "Be grateful," he advised his firstborn. "I wanted to call you Slugger."

For the first time he thought of his unborn child and was swept with sudden fierce loyalty. He had to make Pip stay.

"Daaad," Kaitlin complained.

Belle laughed, drawing her father's attention. "We

called her Belle," he answered Kaitlin, "because she was so beautiful."

Flustered, Belle stopped laughing. It was probably the first compliment her old man had ever paid her.

"Like you, young lady," Sam added gallantly. "Obviously, you take after your mother."

Joe narrowed his eyes and Belle said hastily, "Dad, let's get you a drink."

Daniel strolled over after they left for the bar. "So, are we having fun yet?"

CHAPTER SEVENTEEN

PIP WAS ABOUT TO ASK the bartender for another cranberry juice when the latecomer beckoned from the other end of the bar.

Close up, he had the light tan of a regular golfer, while the faint white band on the ring finger of his summoning hand proclaimed recent singledom. Certainly he felt free to run a connoisseur's eye over her curves.

"Try one of these, little lady. I got the bartender to mix one of my Thanksgiving specials." He filled her empty glass from a jug brimming with ice and lemon slices.

Giving him a friendly smile, Pip inspected the pale cinnamon-colored contents with its bobbing mint leaves and lemon slices. "As long as it's nonalcoholic."

In the midst of handing over the glass, the man paused. "You're not pregnant, are you?"

Her smile faltered. "What m-makes you ask?"

"Isn't that why most women give up drinking?"

"Oh, right." Pip laughed shrilly. "No, I'm not pregnant. Goodness me, no!" A terrible liar, she could feel the heat suffusing her face.

"That's all right then. It's iced tea with a twist."

Pip hid her burning face in the glass. She hadn't developed the Americans' partiality for iced tea, but with her first sip it proved surprising palatable. Very lemony, with an aftertaste she immediately recognized. "You've got Angostura bitters flavoring this, haven't you?"

Joe's relative roared with laughter. "'Bite-ters,'" he repeated. "What's your accent, honey? Because it sure isn't from here." Grabbing a bottle of whiskey at his elbow, he refilled his empty glass.

His rather patronizing endearments were starting to annoy her. "New Zealand."

"You're a long way from home." He glanced around the room, disdain on his face. "So who do you belong to in our mongrel litter?"

"Myself." Pip took another sip. "Who owns you?"

For a moment he looked startled, then gave a dry chuckle and held out his hand. "That's very amusing. I'm Sam Carson."

Pip racked her memory banks. "You're Adam's brother," she said triumphantly, taking his proffered hand. This wasn't so hard.

"Half brother," he corrected coldly.

"I'm Philippa Browne, Kaitlin's teacher and Joe's... girlfriend."

His grip tightened. What was it about these guys and their handshakes? "I'm the one everyone blames for Adam's second stroke." Releasing her hand, Sam took another slug of his drink. Despite his nonchalance, the whiskey in the glass had trembled when he said Adam's name.

"If that was true you wouldn't have been invited today, would you?"

He laughed, a dark humorless sound. "I never back down from a fight." Staring into his glass, Sam added cryptically, "And Adam instigated that one at the golf club. Damn sick fool threw a punch."

He took another gulp of whiskey, then glanced somberly at Pip. "Now that I've seen him, I wonder if I did the right thing, resuscitating the poor bastard when he collapsed after hitting me. I wouldn't wish his condition on my worst enemy."

Pip stared at him in dismay. His assessment of Adam's recovery was so different from Joe's.

"And Adam is my worst enemy right now, but—" Sam tapped the side of his patrician nose with a finger that was slightly off target "—we can't mention *that* today. Today I'm here to talk sense into my wife."

He gestured to one of Joe's aunts, a woman Pip recalled as very sweet but fragile, who stood with her back to them. "Emily left me, apparently because I'm a son of a bitch. I keep waiting for her to come to her senses and come home but..." He shrugged. "So here I am. Now she says this isn't the appropriate forum."

Sam emptied his glass in three swallows, grimacing at the taste. "I said, what is the right forum when you won't return my calls, goddammit? I thought leaving my wedding ring at home would shock her into talking. Instead, Emily told me not to be childish."

Pip didn't know how to reply. He was obviously hurting, but his bitterness made it easier to sympathize with his wife. Still, when he reached for the whiskey, she instinctively caught the bottle's neck. "You'll make a better case for yourself sober," she suggested gently.

"And you'll do much better if you butt out of what's none of your business," he said, equally dulcet. Jerking the bottle from her grasp, Sam refilled his tumbler.

Pip took the hint and left, thinking that if she included Daniel and the baby, that was *three* new friends she'd made today.

Across the room, Joe's cousin Belle stood with her fiancé. "Come join us," the curly-headed blonde invited.

Pip was so grateful, she could have hugged her. Instead she gushed, "I just love your earrings," even though they were gaudy monstrosities, encrusted with crystal and rhinestone.

Belle caught Matt's eye and they burst out laughing. "Sorry," she said, "it's a private joke. Matt dared me to wear them. I do know they're ugly...."

And Pip had just shown herself as either insincere or having appalling taste. Taking a nervous gulp of her iced tea, she caught sight of Sam sloshing more Scotch into his glass. "Listen, that man at the bar—Sam—is hitting the sauce pretty hard. Maybe someone should keep an eye on him."

Belle stopped smiling; Matt squeezed her shoulder. "I'll go," he offered.

"Sam seems pretty cut up," said Pip tentatively. "Do you know if there's any hope of reconciliation with his wife?"

The other woman stiffened. "Did Dad send you here to ask me that?"

Dad. "I didn't know you were his daughter," said Pip. Making friends came to her as naturally as breathing, but this family gathering was proving an emotional minefield, chiefly because Joe had told her nothing about ongoing family dramas. "If I've come across as intrusive I'm sorry."

"No, *I'm* sorry." Belle touched Pip's arm in apology. "I've recently stopped being my parents' go-between—they need to work this out themselves—but Dad's not above subterfuge."

They watched Matt go up to Sam and exchange a few words. The two men went outside. Sam's drink stayed on the bar. "Matt's probably taken Dad out to see his new car," said Belle, "which I'm sure Dad will tell him he paid too much for."

Turning back to Pip, she added awkwardly, "Dad's not usually a heavy drinker, but he's taking the separation hard."

"That's okay."

Belle raked a hand through her springy blond curls, her blue eyes rueful. "Except that Joe so wanted us to make a good impression."

"He did?" For a moment, Pip's heart lifted, before she remembered Joe was doing this for their unborn child, not her.

A baby-free Sue joined them, lifting her wineglass. "It's so great to meet you, Pip." The three women clinked glasses.

"I'm surprised you prefer Dad's concoction over Joe's wine," commented Belle. "Especially when he had a hand in making this zinfandel." She rolled the red wine around her glass, then sniffed appreciatively before taking a sip.

"He did?" Pip asked. She was starting to sound like a parrot. "I knew Joe was a wine buff, but not that his interest ran this deep."

"He and his Napa vineyard buddy, Scott, experiment with a dozen bottles every year," said Sue. "Joe was studying to be a winemaker at Fresno State when he met Nadia. Of course, the pregnancy changed everything for them."

Pip's throat tightened and she took a long sip of her iced tea to loosen it. "Pregnancy seems to do that," she murmured.

At lunch, Pip sat between the Fraser men and opposite Belle, Sue and their partners, who definitely fit the mold of charming Californians. Rick was also in education, which made conversation easy, while Matt quizzed her on surf spots in New Zealand.

Both men so obviously adored their women that by the time they'd finished their entrées Pip could have laid her head on the table and cried. She and Joe weren't making progress, not compared to the real thing.

He was still a closed book, double padlocked and booby-trapped. No girls allowed. It amazed her that Joe even had a close female friend.

But then someone as serene and self-contained as Sue wouldn't dream of trying to pick his locks. Feeling pint-size and pugnacious, Pip sipped her iced tea and brooded.

Joe turned from a conversation with Kaitlin, who sat on his right. "You okay?"

"I didn't know you wanted to be a winemaker."

Immediately his expression closed. "I gave up on that dream a long time ago."

"Sue said you've been considering going back to it."

"I was, but what with Adam and other things—" his gaze took in her stomach "—it's not realistic."

"Well, if there's any other dream I can crush, please tell me," she said tartly.

"Pip, I didn't mean it like that."

Shoving back her chair, she stood up, gripping the table to counter a slight dizziness. "That was delicious," she said to Sue. "Shall we get dessert?"

The other woman looked a little taken aback by her heartiness, but smiling, she also stood. "Sure."

Standing at the buffet, it occurred to Pip that Sue could offer insights into Joe's character. "Were you two really as close as Joe says you were all those years ago?" He was probably exaggerating, like he'd exaggerated his happy family.

Sue shot her a look. "Well, it was before we knew we were cousins."

Pip went to pick up a dessert plate, then realized she was still holding her glass. Draining it, she plonked it down next to the vanilla ice cream. "I need to know more about the heartless trollop who soured him for future relationships."

Sue's face went white, then red. "He got over her," she said.

"The woman, yes." Recklessly, Pip helped herself to both types of pie. "Let's face it, most of us shudder recalling our first loves, but hit some guys at a vulnerable age and they never come out of their shell again. Joe's a classic case." Pip became aware that she was talking way too loudly and speaking way too frankly to someone who was essentially a stranger.

Part of her wondered at that.

Sue opened her mouth, but nothing emerged. Come to think of it, even the ambient noise had fallen away. Pip turned back to the table. No one was eating. Everyone was staring at her in varying degrees of discomfort and amusement. Joe's eyes blazed.

"Any other of my emotional defects you want to share with my family?" he inquired in a tone like chipped ice.

"Well, it's true," she said defiantly. *Whoa, shouldn't she be embarrassed by this?* Pip prodded her feelings. Nope, still defiant. "You let some bimbo in high school ruin you for other women. Isn't that right, Nadia?"

Looking at her, Pip was buoyed by an unexplained rush of affection. Nadia—her sister in misfortune, someone else who'd suffered through loving Joe bloody Fraser.

Nadia shook her head in small jerks, then her brown eyes shifted to Sue.

Recent comments coalesced in Pip's brain.

Doug's aside that Nadia was "still intimidated by Sue" and his speculative "You don't know?"

Joe's expressionless "Nadia was jealous over my friendship with Sue."

And finally Sue's embarrassed "It was before we knew we were cousins."

"Oh, hell," said Pip. The truth was very different to the one her overwrought imagination had conjured. And so much more complicated.

Awkwardly, she faced the other woman. "Sue, I'm so sorry. I didn't know it was you."

"And now my whole family does." Sue swallowed. "Trying to find a bright side, at least I'd already told Rick and my parents."

Pip glanced at the shocked faces around the table, winced and closed her eyes. "Well, they say that the more secrets a family has, the more dysfunctional it is." Her small laugh lacked conviction. "I've just made you all less…" She trailed off.

"Have you been drinking?" Joe demanded.

Incensed, she opened her eyes. "Of course not. How could you suggest such a thing when I'm…I'm on a diet?" Everyone looked at her plate, piled high with apple and pumpkin pie.

"Didn't you have one of Dad's Long Island iced teas?" ventured Belle.

"Yes, but I spefic…*specifically* asked for nonalcoholic." Pip glanced at Sam for confirmation, but his gaze shied away.

"One wasn't going to hurt her."

Joe strode over, picked up her empty glass and sniffed. "How can you not taste alcohol in one of those things?"

"I thought it was the bitters." Pip tried not to panic, but

her hand fluttered over her stomach. "So what are we talking about here? A splash of gin?

"And vodka," he snapped. "And tequila and rum."

"Excuse me," said Pip weakly, and hurried to the bathroom, breaking into a run as soon as she was out of sight.

Bending over the toilet bowl, she jammed a finger down her throat and forced herself to throw up until her stomach was empty. Fear and self-disgust made the task easy.

Tears filled her eyes. She really had to stop throwing up in strange bathrooms. With a shaky hand, she wiped her mouth with toilet tissue. Surely one drink, even a *strong* one, wasn't enough to harm the baby?

The tears started to fall. She didn't know that for sure because she didn't know anything about babies. Like she didn't know anything about Joe's family or what really mattered to him.

A sob convulsed her as she dropped the tissue in the toilet and flushed. In fact, she was so stupid she couldn't even distinguish an alcoholic iced tea from a nonalcoholic one. If she couldn't look after her baby in the uterus, what on earth was she going to do when it arrived? Pip slid down the stall door and wept.

There was a heavy-knuckled tap on the restroom door, then Joe's anxious voice called, "Pip, you okay?"

He'd never seen her cry and he never would. She rubbed her eyes dry with the sleeve of her angora knit. The tears glistened dewlike in the brushed cherry wool. "Go back to your guests. I'll be out in a minute."

Pip waited until she heard him leave before coming out of the cubicle. At the sink she rinsed her mouth and eyes, then, hearing murmured conversation, opened the ladies' room door a crack. Joe and Sue were in the corridor, talking quietly. Pip closed the door again. She couldn't face

Sue, she just couldn't. What must the other woman think of her?

Upending the trash can under the restroom's window, she climbed onto it and hoisted herself to the sill, where she sat gauging the distance to the ground. It was five, maybe six feet down, an easy jump. Unless you were pregnant.

As Pip hesitated, Daniel came around the corner of the building, car keys swinging in his hand. He stopped. "Looks like I'm not the only one making a getaway."

"Despite all evidence to the contrary," she replied with great dignity, "I'm a very sensible person, a shaper of young minds, a respected teacher. Meeting your nephew has made me an idiot. Can you help me down, please?"

He shook his head. "I don't get involved in family dramas."

"I'm not family."

Sighing, he raised his arms and she dropped into them.

"Thank you. Would you—"

"No. I'm not giving you a lift anywhere. What loyalties I do have are to Joe, which is why I think you should go back in there. He's worried about you."

"It's not me he's concerned about, it's the—" Pip stopped herself in time. "Have you ever been in love?" she asked miserably.

"Nearly," said Daniel. "Fortunately, I pulled back in time."

She frowned. "You and Joe are so alike. And that's not a compliment, Red."

He smiled, a real smile, and became a very attractive man. "I'll ignore that because your momentary death wish will pass. And, no offense, but you don't make putting your heart on the line look very appealing."

She smiled weakly at that. "No, I don't, do I?"

"You want to go back inside now?"

"No." She took her cell phone out of her pants pocket. "I'm going to walk a couple of blocks, then call a cab." Her bag was still inside, but she had money at home.

Five minutes later, as she marched along the highway, a four-wheel drive pulled in front of her. Daniel reached over and opened the passenger door. "Hop in."

"I don't want to cause you trouble with Joe."

"I'll be into more trouble if I abandon you in this neighborhood. Now get in."

One look at his aggravated expression and Pip did as she was told.

Daniel surveyed her through narrowed eyes. "I want no tears, no confidences…in fact, after you've told me your address, no talking. I'm not getting involved."

"Joe was right," said Pip. "You can be charming when you want to be."

One corner of his mouth lifted. "Seat belt," he growled.

CHAPTER EIGHTEEN

"IT'S NOT TRUE," Joe said quietly to Sue as they waited outside the bathroom. She'd joined him a couple of minutes earlier, thinking Pip might need more than his reassurances that his family didn't hate her. "You didn't ruin me for other women."

"No," she agreed. "I was only an excuse."

Joe tore his gaze away from the door and stared at her. "What the hell's that supposed to mean?"

"You were already in the shell, Joe." Usually so affectionate and accepting, he read an uncomfortable challenge in her dark brown eyes. "You'll have to come out if you want to keep her."

Women. "You have no idea how complicated things are." Pip needed him. Joe mustered his patience and banked his righteous anger for later.

"Actually," said his cousin, "with the right person, things are pretty simple."

But his attention swung back to the door. Joe wasn't listening. "She's taking too long. I'm going in there." He started forward, but Sue caught him by the arm.

"Pip will come out when she's ready. Maybe it's better if we give her some space instead of hovering."

Reluctantly, he allowed himself to be steered back to the table, where the rest of the family had abandoned dessert and stood talking. Except one, Joe noticed. "Where's Daniel?"

"He remembered an urgent appointment." Belle's tone was uncharacteristically sarcastic.

"How's Pip?" said Aunt Emily.

Joe glared at Uncle Sam. "Throwing up."

"Well, that's all we need!" Sam rolled his eyes. "A bulimic in the family."

In two strides, Joe stood over his uncle. "You damn fool, she's not bulimic, she's pregnant." It took every ounce of self-control not to hit him. "What the hell were you thinking, palming off alcohol?"

"Pregnant!" Nadia was the first to react. "How could you be so irresponsible *twice?*"

Joe thought there wasn't a spare inch of psyche he hadn't already flayed raw, but his ex-wife found one.

Sam looked genuinely shocked. "But I asked her if she was pregnant and she denied it."

"Because we're keeping it a secret, you moron!" Joe roared.

The absurdity of that remark brought him back to his senses. He looked around at his relatives, all displaying varying degrees of amazement, and sighed heavily. "At this rate we're going to be the least dysfunctional family in the entire country."

Smiles broke out, handshakes. "Congratulations!" Belle gave him a warm hug. Sue's embrace was reassuring, but Nadia simply shook her head.

"We'll talk later," he promised.

Kaitlin danced around him. "I'm gonna have a baby sister or brother!" The enormity of his disclosure struck home. Oh, God, what had he done? His daughter tugged on his hand. "Does this mean you guys are gonna get married?"

"We're talking about it, honey." Joe tried to sound enthusiastic, but he was wondering how Pip was going to react when she heard he'd blabbed.

He had to tell her first. Suddenly aware that she was taking far too long, Joe turned toward the corridor.

Sam caught up with him. "Listen, I'm sorry." His so-called uncle actually seemed humble. "I would never have given her alcohol had I known."

Joe lengthened his stride. "Yeah, well, you can make your apologies to Pip." She didn't answer his rap on the door and he pushed it open. "Anyone here?" No answer. He checked all the stalls. They were empty. But she couldn't have left through the restaurant.

Swaying in the breeze of an open window, the net curtains caught his attention. Joe narrowed his eyes. No, not even Pip...

His cell beeped an incoming text. Incredulous, Joe stared at Pip's message: *Dan's taking me home. Please grovel on my behalf.*

BETWEEN PLACATING HIS ex-wife, calming his excited daughter, dodging uncomfortable questions from his relatives and settling the bill, it was two hours later before Joe inserted his key in the lock of Pip's apartment. Before turning the handle, he paused, gathering his composure. He didn't want to yell at Pip. On further reflection he'd decided that part of this fiasco—a very small part—was his fault.

He should have warned her to be careful around Sam. Maybe mentioned that Sue was the woman who'd sent him off the rails in high school. Still, Pip had no business—even under the influence—psychoanalyzing him.

On the drive home he'd phoned a doctor friend who'd

confirmed what Joe already knew in the logical part of his brain. The baby would be fine.

"I know," said Pip. "I made my own inquiries."

Feet tucked under her, she reclined on the candy-striped couch next to her balcony window, almost lost in her fleecy bathrobe, her fair hair damp from a shower.

She'd sent him a cool "Hello" when he'd come in, and returned to her book, *Pregnancy and You.* The late-afternoon sun gilded her hair and skin and blazed white on the lambs marching around the hem of that ridiculous robe.

Joe had expected repentance. He'd expected Pip to be appalled by her actions. He'd come home magnanimously prepared to forgive and console her. "Tea?" he said through gritted teeth.

She inclined her head, as gracious as a queen. "Thank you."

While he made hot drinks, Pip concentrated on her book. Through his irritation, Joe was acutely conscious of the fragrance of lavender soap and warm woman, and the curve of dark lashes over her smooth cheek. Only when he was stirring sugar into his coffee did he realize that she hadn't turned a single page.

Some of his magnanimity came back.

As he handed her a mug of tea, he said brusquely, "I told them about your pregnancy."

She turned the book upside down on her lap. "I guess you had to, given the circumstances."

Joe wrestled with his conscience. "Actually, I hadn't meant—"

"How did Kaitlin take it?"

"Excited...already choosing names." Maybe it was better not to make his apology before she'd made hers.

Raising her mug, Pip paused, looking at him across the rim. "And Nadia?"

"Furious at both of us." Joe sat down beside her. "She calmed down when I explained the circumstances."

Without taking a sip, Pip placed her mug carefully on the gilt-and-beveled-glass coffee table. "And how many think I did it deliberately to get a green card?"

He'd wondered if that had been bothering her. "Sam raised the possibility."

The man hadn't even seen the question as offensive. "I tell it like it is," he'd said when his wife and daughter objected.

He was such a hopeless case that Joe hadn't wasted any more time on him. The guy was more than capable of hurtling to hell by his own efforts.

Pip untucked her feet and sat up straighter, and the book on her lap hit the floor with a thud. "I made such a fool of myself!"

Now they were following Joe's script. He patted her hand, feeling a return of the extraordinary tenderness she always roused in him.

Standing, she swung around and pointed a finger at him. "And it's all your fault."

"*My* fault?"

"And don't you ever use our child as an excuse not to be a winemaker."

He couldn't follow her logic. "What the hell has that got to do with anything?"

"I have absolutely no intention of being a financial burden to you," she said impatiently. "If it comes to that, I'll go back to work six weeks after the birth and—"

Joe sprang to his feet. "No stranger's looking after our baby."

"If I'm home, Mum will look after it."

His temper flared. "Are you even keeping an open mind about this?"

"Are you?" she countered. Pip carried her mug to the sink and tipped the tea down the drain. "There's a strong possibility I'll go back to New Zealand, Joe, so keep that option open, too."

Eyeing her stiff back, he jammed his fists in the pockets of his pants. "Look, if it's the family...Sue and I..."

"Your family's great. It's *you* I'm having trouble with. None of this fiasco would have happened today if you'd shared some information." Her sheepskin slippers slapped the parquet floor as she returned to the living room. "But, no, you can't disclose anything, can you, Joe, that might reveal any vulnerability?"

He cloaked himself in icy detachment. "That's ridiculous and you know it. What about Kaitlin? I accepted your help then."

"Because you were desperate and I was a stranger, someone transient in your life." Pip picked up a couch cushion that had fallen on the floor, and clutched it protectively to her breast. "As soon as that changed, you had to wrest back control, challenge me to a duel and prove you were the tough guy again."

He shook his head in mute protest, but she kept up the attack. "You dropped your guard again when you discovered I was leaving, but since the pregnancy I'm back to arm's length." Her voice rising in frustration, Pip flung the cushion back onto the couch. "And you have the gall to tell me to keep an open mind about staying. You can't even admit to yourself that you love me, let alone—"

"Yeah?" Joe was stung into a reply. "Well, I haven't exactly heard you shouting it from the rooftops."

"Because I know you'll see it as a weakness and use it to manipulate me into doing what *you* want!" Eyes flashing, Pip stormed closer until they stood toe to toe. "We're supposed to be making an honest attempt to find a way forward together. Instead I feel like I'm in a war." She jabbed a finger into his chest. "Fighting for my independence—" another jab "—fighting over this baby—" jab, jab "—fighting to know you!"

He heard the catch in her voice. Joe clasped her shoulders. "Truce."

Pip was breathing hard, breasts rising and falling rapidly, hair drying in wild tendrils, cheeks flushed. He'd never fought with Nadia. Even at the end they'd kept things civilized.

But this stubborn, insightful, infuriating woman made him feel anything but civilized, effortlessly provoking all the emotions he'd be a fool to trust—passion, possessiveness, recklessness.

"Truce," he repeated, and kissed her.

It had been so long, too damn long since he'd held her like this, tasted her like this—toothpaste, sweet tea and passionate woman. With an angry moan Pip submitted to the kiss, her hands fisting in his shirt as she hauled him closer and answered the thrust of his tongue. Heat arced between them. Joe's heart pumped harder, his blood fired.

How could such a small woman have so much power to move him? She only had to quiver to disarm him, gently nip his lower lip to make him shudder with need. Every nerve ending responded to her; with one fingertip caress along his jaw she owned his body.

Pip broke the kiss. "A truce is not a resolution." She let go of his shirt, but only to undo it and push it off his shoulders. Joe opened her robe and exposed her breasts, pale and beautiful, already fuller with pregnancy. The sight made him feel protective and fiercely possessive.

"So negotiate." Sliding her robe to her waist, he lifted her half-naked body and suckled on one pink nipple.

"Ohh." Her cry was astonished, doubtful. Immediately, Joe stopped. "Too tender?"

She swallowed. "Too good."

He returned to his work, losing the last of his rational mind with every soft cry, drunk with the taste and scent and warmth of her. Joe stumbled toward the couch and sat Pip down, then knelt before her and untied the sash of her robe while she wrestled with his belt buckle.

She pushed down his jeans; he felt cool air, then hot hands on his erection as she guided him into her, so wet, so inviting that his mind seized.

His body began the instinctive thrust and withdrawal while Joe fought the urge to plunge deeper, to go past the point of no return. "What do you want from me, Pip?"

"Stop hiding from me," she panted.

With an immense effort he stopped, even though it made everything ache, not the least his heart. "Then say you'll stay." He would give, but only enough to keep her.

Pip shuddered around him and he couldn't hold back, clutching at the pieces of his soul, knowing that some of them would never return. And that was a horror to him. Afterward, he made himself hold her. "Stay."

Sitting up, Pip reached for her robe. "I need more time to make a decision. Please understand."

"I'm trying, but I've got a vested interest, remember?" Drained and frustrated, Joe started to dress. "My child."

Pip dropped her head in her hands. "You think I don't know that?"

Like he knew, deep down, the sacrifice she'd have to make to stay. Looking at her bowed head, Joe stopped pretending there was an easy answer. He gathered Pip in a bear hug and gave her the comfort they both needed. "Okay, let's try this your way. What do you want to know?"

Her arms tightened around him. "Not what," she said. "Who."

"ADAM, MEET PIP."

"Hello, Mr. Fraser."

His father grunted, a sound conveying the opposite of the welcome Joe knew Adam intended. Joe started to sweat, but Pip approached the bed and took the clumsily proffered hand without self-consciousness. "I've been nervous about this meeting," she confessed, and Adam's half smile faded. "Knocked up isn't how I wanted to meet you."

His father snorted a laugh and Joe breathed a silent sigh of relief. He pulled the two chairs up beside the bed. "I guess I should have mentioned her bluntness."

Adam frowned at him. "Bad…habit…pregnant…"

"My fault this time, I'm afraid," answered Pip as she sat down. "I was on the pill, but—"

"Can we please not discuss our contraceptive failures with my father?" Joe interrupted her.

Pip and Adam exchanged another smile, then she began a casual monologue about New Zealand and her family, encouraged by fragmented questions from Adam.

Only when he felt his shoulders relax into the chair did Joe realize how tense he usually was around visitors, even Daniel, Sue and Belle. Every family connection felt like a fuse, all too easily ignited. But Pip didn't carry that baggage and she also had an extraordinary ability to read people and respond accordingly.

Within five minutes she was telling Adam what a great student his granddaughter was. Joe looked away, unable to bear the yearning in his father's eyes.

Kaitlin sat downstairs at the nurses' station, drawing her grandfather a picture to join the dozen already papering the walls.

Joe had expected Pip to protest when he'd told Kaitlin to stay put, but she'd said nothing. His gaze fell on the latest painting, pinned beside Adam's bed.

Made up of three panels, it showed a guy progressing through what looked to be a heart attack. Joe winced. Leaning closer, he read the caption. *Three things to help you get better: 1. Smile. 2. Giggle 3. Laugh.*

For fully five minutes, Joe stared at the picture before he moved. "Excuse me a minute, will you?"

His daughter's head was bent over a drawing, the tip of her tongue poking out in concentration. As he came closer, he saw the picture was of a clown with enormous feet. The text in the speech bubble came into focus. *You think you got troubles? Try walking in* these *shoes.*

"Kaitlin?" He held out a hand. "You want to say hello to Grandpa?"

She was on her feet in a second, the crayons tumbling from her lap. "*Do* I!"

Ascending the stairs, he tried to prepare her, but she interrupted him. "Yeah, Dad, I know. Pip told me what to expect."

He stopped. "Pip."

"Yeah." Kaitlin tugged him forward. "She said you'd

probably come round if we left you in peace to think about it." Okay, it was fine that she read other people, but Joe didn't like the idea of Pip reading him. Half exasperated, half amused, he halted Kaitlin at Adam's door and heard her quick intake of breath. His heart stopped. He'd got this wrong. But then she rushed forward. "Grandpa."

Unaware she'd chosen Adam's paralyzed side, Kaitlin clutched at his arm and kissed his cheek.

"Kaitlin."

Joe steered his daughter to the other side of the bed and picked up Adam's good hand to place it in Kaitlin's. But before he could, Adam's grip tightened. With a shock, Joe saw his father's eyes were moist. "Thanks...son."

Joe dropped his hand as though it were a hot coal. "You're welcome, Adam."

Adam turned his attention to Kaitlin, who was checking him over with great interest.

"You look better than you used to," she confided naively. "You were a little bit fat before, Grandpa."

Adam expelled a laugh. "Missed...you."

"Is that the only way you talk now?"

Joe led the conversation into safer channels, encouraging Kaitlin to chat so Adam didn't have to. Underneath, his will fought his father's. *I can't give you what you want.* He became aware that Pip was studying him, but when he glanced over she looked away. Still, Joe sensed disapproval, and it made him angry. She had no right to judge him.

When Kaitlin ran out of things to say—"it's only nineteen days until Christmas, Grandpa. I'll make you some decorations"—Pip took over. Mercilessly she began lampooning Joe's experiences at camp, until Kaitlin was giggling and Adam had tears of laughter running down his face.

Joe barely cracked a smile. He should have told Adam these stories. Stewing over Pip's rejection and resentful about losing his apartment, he'd shared only the barest details of the camp experience.

And when had he last heard Pip laugh like this? Frustration boiled inside him, all the more lethal for being contained. It didn't matter what Joe gave, people always wanted more. He'd all but bankrupted himself for his father and still Adam wanted some mawkish father-son bond.

Joe shifted restlessly in his chair. He was prepared to do his duty by Pip, but oh, no, that wasn't good enough. He had to buy access to his own child by coughing up love like a goddamn fur ball. Give her a family to replace the perfect one she'd left in New Zealand.

Pip was no different from Nadia, picking away at him, asking for more than he wanted to give. And making him feel bad for withholding it.

Watching the three of them enjoy a joke at his expense, Joe became furious. No, Pip was worse than Nadia because she held up a mirror to his failings and made him mourn for the guy he could never be—inclusive, trusting, openhearted.

Suddenly he couldn't bear to be around her, this woman with her limitless capacity to love. This woman who made him need her in a way Joe didn't want to need anyone.

He couldn't let his life revolve around her as it had once revolved around Sue. With all that potential for hurt.

Abruptly, he stood up. "I'm going to get a soda." Joe left before they could answer.

CHAPTER NINETEEN

"HE DIDN'T ASK IF we wanted sodas," Kaitlin said, puzzled. It wasn't like Dad to forget his manners. "I'll go tell him."

"I'll go," said Pip. "You stay and talk to your grandpa. Want one, Mr. Fraser?"

Grandpa shook his head. "Adam," he stressed.

Smiling, Pip nodded. "Adam."

There was a silence after she left. For the first time, Kaitlin felt awkward in her grandfather's presence. Sneaking a peek, she saw he looked worried. "Are you okay, Grandpa?"

He grunted. "How…Dad…money?"

"Okay since he sold his apart—" Kaitlin squirmed. Keeping secrets was harder than she thought. "His company's having their Christmas party at the Aquarium this year so the kids aren't bored," she finished, proud of her recovery.

"Need…help," said Grandpa.

Petrified, she started to the door. "I'll get someone."

"No!" He panted a little. "Your…help." He held out his hand. "Secret."

Though she was flattered, Kaitlin felt compelled to warn him, "I'm not great at secrets, Grandpa. I mean, I don't go and tell people on purpose, but sometimes it just comes out."

"Try."

His faded blue eyes were so serious she nodded. He gestured to the bedside table. "Drawer."

Kaitlin opened it, holding up the contents one by one until he grunted. It took a long time for Grandpa to tell her what he wanted, and his eyes kept sliding toward the door, but she'd got the gist of it by the time Dad came back. He was alone.

"Didn't Pip find you?"

"No." He didn't look happy. And he was empty-handed.

"Where are the sodas?"

"Right here." Pip walked in behind him, holding three cans. She handed Kaitlin a cherry Coke, gave Joe a Sprite. "I couldn't find you."

"I needed some air. Thanks for this." But Dad didn't look at Pip. Instead he looked at her. "Time to get going, honey."

"But we haven't—"

"Listen…to…father," Grandpa growled, then winked.

Kaitlin leaned over and kissed his hollow cheek. He smelled of shaving lotion, ointments and old age. He'd never smelled old before.

She felt very important and brave and scared in case the task he'd given her was too hard for someone who was ten. Princess Belle would have felt like this, setting off to ask the Beast to spare her father.

But Pip had said the more secrets a family kept, the more dis-something they were. Kaitlin didn't know what that meant, but figured it had to be a good thing. And if keeping secrets was in her genes, she'd try to be better at it.

When Pip shook hands with Grandpa, he lifted her fingers to his lips. "Fine…woman."

"Grandaaad!" Kaitlin had forgotten he could be embarrassing sometimes.

But Pip only laughed. "Don't your Disney princes ever do that in the movies?"

That reminded Kaitlin of something she'd been meaning to tell Grandpa when she'd started choosing names for the baby. "Did you know that the Beast's name was Adam before the witch put a spell on him, Grandpa? And he was Prince Adam when he turned back. I think we should call—"

"We're going *now*, Kaitlin," Dad interrupted in a tone she always obeyed. "See you tomorrow, Adam." Man, he was grumpy suddenly.

Sitting in the back of the car on the way home, Kaitlin thought about Grandpa and how he'd looked and how he'd smelled. "Will Grandpa die, Dad?"

"No," he said. "He's going to be okay."

But she saw Pip's sadness as her teacher glanced at Dad, and had her real answer.

Kaitlin stared out the window as the car crawled across the Golden Gate Bridge. Pedestrians and cyclists—probably tourists—were being buffeted by a high wind.

Thinking about Grandpa dying was like losing a tooth. Even when you knew it made you feel funny you couldn't stop yourself from poking at the spongy hole. But Grandpa must hate not being able to move much, or talk properly. And he was already old. Old people died.

Kaitlin straightened in her seat. "How old are you, Dad?"

"Nearly thirty, why?"

"Promise you won't die until I'm at least twenty."

His eyes met hers in the rearview mirror. "Is this because of Grandpa? I told you—"

"I have to be a grown-up, Dad, before you leave me."

There was silence in the car, only a thin whistle where the wind had found a gap in one of the windows. Then Pip laid a hand on Dad's knee. "I promise," he said.

Her primary concern addressed, Kaitlin thought about what she needed to do for Grandpa. Now that she knew he was dying, it was more important than ever not to let him down.

"WHY DIDN'T YOU TELL Kaitlin the truth about Adam?"

Joe and Pip were making dinner together an hour after dropping Kaitlin home. He'd known this confrontation was coming, and welcomed it.

"You were the one who said a cynic is an idealist who gives up." Shaking the water out of the lettuce, Joe began breaking the leaves into a salad bowl. "Doctors aren't always right."

Lamb chops sizzled in the pan, fragrant with rosemary. Pip stopped turning the meat. "Joe." So much empathy loaded in that one word. It made his heart ache.

"Look, I don't need negativity right now. It's hard enough—" He caught himself. "If you want to disapprove, fine. But don't judge me, Pip." Joe realized he was shredding the lettuce in smaller and smaller pieces and stopped.

"I'm not," she said quietly. "Your relationship with your father is your business."

He needed a fight and she chose to be understanding. In two knife strokes he quartered the tomatoes and tossed them in with the lettuce. "What father? You mean the guy that showed up ten months ago after a lifetime of neglect, expecting to pick up where we left off? That guy?"

Picking up a cucumber, he started dicing it with ruthless efficiency. "He dumped me with Nana Jo a week after my mother died, then spent the next twenty-five years drowning his sorrows. Because let's face it, wallowing in grief takes precedence over raising your son. So don't expect me to get sentimental now."

Joe glanced over, waiting for her to argue with him, but Pip didn't say a word. Her compassion smothered him like a blanket. He threw down the knife. "I'm going to move back to the hotel for a couple of nights." He knew he was hurting her—hell, he was hurting himself, but Joe couldn't stop. "I need some space."

In the bedroom, he packed his suitcase, throwing everything in as quickly as possible. Pip appeared in the doorway. "Please don't do this."

"I'll call you in a couple of days."

As Joe went to move past her, she barred the door with one slim arm. "Please let me in."

"I can't."

Pip dropped her arm and he left. She listened until the last echo of his footfall on the stairs fell away, and all she could hear was the sizzle of meat in the pan. Her appetite gone, Pip turned off the stove, then stood uncertainly in the kitchen. What the hell had just happened?

Shell-shocked, she wandered over to the couch and sat down, straight-backed, her hands in her lap. They'd made love on this, only twenty-four hours earlier. The phone rang beside her and she dived for it. "Joe?"

"Hi, Pip, it's Sue."

She struggled to sound normal. "Hi, Sue. I'm afraid—" *no, not afraid* "—Joe's not here right now."

Maybe he was sitting in his car, regretting his meltdown, too embarrassed to come back. Pip pulled the curtain aside.

"Actually, I'm calling to talk to you. How are things?"

No sign of his BMW. She let the curtain fall. "Great." Pip wasn't going to confide in Joe's best friend. "Listen, I'm really, really sorry about Thanksgiving." She tried to walk off her growing panic. How could Joe do this to her?

"Don't worry, I chewed him out about that. What on earth was he thinking, sending you into one of our first family gatherings unprepared? I hope we didn't ruin his chances with you?"

She couldn't stop herself. "No, he's doing that on his own."

There was a brief silence, then Sue sighed. "I guessed as much. This is awkward, and Joe would kill me, but I have to say it in case you have doubts. He does love you."

Pip stopped pacing. "Did he tell you that?"

"No," Sue admitted, "but it's obvious by the way he reacts to you."

Did Sue mean the emotional withdrawal, the irrational defensiveness or the running away? A lump came to Pip's throat. "You know what I miss most about family? The way they champion your cause no matter how badly you behave."

"That information is for you, Pip. Joe told me you're still making up your mind, and it might help when you're weighing your options."

Except how did you live with a man who hated being in love with you?

"And if you ever want advice or help with babies, call me. None of us start out experts."

Tears pricked Pip's eyes. "Thanks for your call." She hung up and burst into tears. What did it say about her life lately, that a few kind words could reduce her to a blubbering wreck? But she was through pretending that she could cope with any curveball Joe threw her.

Wiping her face with her sleeve, Pip took a deep, sobbing breath, then fetched a box of tissues from the kitchen cupboard and blew her nose hard. It was time to stop wimping out on the truth.

Joe was never going to change.

Every time they came close to a breakthrough he pulled back. And with every withdrawal, Pip's confidence crumbled under the weight of loving someone who wouldn't—or couldn't—love her back. The situation was tearing her up inside, undermining her independence, her self-respect and her equilibrium. Every quality she was going to need in abundance to raise this child.

Tears brimmed, but she blinked them away. She refused to settle for scraps. Well, if she couldn't beat Joe, she'd join him. From here on in, her only priority was self-preservation.

"I HAVE TO BE HOME by five," Kaitlin instructed Great-Uncle Sam when she climbed into his Mercedes after school the following Tuesday. Except he'd told her to drop the "Great" from Uncle Sam. She was happy to.

"It would have been a hell of a lot easier to meet at the hospital," he said impatiently. "Why couldn't your mom take you?"

"Syphilis." Kaitlin had worked out her lie beforehand. "She's at the doctor's."

About to pull into traffic, Uncle Sam stalled the car, then got all flustered and red when someone honked at him. He didn't say a word all the way to Grandpa's rehab center.

Kaitlin didn't mind; she didn't like him very much.

In the corridor outside Grandpa's room, Uncle Sam

stopped. "What I don't understand is why you need to be here?"

"I'm the negotiator." Before he could ask any further questions, Kaitlin pushed open the door. "Hi, Grandpa." She bent to give him a kiss and felt his hand on her hair.

"Hello, Adam," Uncle Sam said brusquely. "How are you feeling?"

A glint came into Grandpa's eyes. "How…look?"

Uncle Sam opened his mouth to say something, then glanced at Kaitlin and coughed. "Fine," he said gruffly. "If this is about the solicitor's letter, you're wasting your time. I'm not backing off from legal action simply because you're incapacitated."

Grandpa nodded to Kaitlin. She cleared her throat. "Do you still want to buy that medal?"

Uncle Sam appeared confused. "My great-grandfather's Medal of Honor," she clarified. When he continued to look blank, she added helpfully, "You know, the one you wanted for your medal collection a long time ago because Billy Fraser saved your dad, only Grandpa said no. Way before you knew you were related. He'll sell it now because he needs the money."

"Kait!"

"Shouldn't I have told him that?" Anxiously, Kaitlin slipped her hand in Grandpa's, but though he squeezed it reassuringly, he kept staring at Uncle Sam.

"Well, I wasn't expecting that." Uncle Sam frowned, then straightened his tie. "Of course, it's hardly surprising you've lost any sentimental attachment, given Billy Fraser isn't your father anymore—"

Grandpa made an angry sound. "Twen…thou."

"What did he say?"

"Thirty thousand dollars!" Her grandfather's hand

jerked in hers and Kaitlin gave it a warning pinch. Dad always said to start the bidding high.

Uncle Sam snorted. "You obviously haven't done your homework, Adam."

"How would he?" she said hotly.

Uncle Sam looked embarrassed. "Aside from the fact that it's grossly overpriced, there's another—"

"What's this, early visitors?" Pushing a meds trolley, Nurse Elaine entered the room. She smiled hello at Kaitlin, who tried not to act guilty. This meeting had been arranged in off-hours so Uncle Sam didn't run into Dad.

Nurse Elaine turned to him. "I'm afraid only immediate relatives are allowed outside visiting hours."

Uncle Sam sighed. "We're related."

"In that case, I'm happy for you to stay. But I'll need ten minutes alone with Adam, if you don't mind." It wasn't a request.

"Bossy...one," Grandpa murmured, and Kaitlin got the giggles.

Nurse Elaine shook her head. "I heard that, Adam." She winked at Kaitlin.

Outside the room Kaitlin stopped giggling when Uncle Sam narrowed his eyes at her. A crocodile at the zoo had looked at her like that once. "Does your father know about this?"

Kaitlin crossed her fingers behind her back. "Of course he does."

Uncle Sam pulled out his cell. "What's his number?"

"I...I don't know."

"Then I'll call Directory."

"Don't!"

Uncle Sam started punching in numbers. "Hello? I need—"

Kaitlin grabbed the hem of his jacket. "Dad sold his apartment to pay hospital bills, and Grandpa wants to sell the Medal of Honor and pay it back."

"Cancel that." Uncle Sam ended the call.

Kaitlin started to cry. "I told Dad's secret to Grandpa and now I've told Grandpa's secret to you."

"Well, crying about it won't un-tell it," he said. "Come away from the door before your grandpa hears you."

Gulping, she followed him down the corridor, where he pulled out a large white handkerchief and ordered her to get cleaned up. "You made a good start in negotiations. Don't ruin it by turning female on me."

Kaitlin sniffed. "Yes, I did."

"Unfortunately, the medal's not worth half that." He rubbed his chin. "Does Adam have a plan B if I don't buy it?"

"We're gonna put it on eBay."

"Then prepare to be investigated by the FBI, young lady."

Kaitlin checked to see if he was joking, but Uncle Sam's face was very serious.

"In the last few years, U.S gallantry medals have come under the protection of the Stolen Valor Act. Although its primary purpose is to stop people wearing medals they're not entitled to, it also means gallantry medals can no longer be sold."

His chest started to puff out and Kaitlin had to swallow a nervous giggle. She'd already noticed Great-Uncle Sam inflated like a rooster whenever he was *telling* people something. "In fact, it's a federal offense punishable by fines of up to one hundred thousand dollars and a prison sentence of up to one year."

"Oh," she said faintly. Kaitlin lost the urge to giggle. "I don't think Grandpa knows that."

"I couldn't buy it even if I wanted to."

Kaitlin slid down the wall to sit on the carpet. "You can just give him the money, anyway."

He snorted. "Thirty thousand dollars…just like that."

"You have plenty, don't you?"

"Not by giving it away."

"But he's your brother."

"Half brother. And he's trying to steal my inheritance."

"No wonder Auntie Emily doesn't want to live with you anymore," Kaitlin said hotly. "You're so mean."

"Don't disrespect your elders, young lady."

She glowered. Grumpy old grump didn't scare her.

Then Uncle Sam did a surprising thing. He sat on the floor beside her, using the wall as support when one of his knees clicked. "I want my life back. My wife, my daughter, everything the way it was before Mom's letter blew it apart."

"Then start being nice to people," said Kaitlin, still bristling.

He grunted. "That simple, huh?"

She thought about it, then admitted, "Not for you."

Uncle Sam barked a laugh. "You remind me of my daughter." They were silent for a few minutes. "I don't think Adam would take it, anyway. The old fool has too much pride."

"He's not a fool and you're older than he is!"

"No, I'm a few months younger." He looked pretty sour about it.

"It must be hard to think you're oldest and then find out you're not," she conceded. Melissa was always trying to be in charge just because her birthday was a week earlier.

"Thank you, Kaitlin," he said. "You're the first person in your family to understand that."

Uncle Sam's face grew red as he used the wall again to push himself up. He straightened his suit, then reached down a hand and pulled her to her feet. "Maybe there is a way for both of us to get what we want."

The nurse popped her head into the corridor. "You can come in now."

"Follow my lead," said Uncle Sam.

Obediently, Kaitlin trailed him back into the room.

Grandpa looked tired, even though he'd only had to take medicine.

"I'll give you thirty thousand dollars," said Uncle Sam, "on two conditions. One, you sign it over as a gift, with that nurse witnessing, and two, you renounce all claim to the Carson necklace."

Kaitlin decided Uncle Sam was a very clever man, but thought it only fair to point out the flaw in his plan. "But you said the medal wasn't worth half that."

Uncle Sam frowned at her. "Sentiment can inflate the market value."

"You...feel...that...much...?"

"It astonishes me, too, Adam." Fastening his suit jacket, Uncle Sam said briskly, "My father was one of the men Billy saved that day."

"Mores...pity..." Grandpa sniffed.

"Well, it's not just me who wouldn't be here if he hadn't," snapped Uncle Sam. "Now do we have a deal or don't we?"

"Necklace...back...Jenny." The two men glared at each other.

"Fine," said Uncle Sam. "I'll go back to suing her."

Dad and Grandpa were only borrowing the necklace, anyway. Kaitlin opened her mouth to remind Grandpa, then closed it. Maybe Uncle Sam wasn't the cleverest person in the room.

Grandpa gestured to the drawer, and Kaitlin opened it and took out the large velvet box holding the medal. Uncle Sam borrowed some paper from reception and used hospital letterhead and his gold pen to write out all his conditions, then got Grandpa and Nurse Elaine to sign it. "I'm assuming you're of sound mind," Uncle Sam grumbled as he wrote out a check to the rehab unit.

Grandpa winked at Kaitlin.

She presented the box to Uncle Sam, who took out the Medal of Honor. The gold star spun on its navy ribbon before he carefully laid it on his palm. He looked at it the same way Grandpa did—like it was very precious.

"You know all about it, right?" she asked. "Around the star is a laurel wreath, and above that is an eagle." Gently, Kaitlin stroked the bird's outstretched wings. "And the lady in the middle is Minerva, the Roman goddess of warriors."

Uncle Sam was staring at her funny. Kaitlin withdrew her hand. "Well, if you collect medals you must know that stuff," she said awkwardly.

"Did your grandpa teach you all that?"

"Yes, sir."

Uncle Sam looked over at Grandpa. "Adam, are you sure you want to do this?"

Grandpa's bony shoulder lifted in a shrug. "Like... said.... Not...my...father." His voice was croaky; he must have a sore throat.

Uncle Sam repacked the medal, then put the box in his jacket pocket. "I'm sorry. I forgot that my family wasn't the only one screwed up by this."

"Emily...back?"

"No. After the Thanksgiving debacle she filed for divorce." Uncle Sam cleared his throat. "Your grand-daughter suggested I start being nice."

Grandpa laughed, which made Uncle Sam grumpy again. "Let's go, young lady. I need to get back to the dealership."

As they were leaving, Uncle Sam looked over his shoulder like he wanted to say something, but didn't know what.

"It's...okay," Grandpa said, and Uncle Sam nodded.

On their way out to the car Kaitlin said tentatively, "Grandpa's dying."

Uncle Sam put a hand on her shoulder. "Yes."

She was glad that someone had told her the truth. He opened the car door for her and Kaitlin decided she liked him a little bit. "Um, Uncle Sam, you can drop me off at the end of my street."

He sighed. "So your mother doesn't know about this, either?"

"No, sir." Getting in the car, Kaitlin pulled the seat belt across her lap and grinned. "It's our secret."

CHAPTER TWENTY

"PIP?" said Adam.

Because each labored word was laden with meaning, Joe had learned to interpret the nuances of his father's speech. For the first day after Pip's visit his father's grunt had meant *I like her. She's wonderful. You're a lucky man.*

Now Adam was concerned. The translation: *What's wrong? Why haven't you brought her back to visit me? Why are you so unhappy?*

Joe pretended not to hear. Why did his flight-or-fight mechanism kick in every time she got close? And how was he going to manage these feelings so he could live with them? Because if he didn't, he'd lose Pip and their baby. Two nights of staring at the ceiling of his hotel room hadn't produced any answers.

In stocking feet, he stood on one of Adam's two visitors' chairs, tacking Kaitlin's homemade Christmas wreath above the door and trying not to knock off any of the precariously glued plastic holly or gold-dusted pinecones.

As long as he concentrated on practical tasks he had a sense of being in control. Glitter floated to the floor. "Hopefully nothing falls off this thing onto someone's head," he commented.

He missed Pip with a gut-wrenching ache, but without

answers Joe knew he'd only make things worse, not better. And he only had one shot at this. Fortunately, she'd asked for one more night apart.

Jumping off the chair, he surveyed his handiwork. No amount of adjustment would ever make that thing symmetrical. Luckily, it only had to hang for thirteen days. He'd take it down on Boxing Day.

"Kaitlin would have come tonight," he said, "but she and a few friends are going caroling at the local old folks' home." Joe packed away his hammer in the red tool kit he'd brought with him. "For their sake, I hope the seniors are all deaf, because not one of those girls can hold a tune."

He'd got used to talking to Adam over his father's three months in rehab. At first it had been small talk: "How 'bout those Giants." When that ran out Joe had been forced to dig deeper. Adam's response to a casual childhood memory had led to other recollections. Slowly, he'd filled his father in on the missed years.

Sometimes Joe wondered if he was trying to rub salt into the wound with these stories. He only knew he needed to tell them.

"Pip," Adam persisted.

"Okay, we had a fight." Joe brushed glitter off his navy polo shirt and discarded the light sweater tied around his waist. It was always too hot in here. "Nothing serious, but I've moved to a hotel for a couple of days to sulk effectively." Pip had given him this, the self-awareness to mock his failings.

Adam frowned. "Don't...blow...it."

"Yeah, well, when I want relationship advice from a guy who's been single for twenty-five years I'll ask."

"Couldn't...replace..." Adam stopped.

His father didn't need to finish. He couldn't replace Francis, Joe's mother.

With an all-too-familiar tension tightening his gut, Joe changed the subject. "You look tired, Adam." There was a gray tinge in his father's complexion that hadn't been there yesterday, and he was struggling more than usual with words.

"Shit...happens."

"Ain't that the truth." Joe returned the blue plastic chair to Adam's bedside and sat down. His father's breathing seemed labored. Joe put a hand on Adam's forehead. Clammy. "You okay? Want me to get a—"

"No!" The response was explosive, even for Adam.

"Okay, okay, keep your shirt on. I'm not going to fight about it. On that subject, I hear through Aunt Jenny that you've decided to quit torturing your little brother. That you've stopped pretending to covet the Carson necklace. Why?"

The corner of his father's mouth lifted. "Good... will...all...men."

"Let's hope the bastard appreciates it." Joe remembered the card in his pocket. "Speaking of Christmas, Kaitlin wanted me to give you this."

It was a Christmas card with faces superimposed on the Christmas tree ornaments. Joe could pick out his mother and grandmother, as well as the Carson clan. And Pip.

He cleared his throat. "I was thinking about Nana Jo last night, and this whole thing with Robert Carson." Looking for answers to his dilemma with Pip, and finding nothing but deceit and disappointment and bereavement in his family tree. "We seem to have a tradition of being unlucky in love."

"I...wasn't."

Joe couldn't help laughing bitterly.

Adam glared. "You...should...be...so...lucky."

"Lucky?" Something held tight for too long suddenly snapped inside him. "Are you so deluded to think you're a role model for a happy-ever-after? Do you honestly think I'd want to feel about Pip the way you felt about Mom?" He remembered his father's grief as painfully as his own. "Your life turned to shit when she died. Hell, even as a kid I swore I'd never—"

Joe stopped as reality shifted. He felt as though a lifetime of fog had cleared—and the view wasn't pretty. His mistrust of love originated from Adam's response to Francis's death, not Sue's rejection. That had only reinforced his conviction that emotional intimacy led to loss.

He stared at his father. And the irony was that he'd lose Pip precisely because he couldn't bring himself to acknowledge how much he loved her.

Every failure in his life came back to this man.

Adam reached out a hand. "Son."

"Don't call me that." The chair toppled as Joe shoved it back to move out of range. "You abandoned me. I lost a mother and a father when Mom died. Can you even imagine how that felt to a four-year-old? You were my hero and suddenly you couldn't stand to be around me anymore."

"No..." Adam struggled to a semi-upright position. "Couldn't...stand...me...around...you." He fell back on the pillow, exhausted. "Best...leave..."

"I missed you." Emotions, felt but never admitted, welled like fresh blood from an old wound.

"Here...now..."

"It's too late." Joe's chest hurt. "I can't give you what you want."

"I...give...*you*.... Listen!" Face shining with perspiration, Adam strained to get the words out. "Learn... my...mistakes." His throat convulsed. "Don't...shut-out...loves...you. Pip...me..."

"Then don't die," Joe said harshly. To his horror, his vision blurred, all the emotions, all the needs he'd suppressed over the years welling up. "Don't leave me again."

He waited for the empty promises, like the ones Adam had fended him off with over his childhood.

I'll see you soon, son.

One more season crab-fishing and I'll have enough money to settle back in San Francisco.

Sure, I want you with me...maybe next year.

Adam's lips moved, the sound barely a whisper. "Forgive...me."

Joe closed his eyes, four years old again and watching in bewilderment as his father walked away. Now, twenty-five years later, he was still helpless to do anything about it.

He dropped his face in his hands and wept silently. Wept for everything he'd lost and found, only to lose again. Finally, he became aware of his father's hand patting his knee. It was the only part of Joe he could reach. "Son?"

Joe walked to the sink and washed his face—Robert Carson's face, with nothing of Adam in it. It didn't matter. In the end a man had to decide for himself who he was going to be, and how he was going to live.

He picked up the fallen chair, sat down and clasped his father's hand. Adam's grip was weak, the love in his eyes strong.

"Dad."

Adam sighed and shut his eyes. Joe could almost see

the tension leave his body. His father's grip relaxed as he drifted into sleep. Through the window, the sky faded to pink and gold, leaching to gray and finally black. Yet Joe was strangely reluctant to move. There was something peaceful about this dark room.

He awoke with his head resting on the bed and his father's hand heavy on his outstretched arm. Heavy and cold. Joe closed his eyes again, holding back awareness by concentrating on the stiffness in his neck, the weave of the blanket under his left cheek, the receding clatter of a meds trolley.

But instinctively he'd already grasped his father's lifeless fingers.

Slowly, he sat up. Adam had moved on. But for the first time in his life, Joe couldn't resent it. With great care, he positioned his father's arms by his sides, then smoothed the covers.

"Give Mom and Nana Jo my love," he said, then put on his sweater and coat and walked into the corridor, where he stopped, momentarily disoriented. Bing Crosby was crooning about a white Christmas; a fir tree at reception blinked with colored lights. He felt as if he'd been on a long journey and come back to a changed world. Except he was the one who'd changed.

"Hi, Joe," Elaine said over the meds trolley. "I popped my head in around dinnertime and saw you sound asleep. Your father shooed me away. He must be starving."

"I left him sleeping." Joe wasn't ready for the fuss, the condolences and papers to sign. It seemed disrespectful somehow. Let his father rest.

"Then I won't disturb him until I have to. Good night."

Outside, a chill wind blew off the Pacific. Buttoning his winter coat, Joe illuminated the face of his Rolex. It was 8:00 p.m. Kaitlin would be getting ready for bed. Hell, he wasn't ready to tell her, either. Tomorrow. But in the car he took a deep, steadying breath and called Daniel.

"Are you okay?" was his uncle's first response to the news.

"Yeah, we'd sorted a few things out." Joe hesitated. "*You* okay?"

"For Adam's sake I wanted it to be over, but—" Daniel's voice broke. There was a long silence, which Joe knew not to fill. "I'm in El Granada, but I'll drive back first thing in the morning."

"Listen, do me a favor and phone Sue. She can tell the rest of the family." After giving Daniel her number, Joe started the engine, cranking up the heat. There was only one person he needed right now.

Joe drove to the pink palace and knocked on the door.

Pip opened it, buttoning her red coat. "You're a little early. I'll just get my..." Looking up, her eyes widened.

Two suitcases sat in the middle of the living room. It took a few seconds before Joe realized their significance. Somehow he managed to speak past his tight throat. "You're going back to New Zealand."

She lifted her chin, swallowed. "I can't do this anymore. I'm sorry."

The intercom buzzed and Pip turned her back on him to answer it. "Hello."

Joe stared at the suitcases. *Leaving.* He tried to think, but his brain was blank with shock, exhaustion and grief.

"ABC Cabs for a Miz Browne."

"Come on up." Her face pale, Pip turned back to him, desperation in her red-rimmed eyes. "Please don't make this harder than it is."

A fat guy lumbered up the stairs, breathing hard from

that slight exertion. Joe pulled a fifty out of his coat pocket. "Your services are no longer required."

"Yes, they are!" Pip picked up one of her suitcases. "Nothing you can say—"

"I'll take you to the airport."

The cabby shrugged, took the fifty and left.

Pip bit her lip. "You're not going to try and talk me out of this?"

"No." Joe took the suitcase from her, and picked up the other. He was grateful for the numbness, grateful because it allowed him to do the right thing. Put Pip first.

He could never compensate for what she'd have to sacrifice to stay. Only arrogance had allowed him to think he could. So he loved her, so what? He'd always be a man who had difficulty expressing emotions, who got it wrong more often than he got it right.

Joe wouldn't stake her future on an hour-old belief that he could change. While Pip locked her front door for the last time, he stacked the bags in the trunk.

The only thing Joe knew for sure was that if his child was born here, Pip would never move back to New Zealand. Because once he'd bonded with the baby her soft heart would never allow her to part them. He slammed the trunk, and the metal was icy cold under his fingers. Hadn't he been banking on that?

But if he was going to put Pip first, he had to do it now. Because once he kissed his newborn's face, he'd never be able to let the baby go.

Sensing Pip's troubled gaze on him, he forced a smile. "Ready to go?"

She was silent through the trip, answering him in monosyllables. Waiting for his reproach. "One day I'll move out of the city," he said conversationally, "somewhere inland where the weather's less erratic."

Pip cleared her throat. "Somewhere between the city and Napa Valley would be nice."

When he sensed she could handle it, Joe said quietly, "You know it's important to me that you accept child support, don't you, Pip?"

"Yes." She turned her head to look out the window, even though there was nothing to see but cars and freeway. "And visit whenever you want. I'm not denying you any rights as a father, Joe."

His vision blurred. He blinked to refocus on the road.

"We'll come for visits, too." Pip's voice was thick. "I haven't forgotten our baby has a sister here."

Always fair. But so much depended on variables, on finances and future relationships. On whether they could raise a child together, living thousands of miles apart.

The airport loomed out of the dark and Joe gripped the steering wheel.

Pip stiffened, too. "You can drop me off at the terminal."

"And have Nana Jo turning in her grave?"

Two weeks before Christmas, the exodus had begun. It took Joe another fifteen minutes to find a place to park in the multistory lot. Then he had to locate a cart for Pip's bags. Neither of them spoke.

The terminal was warm and so brightly lit it hurt his eyes. Festive music played between flight announcements. Colored tinsel decorated the check-in counters.

Joe took a seat and waited while Pip joined the snake chain of passengers waiting to check in. *You're doing the right thing.*

"I'm done."

Joe forced himself to stand. "That's good."

"All that's left to do is go through security." Avoiding his gaze, Pip fumbled with her handbag, then pulled out an envelope. "I was going to post this. It's a letter for Kaitlin."

Their fingers touched as he took it. Hers were chilled. "I'll make sure she gets it."

"And explain things to your dad?" Her voice was small, caught in her throat. This wasn't easy for her, either.

Joe nodded. If he told her about Adam he knew she'd postpone her flight. He wouldn't resort to emotional blackmail.

It was time to end the torture for both of them. "Safe journey, Pip." Over her shoulder he watched a young father sweep his small son in his arms and throw the laughing child in the air. "Call me when you get there."

"One question," she said before he'd made a move to leave. He forced himself to meet her gaze. "How did you know I was leaving?"

"I didn't."

"Then why did you come to my apartment tonight?" When he hesitated, she said, "Honesty, no matter what."

Joe let everything he felt for her show on his face. "I came to tell you I loved you."

Pip froze. "It won't work, Joe." Her lips barely moved. "The last-minute declaration of love to stop the girl taking your baby away."

"You asked."

She gulped and came to life. Took two quick steps backward. "No, I can't do this anymore, *feel* like this anymore. I'm going home."

"It's okay," he reassured her. "I know it's too late for us."

Gently knuckling her cheek, Joe walked to the exit and out into the night, where he stopped to suck in deep breaths of chilled air. The cold seemed to fan out from his lungs into his limbs. He started to shiver.

An old lady stopped in front of him. "You okay, son?"

Joe slowed his breathing. "Fine, thank you."

But her kindness released something in him. As he walked on, tears stung his eyes. Before today, the last time he'd cried was at Kaitlin's birth.

Pip's perfume lingered in the car. Joe pillowed his arms against the steering wheel and buried his face. He'd lost three people he loved tonight—his father, his soul mate and their child.

Nothing will hurt this much again, he promised himself. *No day will ever be worse.* In a moment of illumination Joe understood the self-sacrifice behind his grandparents' decision to give up two of their children.

Adam had had a future as the son of a dead war hero, none as the bastard of a married man. However much Robert Carson might have wanted to acknowledge his son.

And Josephine had spared her daughter the stigma of illegitimacy, with all the prejudice that entailed at the time. His grandmother had taught Joe a lot in life; she was still teaching him in death.

Selflessness sucked. Joe managed a shaky laugh, then started the engine and drove to the exit, where he shoved his ticket in the slot and waited until the barrier lifted. As he accelerated, he did a routine check in the rearview mirror.

Waving her arms, Pip was running after the car.

CHAPTER TWENTY-ONE

PIP STOPPED RUNNING when Joe slammed on the brakes, and bent double to catch her breath, which escaped in foggy gasps.

She was winded by the desperate surge of adrenaline that had slammed her as she'd watched Joe's car pull away. Overheated, she pulled open her coat, letting the cold air snake around the summer dress she'd worn for the New Zealand climate.

Joe leaped out of his car and ran back toward her. "Are you okay?"

Planting her hands on her hips, Pip glared at him. "Why didn't you tell me?"

In the middle of reaching out to her, Joe dropped his arms to his sides. "How did you find out?"

"It doesn't matter. What matters is that you didn't tell me."

She'd just finished going through customs when Daniel called her cell. Thinking it was Joe, she'd resisted answering, too lacerated by his expedient declaration of love to have anything more to say to Joe bloody Fraser. Except when she finally checked, she hadn't recognized the number.

She was still angry. "You really think I'd leave you on the day your father died?" Pip accused him.

Joe backed away, his hands raised. "This is exactly why I didn't tell you. I don't want pity swaying your decision."

Pip stared at him. "My God, you were telling the truth." Joy swept through her from the toes up. "You do love me."

"No." He shook his head. "You were right, I was trying to manipulate you into staying."

"In that case you would have told me about Adam."

He passed a hand over his face, obviously too shell-shocked to sustain a logical argument. "I'm doing what's right for you, Pip," he said doggedly. "Walking you back to the terminal and putting you on a plane home to your family."

She had never loved him more than she did at this moment. Never been so confident that they could make this work.

"You're a damn fool, Fraser." Stepping forward, Pip wrapped her arms around him, buried her face in his shoulder and held on tight. "*You're* my family."

Of course Joe didn't believe her. Because that would be too easy, and nothing about this man was easy, what with his ridiculous aversion to being happy.

"At least," he said carefully, when he realized he wasn't going to persuade her to catch her flight, "you still have your original flight booking, next week."

Pip didn't argue. So they weren't going to have their happy-ever-after moment in the airport car park. That wasn't her priority right now.

"Let's get you home." She led him to his car, where she dumped him protesting in the passenger seat, then got behind the wheel.

Joe fell asleep almost immediately. As she drove, Pip thought of Adam, and her tears flowed as she mourned the opportunity to know him better, for him to know her unborn child.

Halfway home she remembered her bags were still at the airport, and rang to stop them from being blown up. Since neither of them had clothes at her apartment she drove to Joe's hotel, where she roused him enough to get him upstairs. He collapsed on the bed, asleep again before his head hit the pillow.

Pip made hot tea and sat quietly, composing herself. Then, taking a deep breath, she called her family.

"BUT I DON'T SEE WHY you won't marry Pip," Kaitlin said. She'd decided her special skill lay in uncovering secrets, not keeping them.

Though she hadn't told Dad about Grandpa gifting Uncle Sam the medal—not even when he was looking for it when he packed up Grandpa's things—Kaitlin knew she'd let it slip sooner or later. She always did. "Pip said she'll stay, and I know you want her to. I just don't get it."

She and Dad were standing at the back of the funeral home waiting for people to arrive for Grandpa Adam's funeral. Kaitlin intended to go up to his open casket and say goodbye, but she hadn't quite managed it yet.

It wasn't that she had a problem looking at dead people—wanting to be a missionary, she couldn't—and she'd been to both her other grandparents' funerals. But as long as she didn't look at Grandpa's face, she could still pretend somebody had made a mistake.

"Kaitlin," said Dad, "you've got to stop eavesdropping."

"Just tell me why and I'll quit pestering you."

With a sigh, he sat down in a back pew and drew her close. "What if the Beast stayed the Beast instead of turning into the handsome prince? Would you still want Belle to marry him?"

"But he didn't," she pointed out.

"In real life it's harder for people to change. There's no kiss that breaks the spell."

"How about a blow to the head with a two-by-four?" said Pip, suddenly standing beside them. "Does that sound like someone who'd sacrifice her life for pity?"

Dad frowned. "I don't think we should have this conversation in front of Kaitlin. Or my father."

"Adam was on my side, and *our* family is starting a new trend. No secrets. Kaitlin, I'm going to pay my respects to your grandpa. Do you want to come with me?"

"Not yet."

"Okay, honey, when you're ready."

Kaitlin watched Pip walk up to Grandpa's casket, and bow her head. Beside her, Dad was looking sad, and she put her arms around him. "Are you missing Grandpa?"

He returned her hug. "Yeah, baby, but I'm also happy Dad's not suffering anymore."

Kaitlin sat back and looked at him curiously. "Why did you start calling him Dad?"

"Because he needed me to, and because I wanted to. He ended up being a good father."

"And he was smart," Kaitlin said. She waited for Dad's agreement before she added innocently, "So what did Grandpa say about Pip?"

Dad's eyes narrowed. "Kaitlin Josephine Fraser, you're getting more like him every day. Now go talk to your uncle Daniel."

She saw him with Pip, who'd moved away from the casket now. As Kaitlin approached, she heard Pip say, "I thought you didn't get involved in family dramas?" and she slowed to a dawdle.

"I told you, I rang your number by mistake," Uncle Daniel replied in the dry voice he used for teasing. Deciding they weren't saying anything interesting, Kaitlin went to talk to Belle instead.

After everyone arrived, Dad asked her to shut the chapel door to stop the December rain from blowing into the vestibule, and to keep the cold out. As she started to pull it closed, Kaitlin saw Great-Uncle Sam walking up the driveway, dressed in a black suit and holding an umbrella.

She ran down the steps to meet him, and he drew her under the shelter with him. "Didn't anyone teach you not to run around in the rain?"

"I like the rain," she said. "Why did you come, Uncle Sam? I didn't think you wanted Grandpa Adam as your brother."

"Whether I did or whether I didn't is not your concern. But I have something for Adam's casket, something that belongs to him."

Kaitlin smiled. "So you *are* being nicer."

"Don't be impertinent." Uncle Sam looked into the chapel, saw Dad and hesitated.

"I'll take you, Uncle Sam." Snagging his hand, Kaitlin marched up the steps and into the chapel. Dad stiffened when he saw who she was with, but Kaitlin kept walking straight up the aisle to the casket.

She got all trembly inside as she got closer, and a little scared, but Uncle Sam's hand was big and warm and he didn't seem to mind her squeezing it so hard. Cautiously, she looked into Grandpa's face. "He really died," she whispered, tears coming to her eyes. She'd thought she'd cried out all her tears for him.

"Would you like me to take you out, Kaitlin?"

Uncle Sam's briskness always made her braver. "No." She looked up at her relative. "Can I give it to him?"

Nodding, he handed over the box.

Kaitlin took out the Medal of Honor and gently laid the star over Grandpa's heart, with the blue ribbon and its cluster of thirteen stars diagonally across one shoulder. "It was his favorite, most special thing," she whispered.

"I know."

"Is that why you gave it back?"

He didn't answer because Dad had come up and laid a protective hand on her shoulder. In silence, they all looked at the medal, then Dad said quietly, "Does this have anything to do with the thirty thousand dollars that's been refunded to me by the rehab clinic?"

Uncle Sam said nothing. Kaitlin followed his lead.

Dad sighed. "You can stay, Sam. Not because you're lying to me, and certainly not because you've subverted my daughter. Pip's just told me that you resuscitated Dad after his second stroke at your golf club. If you hadn't, we wouldn't have resolved our relationship before he died. For that I'll always be grateful, whatever you feel about the Frasers."

Squeezing Kaitlin's shoulder, Dad walked away. Uncle Sam waited until he was out of earshot, then said approvingly, "You've learned how to keep a secret."

But later, after the funeral, Kaitlin did tell two people the whole story. Belle and Aunt Emily. Somehow she knew Grandpa would have wanted her to.

NEAR THE END OF THE WAKE, Joe stood in the living room of Belle and Matt's new house and watched Pip trying to flirt with one of Sue's foster babies. She produced a big smile, then pulled a funny face.

Donnie, chewing a toy on the rug, was unimpressed.

Joe wasn't. It felt like the first time he'd smiled in three days. Then Pip glanced up and caught him watching. Embarrassed, she returned to her conversation with the grown-ups.

Joe continued to the kitchen, where he dumped the empty glasses he'd been collecting in the dishwasher.

Since Adam's death, they'd talked once about what should happen next. The morning he'd woken up in his hotel room with Pip beside him. Joe could still remember the surge of happiness he'd felt before recalling that she was there for the wrong reasons.

She'd insisted she was staying, but Joe replied he wasn't a pity case. If he wasn't enough for her before Adam died, he wasn't going to be enough after.

They'd argued back and forth for an hour.

Privately, Joe had other reservations. He'd told Pip he loved her, and she hadn't believed him, hadn't wanted to. That hurt. She didn't trust him with her fears about motherhood, and he was a man who needed to be needed. And she'd never said she loved him.

The disparity between Pip's words and her actions suggested she still had doubts.

And with a funeral to organize, a child to comfort and a father to mourn, Joe hadn't been able to think straight or trust his judgment. So when Pip suggested they wait until after the funeral to talk, he'd accepted the reprieve with relief.

He finished stacking the glasses, turned the dishwasher on, then looked around for his next chore. But Belle and her mother had already cleaned up and the kitchen was spotless. For the first time since Adam died, Joe had time to think.

Sue appeared in the doorway, carrying her wriggling toddler, who'd been causing mayhem pulling decorations off the Christmas tree. "We're burning off some of this energy in the park across the road." His cousin repositioned Carrie onto her other hip. "Come with us?"

"Sure." Taking Carrie from Sue, he lifted her onto his shoulders. "C'mon, monkey." The toddler laughed, her mittened hands gripping his hair with enough force to make him wince.

The December afternoon was cold, the sky a pale blue. A chill breeze nipped at his exposed skin. Sue reached up and put a woolly hat on Carrie, which the toddler promptly pulled off and threw on the ground. Then she caught sight of the playground and started to squeal in excitement.

"Hat first," insisted her mother.

Joe secured Carrie in the baby swing, then gave it a gentle push. Carrie rewarded him with a tiny-toothed grin.

"In another year you'll be doing this with your baby," Sue commented. She sat on the park bench, knees pulled up under her black coat, her long, fair hair pulled back in its customary ponytail.

Joe couldn't allow himself to think about that, not until he'd settled things with Pip. He gave a noncommittal grunt.

"Why are you still holding Pip at arm's length?" Sue said quietly.

He took a while to find the right reply. At some profound level, making his peace with his father had changed him. But old habits died hard. "I need her to be sure."

Carrie vocalized her disapproval at being stationary. Joe gave the swing another push.

"You've always accepted too much responsibility," said Sue. Carrie's hat fell off and she retrieved it, replacing it on the little girl's curls. "We broke up because of my shortcomings, not yours. But you still gave me a job when I needed one. Nadia made a baby, too, but it's always been your fault." Sue dug her hands in the pockets of her coat. "Now you're trying to guess how Pip's going to feel in five years time about giving up her family. Stop it."

Carrie put her arms up for her mother, and Joe stopped the swing. "This playground trip was a ploy, wasn't it?" he accused her.

Sue disentangled the toddler from the harness and faced him. "You're in love with a strong woman who knows her own mind. If Pip's chosen you, let her."

"As easy at that, huh?"

"No, it's not easy." They started back toward the house. "But if you're waiting for your head to catch up with your heart, it's not going to happen."

Joe didn't like the sound of that.

In the hall, Sue wrinkled her nose at her small daughter, then picked up the diaper bag near the door. "Roll on, potty training."

As she headed up the stairs toward the bathroom, Joe called softly, "Sue."

With Carrie in her arms, she looked down.

Neither of them said anything, but then they'd never had to. Smiling, she continued up the stairs.

Joe paused at the living-room door. Most of Adam's acquaintances had gone. Only family remained. Next to the Christmas tree, Kaitlin played peekaboo with Donnie, who gurgled at her adoringly.

Across the room, Daniel was saying his farewells to Aunt Jenny and Luke. He gave Joe a "you'll be okay" shoulder squeeze on the way out. His loyalty had been the rock at Joe's back since he was four years old. But,

Joe realized, his uncle's solitary path was no longer his—if it ever had been.

His gaze shifted to Aunt Jenny and Uncle Luke, still committed, still happy after thirtysomething years together.

He looked at Uncle Sam, who was too damn stupid to realize pursuing the necklace was costing him everything that really mattered, and yet was still capable of making a poignant gesture. If Sam could change, even a little bit, surely Joe could.

Finally, he looked at Pip, who was chatting to Sue's husband, Rick, by the fireplace. Joe stopped thinking and allowed himself simply to feel. The message was unequivocal. *She's the one.*

And he smiled because Sue was right. When he led with his heart he knew exactly what he had to do.

CHAPTER TWENTY-TWO

THE KING'S ELEMENTARY Nativity play was in full swing. So far Mary had dropped baby Jesus on his head, the donkey had decided he was a comedy act, and the three wise men were currently ad-libbing a sword fight with weapons they'd insisted on carrying. Now Pip knew why.

But a sword fight made things so much more exciting, the three wise men argued after they'd staggered into the wings, clutching their chests.

"You conned me," she said sternly, then lectured them on their characters' motivation, and sent them back on stage subdued and suitably wiser. Standing in the right wing, next to the curtain, where she could troubleshoot as necessary, Pip allowed herself a quiet chuckle.

Suggesting to the principal that she return to finish out her last week had been a great idea. She got to say a proper goodbye to her class, and was too busy to brood over Joe.

After the funeral he'd asked for a few more days to get a couple of things settled. And because she loved him, because Pip understood what it was to lose someone you loved, she'd said yes. Inside, she wanted to scream with frustration.

The *waaa-waaa* of a ten-year-old offstage pretending to be a newborn dragged her attention back to the play.

In the opposite wing, her sound effects guy was building up to a full-blown tantrum. Pip sliced a hand across her throat and he broke off mid*waaa*.

In two days the lease was up on her apartment, and in another week her working visa for the States expired.

Time was running out.

Checking her script, Pip turned and whispered, "Everybody ready?" Tinsel halos nodded in unison. She smiled at her most responsible student. "Kaitlin, lead them on."

"Okay, Pi— Miss Browne."

Homemade wings flapped and jigged on white sheet robes as her choir of angels—everyone in the class without a formal part—trooped on stage for the grand finale. Below the front of the stage, Anita struck a note on the piano, and after a wobbly start, the choir settled into "Away in the Manger."

Pip got a lump in her throat and blinked furiously. A hand proffered a handkerchief. Joe.

"What are you doing here?" she whispered.

He whispered back, "I've got a daughter performing, remember?"

They looked at Kaitlin, who stood with her friends in the front row of the choir, where their appalling singing couldn't throw any of the other singers off-key.

"I meant in the wings," said Pip.

His gaze settled on her. "It's time to talk."

"Now?" He smiled, and Pip's heart started to beat faster.

"Now. Besides, what could go wrong in the last song?"

On stage, one of the choristers backed into the stable and the piece of painted cardboard backdrop started to wobble. Mary shrieked theatrically and the singing faltered. Beside Pip, Joe started to sing in a deep baritone, "The stars in the sky looked down where He lay." Encouraged, the kids picked it up again.

Joe stopped singing and reached for Pip's hand. "I've already kept you waiting long enough," he said, and unaccountably, she started to cry.

"You think?"

He caught her in his arms and kissed the tears away. "You told Kaitlin that one kiss doesn't break the spell," Pip reminded him.

"No." His hold tightened. "It's going to take a lifetime of kisses, but let's not get ahead of ourselves."

The singing stopped; applause signaled the end to the play. Kaitlin called in a stage whisper, "Now, Dad?"

"Now, Katie." Joe released her.

On stage the choristers pulled signs out from under their sheet robes and held them up. Each was a letter. Pip took a couple of side steps left to get a better view.

P-I-P-W-I-L-L-U-blank-*A-R*-blank-blank-*M-E*

"You've lost me," she said. "Who do I arm?"

Joe sighed. "Melissa, Kaitlin, Scooter. Turn your signs around and angle them more to Miss Browne."

Another *M, R* and *Y* appeared. The message sprang into sharp relief: "PIP WILL YOU MARRY ME?" Pip gasped and covered her mouth. From the auditorium she heard oohs and scattered applause.

Joe dropped to one knee. "I figured my humiliation should be public."

Pip tried to speak, but emotions overwhelmed her.

He took her hand. "I love you so much," he added huskily, "that I can't separate what's right from what I want anymore. You choose."

"Say it again," she croaked.

"You choo—"

Tears pouring down her face, Pip grabbed his shoulders and shook him. "The love part, Joe. Tell me now, then tell me every day for the rest of our lives."

"What's happening?" Pip heard Anita call to the performers. Her piano was below stage with the audience, just out of sight.

"Dad's kneeling down," Kaitlin yelled back. "Miss Browne just shook him." The audience hushed; every child on stage craned to see. "But I can't hear what they're saying."

Joe smiled. "I love you." Pip took one deep, tremulous breath and stopped crying. She smiled back. Standing, Joe took back his handkerchief and wiped the last traces of tears from her cheeks, his expression serious again. "And I promise you'll get back to New Zealand at least once a year, and that when Kaitlin's older we'll look at living there for six months and—"

Pip pressed a finger over his lips. "I've never questioned your fairness, only your feelings."

He caught her hand. "And what are yours, Pip?"

Suddenly, she felt nervous and shy. "I love you," she said awkwardly. Joe broke into a grin. Pip smacked his arm. "This isn't a competition."

"She just hit him," Pip heard Melissa report. The audience gave a collective groan.

"You're on." Joe caught her around the waist and pulled her close. "Who loves who the most?"

But Pip knew how to handle tough guys.

"She's kissing him," Kaitlin reported to the audience a few seconds later. "I guess that means yes." The floor vibrated under them as applause thundered through the auditorium.

Pip came up for air, rested her head against his shoulder. "One thing," she confessed. "I'm scared of babies."

Joe's hand made warm, soothing circles on her back. "So was I before Kaitlin. It will pass, I promise."

Pip relaxed into him. This man didn't make promises he couldn't keep.

"I'll teach you about babies," he said, "if you teach me how to be an idealist again."

"That's easy." Softly, Pip quoted her favorite Maori proverb, "'Turn your face to the sun and the shadows fall behind you.'"

There was a moment's silence, then he said, "You're my sun."

She nearly started crying again, but the kids had swarmed offstage and were surging around them. Releasing Joe, Pip bent to hug Kaitlin.

But the girl skipped around her. "Can we give Pip her Christmas present now, Dad?"

"Oh, no," Pip exclaimed, only half joking. "We have to wait until Christmas Day."

Kaitlin looked dismayed. "But where will we *hide* them?"

Joe started to laugh. "Pip, this present won't wait." Putting his hands on her shoulders, he spun her around and steered her forward, where she could see the audience.

Most people had stood up to leave, filing toward the double doors at the rear of the auditorium. Only a group near the back remained seated....

Pip's stunned gaze traveled from her brothers, their wives and a baby, to her dad and...

Her knees gave way and Joe supported her against him.

"I figured your family had to be at our wedding. I'm thinking Christmas Eve."

Rooted to the spot, Pip stared at her mother, unable to believe her eyes.

"You can still change your mind about marrying me," Joe said quietly, and turning her head, she saw he meant it. *I was wrong,* she thought. *This is the moment I'll love him most.*

Pip cupped his face and kissed him fiercely. "You're never getting rid of me." Grabbing Joe's hand, she hauled him down the stairs at the front of the stage and toward her family. "Besides, I can't interfere with your destiny."

He laughed. "Oh, yeah, Miss Browne, what's that?"

They were going to be so happy. "Why, Mr. Fraser, you're a family man."

* * * * *

*Don't miss the next book
in this 60th Anniversary family saga!
Look for* A Mother's Secret
*by Janice Kay Johnson in December 2009
from Harlequin Superromance.*

Celebrate 60 years of pure reading pleasure
with Harlequin®!
Just in time for the holidays,
Silhouette Special Edition® is proud to present
New York Times *bestselling author*
Kathleen Eagle's
ONE COWBOY, ONE CHRISTMAS

Rodeo rider Zach Beaudry was a travelin' man—
until he broke down in middle-of-nowhere South
Dakota during a deep freeze. That's when an angel
came to his rescue....

"Don't die on me. Come on, Zel. You know how much I love you, girl. You're all I've got. Don't do this to me here. Not *now*."

But Zelda had quit on him, and Zach Beaudry had no one to blame but himself. He'd taken his sweet time hitting the road, and then miscalculated a shortcut. For all he knew he was a hundred miles from gas. But even if they were sitting next to a pump, the ten dollars he had in his pocket wouldn't get him out of South Dakota, which was not where he wanted to be right now. Not even his beloved pickup truck, Zelda, could get him much of anywhere on fumes. He was sitting out in the cold in the middle of nowhere. And getting colder.

He shifted the pickup into Neutral and pulled hard on the steering wheel, using the downhill slope to get her off the blacktop and into the roadside grass, where she shuddered to a standstill. He stroked the padded dash. "You'll be safe here."

But Zach would not. It was getting dark, and it was already too damn cold for his cowboy ass. Zach's battered body was a barometer, and he was feeling South Dakota big-time. He'd have given his right arm to be climbing into a hotel hot tub instead of a brutal blast of north wind. The right was his free arm anyway. Damn thing had lost altitude, touched some part of the bull and caused him a scoreless ride last time out.

It wasn't scoring him a ride this night, either. A carload of teenagers whizzed by, topping off the insult by laying on the horn as they passed him. It was at least twenty minutes before another vehicle came along. He stepped out and waved both arms this time, damn near getting himself killed. Whatever happened to *do unto others?* In places like this, decent people didn't leave each other stranded in the cold.

His face was feeling stiff, and he figured he'd better start walking before his toes went numb. He struck out for a distant yard light, the only sign of human habitation in sight. He couldn't tell how distant, but he knew he'd be hurting by the time he got there, and he was counting on some kindly old man to be answering the door. No shame among the lame.

It wasn't like Zach was fresh off the operating table— it had been a few months since his last round of repairs— but he hadn't given himself enough time. He'd lopped a couple of weeks off the near end of the doc's estimated recovery time, rigged up a brace, done some heavy-duty taping and climbed onto another bull. Hung in there for five seconds—four seconds past feeling the pop in his hip and three seconds short of the buzzer.

He could still feel the pain shooting down his leg with every step. Only this time he had to pick the damn thing up, swing it forward and drop it down again on his own.

Pride be damned, he just hoped *somebody* would be answering the door at the end of the road. The light in the front window was a good sign.

The four steps to the covered porch might as well have been four hundred, and he was looking to climb them with a lead weight chained to his left leg. His eyes were just as screwed up as his hip. Big black spots danced around with tiny red flashers, and he couldn't tell what was real and what wasn't. He stumbled over some shrubbery, steadied himself on the porch railing and peered between vertical slats.

There in the front window stood a spruce tree with a silver star affixed to the top. Zach was pretty sure the red sparks were all in his head, but the white lights twinkling by the hundreds throughout the huge tree, those were real. He wasn't too sure about the woman hanging the shiny balls. Most of her hair was caught up on her head and fastened in a curly clump, but the light captured by the escaped bits crowned her with a golden halo. Her face was a soft shadow, her body a willowy silhouette beneath a long white gown. If this was where the mind ran off to when cold started shutting down the rest of the body, then Zach's final worldly thought was, *This ain't such a bad way to go.*

If she would just turn to the window, he could die looking into the eyes of a Christmas angel.

* * * * *

Could this woman from Zach's past get the lonesome cowboy to come in from the cold...for good?
Look for
ONE COWBOY, ONE CHRISTMAS
by Kathleen Eagle
Available December 2009 from
Silhouette Special Edition®

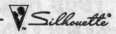

™ *Silhouette®*

SPECIAL EDITION

FROM *NEW YORK TIMES* AND *USA TODAY* BESTSELLING AUTHOR

KATHLEEN EAGLE

ONE COWBOY, *One Christmas*

When bull rider Zach Beaudry appeared out of thin air on Ann Drexler's ranch, she thought she was seeing a ghost of Christmas past. And though Zach had no memory of their night of passion years ago, they were about to share a future he would never forget.

*Available December 2009
wherever books are sold.*

SSE65493

Visit Silhouette Books at www.eHarlequin.com

REQUEST YOUR FREE BOOKS!

2 FREE NOVELS PLUS 2 FREE GIFTS!

HARLEQUIN®

Super Romance®

Exciting, emotional, unexpected!

YES! Please send me 2 FREE Harlequin® Superromance® novels and my 2 FREE gifts (gifts are worth about $10). After receiving them, if I don't wish to receive any more books, I can return the shipping statement marked "cancel." If I don't cancel, I will receive 6 brand-new novels every month and be billed just $4.69 per book in the U.S. or $5.24 per book in Canada. That's a savings of close to 15% off the cover price! It's quite a bargain! Shipping and handling is just 50¢ per book*. I understand that accepting the 2 free books and gifts places me under no obligation to buy anything. I can always return a shipment and cancel at any time. Even if I never buy another book from Harlequin, the two free books and gifts are mine to keep forever.

135 HDN EYLG   336 HDN EYLS

Name _____ (PLEASE PRINT)

Address _____ Apt. #

City _____ State/Prov. _____ Zip/Postal Code

Signature (if under 18, a parent or guardian must sign)

Mail to the Harlequin Reader Service:
IN U.S.A.: P.O. Box 1867, Buffalo, NY 14240-1867
IN CANADA: P.O. Box 609, Fort Erie, Ontario L2A 5X3

Not valid to current subscribers of Harlequin Superromance books.

Are you a current subscriber of Harlequin Superromance books and want to receive the larger-print edition?
Call 1-800-873-8635 today!

* Terms and prices subject to change without notice. Prices do not include applicable taxes. Sales tax applicable in N.Y. Canadian residents will be charged applicable provincial taxes and GST. Offer not valid in Quebec. This offer is limited to one order per household. All orders subject to approval. Credit or debit balances in a customer's account(s) may be offset by any other outstanding balance owed by or to the customer. Please allow 4 to 6 weeks for delivery. Offer available while quantities last.

Your Privacy: Harlequin is committed to protecting your privacy. Our Privacy Policy is available online at www.eHarlequin.com or upon request from the Reader Service. From time to time we make our lists of customers available to reputable third parties who may have a product or service of interest to you. If you would prefer we not share your name and address, please check here. ☐

HSR09F

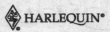

INTRIGUE

FIRST NIGHT
BY
DEBRA WEBB

To prove his innocence, talented artist
Brandon Thomas is in a race against time.
Caught up in a murder investigation,
he enlists Colby agent Merrilee Walters
to help catch the true killer. If they can survive
the first night, their growing attraction
may have a chance, as well.

Available in December wherever books are sold.

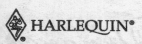

HARLEQUIN®

A Cowboy Christmas
MARIN THOMAS

2 stories in 1!

The holidays are a rough time for widower
Logan Taylor and single dad Fletcher McFadden—
neither hunky cowboy has been lucky in love.
But Christmas is the season of miracles! Logan
meets his match in "A Christmas Baby," while
Fletcher gets a second chance at love in "Marry
Me, Cowboy." This year both cowboys are on
Santa's Nice list!

*Available December
wherever books are sold.*

"LOVE, HOME & HAPPINESS"

www.eHarlequin.com

HAR75292

COMING NEXT MONTH

Available December 8, 2009